CORNERS OF MY MIND

AMERICAN SHORT STORIES

TRAVIS SHORT

To my seven children: Travissa, Jennifer, Jill, Travis, Timothy, Trent, and Lucy. I trust they will enjoy these stories in years to come and pass them on to those who follow.

CONTENTS

PREFACE

I have been writing all my life—mostly short stories, which is the genre I favor. I always wanted to write a novel, and about four years ago, I did just that, a short parody of tough-guy private detectives. Mine was named Pete Pitchfork, a takeoff and spoof of the once-famous private detectives, Sam Spade and Mike Hammer, only my tough guy was tougher. That start led me to serious novel writing, and I have published four novels and an illustrated epic poem since then.

I am in the process of researching historical and legendary reports for my next book, a historical fiction account of murder in the mountains of southwest Virginia and eastern Kentucky. And all the while, ideas for a totally different crime novel are creeping into my subconscious. But I have found that in writing a novel, the author must be totally absorbed with and dedicated to the characters he is creating in that novel. The author has very little time to flirt with distractions or competing ideas. Not so when writing short stories, at least not for me.

PREFACE

I have been asked where I get my ideas. My response is from everywhere, everybody, and everything. From people I have known or been told about, from a dream, a sentence someone spoke, a picture, everyday events, an untimely death, or anything that makes me laugh or cry. I like subjects with the possibility of surprise or unexpected twists. That is what I have tried to capture in the stories contained in this book. They have come from the most mundane or most shocking sources imaginable—right from the corners of my mind.

In *Old Men Cry Too Easily,* you will read of Jacob Monroe who, through the fog of Alzheimer's, celebrates his seventy-sixth birthday.

Julius the Talking Dog surprises his master with his superior intellect but refuses to talk to others.

In *Trimming Trees for God,* a radio minister captures the attention of an agnostic who supports his wife's church only to have her leave him for her pastor.

In *Extra! Extra! Read All About It,* a cheating husband is saved from a painful amputation of his extremity by a timely newspaper headline.

A young soldier who escaped a life of abuse at home is left behind on a North Korean frozen mountain in the story, *In from the Cold.*

A widower is captivated by a pole dancer who bilks him out of his life's savings in *Lap Dance.*

These and other intriguing stories are contained in this volume. I hope you enjoy them.

1

THE CRIMSON SHOES

Starting at the age of ten, Elmer Hatfield apprenticed for his father, Harvey, at Hatfield's Shoe Repair and Emporium. Elmer inherited the thriving business when Harvey succumbed to internal bleeding, caused by swallowing a handful of shoe tacks which he was holding in his mouth while fitting a hunting boot over an iron last. Harvey's longtime friend and former high school classmate, Billy Buttmore, ventured into the shop just at that untimely moment, slapped Harvey on the back, and greeted him with a raucous *hello*. Harvey sucked in his breath, attempting to respond with equal exuberance but swallowed the tacks and precipitously keeled over, never again to regain consciousness.

A mere boy at twenty-two when he assumed the proprietorship of a thriving shoe sales and repair business, Elmer Hatfield promptly became the matrimonial target of many young ladies in Steadfast, South Carolina. Theretofore, he had been characterized by people who knew him best, as a good-natured doofus. But Elmer—victim of a typical male ego—soon bathed in his new popularity, attributing it to his imagined good looks, wit, and charm. He blissfully discounted the attractiveness of his modest inheritance, including a cinnamon-red 1948 Buick Roadmaster convertible with Dynaflow transmission, his late father's single venture into extravagance.

It might be said of Ruby Rhinestone that she also apprenticed in an equally lucrative trade, learning the art of seduction at her mother's knee at an early age. Ruby hailed from the other side of the tracks, having been sired by an itinerant *New World Encyclopedia* salesman and reared by her mother, wickedly beautiful and consummately skillful in the wiles and ways of a wanton woman.

Ruby never knew her father but was briefly attached to each of numerous *uncles* who passed through her life in frequent succession. From these *gentlemen,* she acquired a sense of adventure that, combined with her natural beauty and sensuality, made her a twenty-to-one long shot for being true to any one man. Unfortunately, no one ever warned Elmer Hatfield to be wary of such women.

Still, we should attempt to be objective when assessing Ruby's intentions. In fairness, we might surmise that she had never seen Elmer cruising about town in his convertible Roadmaster, top down, before she innocently wandered into Hatfield's Shoe Repair and Emporium one Saturday afternoon in 1950. And one can only conjecture as to Elmer's delight when Ruby said in her most coquettish low-country dialect, "Would you mind if I tried on those crimson straps in the window?"

Elmer slithered from behind the glass counter, scurrying

nervously toward the small display window, keeping his head turned toward the green-eyed beauty. "Wha... Wha... What size are you?"

"Thirty-eight." She smiled demurely, her eyes fluttering.

"No," he said, holding the patent leather heels by their straps almost daintily, for her to see. "I meant what size shoe do you wear?"

They both laughed flirtatiously.

"Six and a half," she said.

"These should be just right." His voice took on a serious, businesslike tone, belying a palpitating heart inside his chest and the trickle of sweat down his back into the crack of his butt.

The ventilation fan droned above Ruby's head, lilting her raven hair softly in the breeze. She took a seat and crossed her legs, the hem of her dress settling just above her knees. Elmer gasped, then breathed deeply, attempting to contain the composure he felt swiftly slipping away. He cleared his throat as he straddled a fitting stool, scooting it closer to her feet. At the carefully choreographed moment, Ruby slowly uncrossed her legs. He sucked in his breath at the sight of her red garters with miniature black bows. The fatal mistake of his father flashed through Elmer's mind, and he gave thanks to the good Lord above that he was not about to swallow a mouthful of shoe tacks along with his tongue.

Their eyes met in a mutual embrace that endured for several minutes while Elmer fumbled with the patent leather straps, encircling her trim ankles. He fastened the final strap and pushed back the fitting stool to get a good look at his handy work. "My, my, Miss; What did you say your name was?"

"Rhinestone," she said, then slowly wet her lips with her tongue. "Ruby Rhinestone." She extended her hand, which Elmer grasped lovingly between his palms.

He smiled with exemplary satisfaction. "Miss Rhinestone. No doubt, those shoes were made for you."

She extended her legs, first one then the other, raising each to get a good view of the shoes. With each move, the hem of her dress inched its way further toward her garters, almost giving Elmer an equally good view. "These are so pretty," she remarked, getting to her feet. "How much are they?"

"Five and a quarter." Elmer grimaced apologetically.

"My, my. They are expensive; aren't they?" She opened her purse and began to rummage inside. "I don't know if I can afford them." She continued to fumble with the purse's contents, jiggling lipstick, mirror, rouge, and powder compact. After a moment, she sat and began undoing the buckle on one shoe. She sighed, "I just can't do it right now."

Elmer shifted his weight from one foot to the other, contemplating how he might facilitate the momentous decision being considered by his menacingly attractive customer. "Tell you what."

She stopped unbuckling and looked up through half-closed eyes at the shoe store proprietor.

"Yes?"

"Tell you what. I'll let you have them for three dollars ... that's below wholesale."

Slowly blinking her long dark lashes, she sighed again as she went back to unbuckling the shoes. "No. I guess I'll just have to order something from Montgomery Ward."

Elmer moved the fitting stool close to her. He sat and

lifted each foot, his eyes gazing into hers as he adroitly buckled the straps, one then the other. "We'll call it customer relations," he said, "They're just your size."

"It would be a shame for someone else to get them, wouldn't it?" Her eyes twinkled with appreciation. She leaned forward and kissed Elmer, who sat dumbfounded but happy to have been taken by the seductress from across the tracks.

Two weeks later, he drove the Roadmaster to Columbia, Ruby by his side. They returned three days later, a blissfully married couple. Elmer's public relations strategy had worked exactly as Ruby planned.

It was soon apparent that Ruby possessed natural attributes, ideally honed in the art of salesmanship, particularly alluring to the male population of Steadfast. Bachelors and husbands alike abandoned JC Penney's, Walk-More, and City Boot Shop in order to frequent the newly decorated Hatfield's Shoe Repair and Emporium. No doubt, even Montgomery Ward's catalogue shoe sales plummeted in the face of the accelerated competition from Hatfield's, engendered by the presence of one Ruby Rhinestone.

Elmer reveled in his success, intoxicated at the thought of his bold business prowess, which by all accounts surpassed any achievements of his recently departed father. As business boomed and profits soared, Elmer busied himself at the iron last—the one implicated in his father's untimely demise. Elmer, secure in his belief that his much-admired young wife was true to the bone, was too busy to take note of the frequent visits to the emporium by Happy Hanover, heir to the Hanover Hotel chain consisting of three hotels—the latest a twenty-six-room monstrosity newly established in Charleston. Elmer might never have grown suspicious if not for the keen eye of Pudge Parker, a new sales clerk and fellow Steadfast High alumnus. And Pudge might never have brought the matter to Elmer's attention if Pudge's own awkward advances to Ruby had not been spurned—such is the guile of a rejected suitor.

Pudge approached Elmer as he pounded shoe tacks into the new Cat's Paw heels and half-soles he was attaching to Dickey Dilford's well-worn, but salvageable Red Goose oxford loafers. Pudge's bountiful butt cheeks wrestled for room in his too-tight pink pegged pants as he sidled alongside Elmer and whispered into his ear. "As much as I hate it, I have to tell you something, boss."

"Yeah?" Elmer kept right on pounding without missing a stroke. "What's up, Pudge?"

"That Happy Hanover comes in here every day."

"Buying shoes?"

"No," he emphasized, "no, Elmer—sniffing."

"Sniffing?" Elmer stopped pounding tacks and looked up. "Sniffing what?"

Pudge jerked his head toward the front of the store. "That pretty wife of yours."

At that very moment, Happy Hanover honked the horn of his new lemon-yellow 1951 Cadillac Coupe de Ville as he slid it to a stop alongside the curb in front of the emporium. Elmer and Pudge heard the clamor and pulled back the leather curtain that covered the doorway between the shoe shop and storefront. They watched, not making a sound, not even breathing, as Happy got out of the car and made his way through the front entrance, heading directly to the back of the store where a smiling Ruby waited behind the counter, her face alight with an effervescent glow.

Happy cut a handsome, debonair figure in his perfectly tailored vanilla-ice-cream-white summer suit with a matching Panama fedora hat, the brim of which he held nonchalantly between the thumb and finger of his left hand. Elmer, imagining his own face streaked with shoeblack, looked himself up and down from his unpolished brown brogans, past his full-length leather apron, to the small streak of mustard on the rolled-up cuff of his blue chambray shirt. The comparison sent shivers of doubt up his spine, through his brain stem, into his frontal lobe where they awakened the green-eyed monster, the center of envy and jealousy. Not the brightest bulb in the chandelier, he was, nevertheless astute enough to know his empire was in danger of crumbling if Happy Hanover was allowed to sweep Ruby Rhinestone right off her three-inch crimson heels.

That night, after finishing the Friday night dinner dishes, Elmer laid down an ultimatum to the worrisome wench who had shared his bed for nearly a year. "I don't like that Happy Hanover strutting into the store like he owns the damn place."

Versed in subtle subterfuge regarding matters of the heart, Ruby responded with apparent equanimity. "I hadn't noticed."

"From now on, when he comes into the store, I'll wait on him."

"If that's what you want, sweetheart. Better yet, I'll just

tell Mr. Hanover we don't need his business." She tweaked Elmer's cheek. "I think my little hubby is jealous."

"I just don't want people thinking I'm dumb." He pulled the kitchen apron over his head and laid it across the towel rack.

"Oh, I don't think you need to worry about that, honey. Everyone tells me how bright you are."

That night, Elmer sighed with satisfaction as Ruby gently stroked his back, lulling him into a sense of serenity. Moments later, he was snoring. She eased herself from the bed, slipped quietly down the stairs, and dialed Happy Hanover on the living room phone.

THE FOLLOWING MONDAY, Ruby failed to show up for work at the emporium. Elmer offered no explanation for her absence. He took refuge in the shoe repair shop, leaving to Pudge the task of appeasing inquiring customers, eager to get a glance of the long-legged beauty.

By Tuesday, the venerable citizens of Steadfast were atwitter with speculation and gossip—Ruby Rhinestone had probably eloped with another man. And considering her less-than-desirable origins, most people believed the rampaging rumors well-founded. But the tongue-wagging and eyebrow-raising that had followed the marriage of Ruby and slow-witted Elmer were only rehearsals for what was to come. Predictably, the town folk were blessed with a desirably sordid situation when the Thursday morning headline blazed across the banner of the *Charleston Gazette:* **HANOVER HEIR MISSING.**

There was a sliver of satisfaction in Pudge's demeanor as he approached the workbench where a disconsolate Elmer sat. Pudge placed the newspaper, folded in half, headline up, onto the workbench. Elmer glanced at the headline but continued to trim excess leather from the new whole-soles of Clyde Colburn's army boots, survivors of the amphibious landing on Iwo Jima.

After a moment, he set the boots upright on the workbench and looked at the paper. A two-by-three, black-and-white photograph of Happy Hanover smiled back at him. He turned to his prospective new sales manager. "What's it say, Pudge?"

"Says here, 'The son of Harold Hanover, prominent founder and CEO of Hanover Hotels, Inc. is missing. Happy Hanover was last seen on Saturday afternoon according to a spokesman for the Hanover chain. The thirty-one-year-old has not communicated with his family since Friday evening. That is unlike Happy,' the spokesman stated.

The Charleston Police Department is leading the investigation into Mr. Hanover's disappearance. They are following a report that he was sighted at a filling station in Moncks Corner on Saturday afternoon. He was driving a yellow Cadillac Coupe de Ville and was accompanied by a dark-haired woman."

Pudge folded the paper to the back page. "There's more here; want me to read it?"

Elmer shook his head, picked up a bottle of shoeblack, and began staining the edges of the soles on Clyde's combat boots. "No," he said dejectedly, "I've heard enough."

The atmosphere at the emporium took on a morose personality. From behind the curtain, the thud, thud, thud of

Elmer's hammer struck a dirge upon the iron last. Out front, sales slumped as curiosity seekers replaced paying patrons. Absent were the men who once waited their turn for a chance to glimpse Ruby's red garters with tiny black bows as she straddled the fitting stool. Pudge, prissy and precise in his form-fitted pegged pants, his hair combed into a carefully styled ducktail, was poor compensation for the loss of Ruby. Despite his best efforts, he could not fill her shiny red shoes.

Melvin Magineaux backed his 1942 Ford Pickup down the boat ramp on the north side of Lake Moultrie. The slightly overcast sky and calm winds forecast a good Saturday of fishing. Behind Melvin's truck, his fourteen-foot bass boat trailer slowly eased into the lake. As the boat stern touched the water, the trailer came to an abrupt halt. Melvin gunned the engine, but the trailer stubbornly stood its ground. He turned off the engine and got out. As he peered into the translucent water, the sun broke through the clouds like a lightning bolt and reflected off a shiny object two feet below the surface.

By 10:00 a.m., Berkeley County Sheriff, Buford Billings, was on site with a squad of highly trained deputies. By 10:30, a scuba diver confirmed the submerged car contained two bodies, probably a man and a woman. By noon, the lemon-yellow Cadillac Coupe de Ville had been hauled onto the boat ramp and cordoned off to keep away the curious.

That afternoon, Elmer answered a knock at the door. Sheriff Billings doffed his cap and placed it under his arm. "Mr. Hatfield, can I come in?" He entered and stood stiffly as if preparing to make a rehearsed speech. "I'm afraid we have some bad news. We think we've found your wife's body in Lake Moultrie."

Elmer's face contorted with anguish. He sat, silent, his eyes shielded by his hands. A sob, and then another, ebbed from beneath his palms. Somehow, his tongue managed to push the words from his mouth. "What happened?"

"We think she drowned," the laconic sheriff replied. "We need you to come to the morgue in Charleston to make a positive identification."

The *Sunday Gazette* told the story, led by a three-inch bold headline: **HANOVER HEIR FOUND DEAD.** Happy Hanover, heir to the Hanover Hotel chain, was found dead in Lake Moultrie yesterday. He was reported missing on Tuesday. His submerged car was discovered by Melvin Magineaux of Monck's Corner. Berkley County Sheriff, Buford Billings, was called to the scene. His deputies recovered a 1951 Cadillac Coupe de Ville registered to Mr. Hanover. The car contained the bodies of Hanover and a female companion, later identified by Elmer Hatfield as his wife, Ruby Rhinestone Hatfield. Mr. Hatfield is the owner and proprietor of Hatfield's Shoe Repair and Emporium in Steadfast. The cause of death has not been determined.

Elmer read the *Gazette* story continuation on the second page. He took note of each detail, including the probable length of time the bodies had been in the water and the fact that Ruby was not wearing shoes. The paper quoted Mr. Magineaux. "I went fishing last Sunday, didn't pull my boat out until nearly dark. The car wasn't in the water then." The *Gazette* went on to say, "According to Sheriff Billings, Mr. Hanover's car must have been driven into the water Sunday night. The sheriff stated 'It's hard to see how the deaths are accidental. The investigation is continuing."

The town of Steadfast had the scandal it had longed for since Ruby Rhinestone crossed the railroad tracks and made her way to Hatfield's Shoe Repair and Emporium, smack dab into the middle of poor Elmer Hatfield's heart. The public consensus was that Elmer simply lost his simple mind when he learned Ruby was consorting with Happy Hanover, well-renowned playboy and reputed womanizer. People propagated as fact the theory that Elmer had deposited .38 caliber lead slugs in the skulls of Happy and Ruby before releasing the Coupe de Ville emergency brake. Such whispers made their way across Berkley County, into Charleston and its inner harbor, out to Fort Sumter. The suppositions and whispers were confirmed on Monday shortly after the coroner began his autopsies.

Hang down your head Tom Dooley
Hang down your head and cry
Hang down your head Tom Dooley
Poor Boy you're bound to die

- An old North Carolina ballad

JUSTICE MUST PREVAIL, or must it? Three years to the day, following Melvin Magineaux's discovery in Lake Moultrie, Elmer Hatfield received three jolts of electricity, each raising his buttocks off the wooden seat. His final phone call, a few hours before walking the long mile, was to the person he trusted most. "I want you to be here when it happens. You're the only real friend I have."

Pudge Parker's hands shook as he replaced the phone receiver. He nervously combed his ducktail nearly to perfection as he prepared for his two-hour drive to the state prison in Columbia. As he approached the door to leave his apartment, an image in the mirror over the dressing table caught his eye. He followed the reflection to a table by his bed. There, a pair of three-inch crimson heels sat, reflecting brilliant rays from the bedside lamp. Pudge slumped into a chair by the bed. For an instant, he thought of doing the right thing, of calling Sheriff Billings and confessing.

The shoes glistened. Pudge had wiped them clean, all the while imagining the straps wrapped about Ruby Rhinestone's trim ankles. He closed his eyes, clutching the patent leather straps to his chest. There was nothing he could do now but wait to hear of his friend's unhappy end.

Two days later, the professionally painted sign on the window read: PARKER'S SHOE REPAIR AND EMPORIUM. Among the wares on display below the sign was a pair of shiny crimson shoes.

2

IN FROM THE COLD

Say a prayer for all the boys who are men
too soon
Who never sleep on satin sheets nor eat from
silver spoons
Who answer first the nation's call whenever
danger looms
Who fall upon the battlefield and die of
mortal wounds

- Travis Short © 2017

James Curtis (JC) Mullins was vaguely aware of a country called Korea when he joined the Army in the early days of 1950. War on the Korean Peninsula had not begun. Thus, his reason for enlisting at seventeen was not to answer a clarion call, but rather to escape the hell of his existence. Whatever awaited him in the Army would be better than that. As he slipped away from home for the last time that February morning, he had no thought his decision was taking him to the frozen mountains of North Korea.

In the first days of summer, the North Korean Army attacked South Korea in a full-scale invasion all along the thirty-eighth parallel, which divided the two countries. The North quickly captured Seoul and drove UN and ROK, peacekeepers nearly into the sea. A defensive line called the Pusan Perimeter, was established at a radius of about one hundred thirty miles from the port of Pusan. There, United States, ROK, and British forces fought the North Koreans to a standstill for nearly two months. The US Calvary was rushed into battle, coming ashore on the southeast coast of Korea in late June. A few days later, PFC JC Mullins aimed his rifle to the north from somewhere on the Pusan Perimeter.

The Mullins boys trudged through the snow, their frosty breath chaffing their faces as they ran to get home before suppertime. They had lingered too long, warming themselves by the bonfire where the neighborhood kids gathered to ride their sleds. Ethel, their stepmother, waited near the chain-link gate. She wielded a long, willow stick. As the twelve-year-old Leroy ran past, his arms raised to fend off her blows as she slashed the switch across his back. He cried out but never broke his stride. JC continued slowly toward Ethel, delaying the inevitable confrontation as long as possible. By the time he neared the gate, he decided that if she struck him, he would choke her blind.

"Get in here, boy." Ethel raised the stick above her head. She shivered, her angry words turning to frozen mist in the cold evening air. She stepped toward JC, her shoulders hunched like the ruffled neck feathers of an angry wet hen.

God help me. If she hits me with that stick, I'll kill her. She must have seen the defiance in his eyes because she stopped two feet from him and lowered her arm. JC reached for the stick. She resisted, stepping away from the young man who towered above her. He wrenched the stick from her grasp, broke it across his knee, and tossed it into the snow. "No more, Ethel; you ain't goin' to ever hit me again."

"Just wait 'til your daddy gets home. You just wait." She turned and strode briskly to the gate, the snow clinging around her ankles. She stopped just inside the front yard. "You won't threaten your daddy, big boy."

Ethel's shrill words penetrated the walls of the house next door where Heather Bingham was frying chicken on the kitchen stove. She pushed the pan aside and walked to the window. She pulled back the curtain as Ethel was disappearing behind the Mullins's house. JC stood forlornly outside the fence. He shoved his hands into his jacket pockets and futilely kicked at the snow. He lifted his gaze to see Heather motioning for him to come inside.

Normalcy for the Mullins children ended six years earlier when they lost their mother to diabetes. Ethel married their docile father and changed their lives forever. An older brother and sister left home shortly after Ethel's arrival, leaving Leroy and JC to contend with her volatile moods. The severity of retribution for childish infractions increased each year as the boys grew older and more resentful. Heather

Bingham lived in fear that a catastrophe was brewing in the home next door.

She heard his boots on the back porch steps and met him at the door. "Come in, boy. You're just in time for supper."

He removed his wool cap and stood by the coal stove, warming his hands. "No thanks, Miss Heather. If you don't mind, I'll just warm myself 'til Daddy gets home, then I'll be goin'."

"Suit yourself, but I hope you know you're welcome." Heather set the dining room table then returned to the kitchen. "The boys will be coming home any minute. You sure you won't stay and eat with us?"

"I better go home hungry, or Ethel will have a conniption." He let go a deprecating laugh. "No one can stretch a story the way she can, and there's no tellin' what she'll say when Daddy gits home."

"What do you think he'll do?"

"I guess he'll give me a whippin'."

"Why?"

"'Cause he don't want to make Ethel mad at him."

"That isn't right," Heather spoke over her shoulder as she walked back into the dining room. "I feel like I should talk to your daddy."

"Please don't, Miss Heather. It would just make things worse."

"It isn't right," she said. "I won't say anything, but it isn't right."

JC eyed the crisp fried chicken warming on the stove. Its irresistible aroma wafted from the platter. He could almost taste the warm, savory meat. His arm reached toward the platter. His fingers grasped a drumstick. He did not consider the incongruity of his actions. Perhaps he had no capacity to do so. He did not ask himself why he refused Heather's invitation to dinner even though he was hungry enough to take the chicken when he thought she wasn't watching. Pilfering food from home had become a necessary habit, and stealing a piece of fried chicken seemed the natural thing to do. At least it would ease his hunger if Ethel refused him supper. He shoved the chicken into his jacket pocket. Almost immediately, he was filled with shame and regret. He wished he could put the chicken back onto the platter, but Heather returned to the kitchen and carried the plate to the dining room table before he could.

The Bingham family gathered around the table while JC lingered in the kitchen by the stove.

"You sure you won't join us, JC?" Heather bowed her head and waited for her husband to say grace.

"No thanks, Miss Heather. I'd better not."

Moments later, Heather heard the back door open and close. She got up from the table and watched from the window as JC walked slowly through the snow. Her heart ached for the boy, guessing what lay in store for him at home. She smiled as she thought of the drumstick in his jacket pocket. She hoped it might keep him from going to bed hungry.

While the Eighth Calvary and other forces were holding the North Koreans at bay on the Pusan Perimeter, General Douglas McArthur planned for an amphibious assault behind enemy lines. In September, the Americans staged a surprise landing at Inchon on the west coast of South Korea. They captured Seoul and headed north, toward the 38th parallel and the North Korean capital, Pyongyang. The First Calvary regiments were ordered to break out of Pusan and join the march north. With enemy forces scattering before the American advances, McArthur set his sights on the Yalu River lying between North Korea and China. If he could reach the banks of the Yalu, the entire Korean Peninsula would be under United Nations control.

"Get off your asses, boys; we're movin' out in a couple of hours." Sergeant Masters tossed his cigarette butt into a muddy puddle and blew his nose onto the ground, first one side then the other. "Get your vehicles and weapons checked out."

Corporal Kelly stood quickly, lifted his poncho, and straightened his coat. "Christ, I was just gettin' comfortable. Where we goin', Sarge?"

"China," the Sergeant laughed. He fingered a piece of paper in his top field jacket pocket, withdrawing the note with his thumb and forefinger. He shook the paper so it unfolded and waved in the brisk northern breeze.

JC fastened the second buckle on his boots then stood. He rubbed his arms vigorously to get blood flowing, then slipped the M1 strap over his shoulder. "Which way's China?" A perpetual smile belied the sincerity of his question.

"You just go in the direction I point, Mullins, and you'll get there soon enough." The Sergeant motioned with his arm in the air. "Gather 'round boys." The troops moved in close enough to hear. The sergeant was quiet for a moment then he read the paper just taken from his pocket.

"First Calvary has been ordered to break through Unsan and get to the Yalu before the hard winter sets in. Eighth Regiment will move along the main road with H Company out front. Reconnaissance reports only scattered resistance, so it shouldn't be much of a fight. We will take out any batteries we encounter in and around Unsan. Mop up in the city will be left for the infantry."

"How far away are we, Sarge?" Corporal Kelly asked.

"Fifteen miles to Unsan then about sixty miles to the Yalu. When we get into the mountains, weather will be a bitch. There's no cold weather gear to issue. So, if you got extra Long Johns, get them on before we pull out."

Moans went up. "Knock it off, guys. Ain't any use to whine." The sergeant was a no-nonsense soldier. He carried out his orders and expected the same of his men. "We got a job to do. With any luck, we'll be thumbin' our noses at the chinks across the Yalu by the end of November."

JC pulled his wool-lined cap down over his ears and fastened the buckle under his chin. He turned to Corporal Kelly. "What day of the month is this, Charlie? I've lost track."

"The twenty-ninth, I think. What difference does it make, Mullins? You got someplace else you'd rather be?"

"No. No, I don't. I guess that's why I'm here. I guess that's why we're all here."

Engines sputtered and gurgled as they came up to idle speed. "Saddle up." The word rippled across the front line like slow-moving thunder. H Company tanks began to roll along a road heading northwest. JC and Corporal Kelly ran to take their position alongside the forward tank.

On the morning of October thirty-first, US forces

advanced beyond Unsan. That evening, word came down that ROK troops, positioned nearly four miles to the north, were under heavy attack by North Korean troops. By the time the Calvary reached the ROK the next afternoon, they had been pushed back more than a mile and were retreating toward Unsan. The tank formation stopped. A call from the command vehicle sent Sergeant Masters scrambling toward the rear. After a half hour, he returned to the lead tank and called for his crews to gather around. "Word is that PRC soldiers have been sighted fighting alongside the North Koreans. We need to find out what's waiting for us up ahead." He put two fingers to his lips and whistled. Moments later, PFC Art Prevost skidded his Jeep to a halt alongside the sergeant.

"Corporal Kelly, you and Mullins see the hill over there?" The sergeant pointed to a foothill, two thousand yards away. He didn't wait for an answer from Kelly. "Prevost will drive and wait in the Jeep while you guys get up the ridge to see what is on the other side. Look for any troop movements along the road from the north. I want to know what kind of uniforms the yellow bastards are wearin'. Get back before dark. We saddle up at 2200."

It was dusk before the patrol started back down the hill. Snow was beginning to fall. The radio hanging from Corporal Kelly's neck crackled with static. He stopped and pressed his lips to the mike. "Prevost, call the Sarge. Nothing to report. Don't see any movement at all." He hurried his gait in the direction of the awaiting Jeep.

"Hear that?" JC stopped walking, then ran back up the ridge for another look through his field glasses. He was a hundred feet from Corporal Kelly. "Listen. A fox horn." JC pointed over the hill to the north. He had heard the sound many times as hunters called their fox hounds in the hills of eastern Kentucky.

Kelly cupped his hands. "I didn't hear nothin'."

JC peered through the field glasses. Soldiers in black uniforms swarmed like ants three miles ahead of H Company. An amorphous black fog of human forms spread along the roadway and across the valley. JC's heart thumped. *Chinese.*

Corporal Kelly was now two hundred feet away and still heading down the hill. JC called to him and pointed to the northwest. "Chinese, Chinese. Get down."

JC dropped to his knees and crawled to a thicket of small evergreen bushes. When he looked up again, he could no longer see Corporal Kelly. Explosions in the vicinity of the Jeep told him the Chinese had spotted Prevost. JC peered through his binoculars. Prevost sped away. *I hope Kelly made it to the Jeep in time.*

Bugles wailed again as the Chinese swarmed toward Unsan. The lights of American tanks and other vehicles moved back down the road they had traveled the previous night. With deepening shadows obscuring the valley below, JC pressed himself to the ground and waited for his paralyzing fear to pass.

During the night, the wind turned bitter. He shivered under the brush he had pulled over him for warmth. When morning came, he scanned the road toward Unsan for signs of his company but saw only abandoned tanks, armored vehicles, and trucks. Thousands of Chinese troops advanced toward Unsan.

JC turned into the woods and followed the sloping ridge

up the mountain. He thought it would eventually lead eastward and place him behind friendly lines. Then, by going south, he would rejoin the remnants of the Eighth Calvary. He could not have known their hasty retreat was taking them further and further away from his position with thousands of Chinese soldiers in his intended path. Emptiness gnawed at his stomach. He shook his canteen. *A couple of drinks. No use wastin' it.* He put a handful of snow to his mouth. It had been more than eighteen hours since he last smoked. A cigarette might ease his hunger. Slumping against a fir tree, he pulled a pack of Lucky Strikes from his field jacket. Moments later, he got back on his feet and moved up the ridge. In the distance, blasts of the 75MM Howitzers told him the US tanks had slowed their retreat and turned to fight the advancing Chinese attackers.

After sunset, JC stumbled through snow-covered underbrush until darkness made it impossible to go on. Crouching between two large boulders, he covered himself with his poncho. He slept in fits, kept awake by a battle raging somewhere north of Pyongyang and the howl of a cold wind blowing across the ridge. Sometimes, in the dark, he fumbled at his canteen with frigid fingers only to find the water was frozen solid. He attempted to wiggle his toes but couldn't feel them move. The thought of frostbite and amputation spurred him to sit upright. *Keep movin', JC. Keep movin'.* He forced his arms and legs into motion, but gradually grew tired and drifted into a troubled sleep.

With the first light of day, he awoke and stood to get his bearings. Snowfall had continued through the night. Wind whipped at his body like the blade of a cold steel scythe. His eyes searched the surrealistic surroundings as he considered his options. He might not make it through another night on the inhospitable mountain. If he traveled directly south, he would almost certainly be captured by the Chinese. He decided to continue eastward for the remainder of the day, gradually moving down the hillside. The next morning, he would take his chances and begin walking southward, following the retreating American forces toward Pyongyang. The sun remained hidden behind low, gray clouds all day as he pushed through snowdrifts and underbrush. His steps were slow and deliberate as he crossed the rocky terrain. By late afternoon, he was too hungry and exhausted to walk further. He looked around for shelter for the night. Up the hill, fifty feet was a rock formation covered with shrubs and scrub bushes. He fell to his knees and crawled toward the rocks. His hands shivered in the bitter cold as he pushed his body into a crevice under an overhang. The evening sun moved west around the mountain. Cold penetrated his clothing. He readied his rifle, resting it in the branches of the shrub, the trigger half an arm's length away. Maybe he would have the strength to reach the gun if the chinks found him. Then he lost track of morning and night. In his lucid moments, he was unsure how long he had been on the mountain.

He listened for voices and steps in the snow but heard only his own shallow breathing. As his eyelids grew heavy, he attempted to move his arms. He looked at the M-1 poised in the shrubs. *Useless.* He attempted to pray to a God he had not relied on since he was twelve. *The Lord is my shepherd; I shall not want.* He could not think of what came next. His mind turned to frivolous delirium. *She'll be comin' round the mountain when she comes. She'll be comin.* He rested his chin on his chest.

He opened his eyes and realized he had made it through the night. Footsteps sounded in the snow and dry underbrush. "That you, Ethel?" She held a stick over her head. "That you, Ethel?" He waited to hear her shrill voice, but she never spoke. The stick came toward him. He tried in vain to ward off her blow. The cold steel bayonet pierced his chest just below his heart. He grunted at the initial discomfort but was unable to cry out. As the blade was pulled away, he felt warm blood running onto his stomach. Someone smiled at him. *That you, Miss Heather?* The aroma of chicken frying on the stove filled his nostrils. He saw his immobile hand move toward the platter. A second thrust of the Chinese soldier's blade found its mark. JC looked up to see Heather Bingham, smiling, waving at him through the window, beckoning him to come in from the cold.

Author's note: A few months after I wrote this story, I learned that JC's remains had been found in South Korea and received by his brother in North Carolina for burial. I wrote the following tribute to JC:

A Prayer for JC Mullins

Today, I have good news—heartbreaking news, but nonetheless, good news. PFC James Curtis (JC) Mullins, US Army, deceased, came home to rest. After sixty-two years in the ground somewhere near Pusan, South Korea, his bones were recovered and returned to the US. On Friday, November 2nd, he was buried with full military honors in the Sandhills State Veterans Cemetery in Spring Lake, North Carolina. He is survived only by an older brother, Clayton, who also served in the bitter conflict in Korea in the early 1950s.

I was a small boy when JC left home. His younger brother, Leroy, was my best friend; he died at age 44 of diabetes. Over the years, I have remembered Leroy and JC with great fondness, and I was often haunted by thoughts of JC, who was listed as missing in action until last week. My memories of him compelled me to write a story titled, *In from the Cold,* which I posted on FanStory last year, and which was nominated for Story of the Month.

In from the Cold is a fictionalized account of JC's four months of war, ending in the frozen mountains of North Korea. In truth, he died fighting on the Pusan Perimeter on July 22, 1950, twenty days after wading ashore and only a few days after his seventeenth birthday. However, the premise and events of a hellish life at home which drove him to falsify his birth certificate and join the Army, are demonstrative if not entirely factual. Like so many other unfortunate young men who have died in our wars, JC saw the Army as his only hope of escape. That escape was to oblivion until last week.

I began the story, I*n from the Cold*, with the following verse:

Say a prayer for all the boys who are men
too soon

Who never sleep on satin sheets nor eat from
silver spoons
Who answer first the nation's call whenever
danger looms
Who fall upon the battlefield and die of
mortal wounds

The name of Private First Class James Curtis Mullins is inscribed in the Courts of the Missing at the Honolulu Memorial in Hawaii. But he is no longer among the missing. He has come home. If he had lived, he would now be seventy-nine years old. Instead, he will forever be as he appears in the only known picture of him in uniform at age seventeen.

I pray that his young soul is finally at peace.

3

REVIVAL

There I was at nineteen, cold, broke, and hungry, standing alongside a backroad somewhere near Abingdon, Virginia, a beat-up Yamaha acoustic guitar flung across my back and my thumb stuck out. A bearded dude with whiskey breath and nostril-clearing body odor had dropped me off an hour earlier in downtown Abingdon and pointed me up a road that "will take you to Norton and get you back on US 23," according to him. He said his name was Jake. Jake didn't tell me his last name and I didn't ask. Later, out of boredom I suppose, he volunteered that women had caused him a peck of trouble, and he was just happy to be heading toward Abingdon and home. When I asked what kind of trouble, he shrugged and said, "Never mind, my friend. Just be happy no woman has her hooks in you."

The passenger side window of his thirty-year-old Ford pickup truck was broken out. The piece of cardboard, duct-taped to the door, almost prevented a brisk wind from blowing away my face. Still, I was mighty grateful for the ride all the way from Roanoke but happy to breathe untainted air once I was outside the truck.

After more than an hour of dragging along the two-lane highway northwest of Abingdon, I was hoping Jake would happen my way again, and this time, I would be more grateful. At that moment of despair, a white 1997 Cadillac Deville rounded the curve and pulled to a stop thirty feet ahead of me. I sprinted toward the car as the guy on the passenger side reached across his seat and opened the back door. He motioned for me to get in. I was out of breath as I shoved my guitar across the seat and climbed in after it.

"You guys are lifesavers," I grunted.

"Soul savers too." The passenger swung his hand in my direction, and I grasped it gladly.

"Brother Charles Mason," he said, then nodding his head at the driver, "And this is Brother Jim Dickson. Mason and Dixon, he laughed, and I got the connection. We're doing the Lord's work. How about you, Son? What do you do?"

The driver turned his head and glanced at me, kinda checked me out, but didn't speak.

"Well, to be honest," I hesitated, choosing my words carefully, thinking I might be in the presence of two of God's chosen people. I didn't want to shade the truth too much. But I most certainly didn't tell them there was a guy by the name of George Gleason with a shotgun in Murfreesboro, Tennessee, attempting to make me a reluctant son-in-law—me or anyone else he might convince to marry his pregnant daughter, Georgette. "Well, not much right now, just wanting to get back home to Neon, Kentucky. Been up to Nashville, trying to make it big, but ..."

Charlie broke in, smiling broadly. "What's your name, Son? You a singer? Sing any spirituals?"

I answered his questions in succession. "Jesse Black. I am a singer, but apparently not a very good one. I do sing a few spirituals, "The Church in the Wildwoods" and "Old Country Church" and some Hank Williams stuff. Guess I'm too old-fashioned for country fans today."

The driver spoke without looking my way, his voice a deep baritone. "That's good enough for us. Heck, we're just two ole country boys ourselves. I grew up in Chattanooga, Tennessee, and Charlie there comes from Columbus, Georgia." I could imagine his compelling voice holding a congregation spellbound while delivering a fire and brimstone soliloquy.

"Where you guys headed now? Anywhere near Neon, Kentucky? You know where that is?" I asked.

"Sure do. We're going to Whitesburg, Kentucky," Charlie said.

"Great. That's twelve miles from Neon. Can't believe I got so lucky."

He turned to look at me. "There is no such thing as luck or coincidences. Everything is in God's plan. For instance, we just finished a most successful revival in the city behind you, Abingdon. You must believe it was in God's plan that we would happen along just when you need a helping hand. No coincidence. None of it happened by chance."

I pondered that bit of wisdom for a moment.

He continued. "We're holding a revival for a week at the Freewill Baptist Church of Whitesburg. We could use some old-fashioned music for the services if you are up to it." His voice was a little higher pitched than Jim's, but I could imagine him in the pulpit, whipping the church sisters into a frenzy. They were both tall and handsome, well-dressed dudes, and I figured that by the end of the week, there would be singing and shouting and soul-saving and sites worth seeing—sounded like fun to me.

"I might like that, but I'm not much of a churchgoer." It then occurred to me that I might have said the wrong thing to a couple of preachers by admitting I didn't go to church, and I wished I hadn't made that confession, at least not until we reached Whitesburg. But it was too late, and I half expected the car to come to a halt and I would find myself back on the roadside hoping the smelly Good Samaritan from Abingdon would give me another lift, at least to the Kentucky state line.

Jim smiled into the rearview mirror. "Sounds like you just need some working on, and that's the business we're in."

"I'll give it a shot," I said. "Do I get paid?" That was something else I wish I had not said until we got to Whitesburg. But I was broke and desperate, even desperate enough to spend every evening for a whole week in church. So, as a precaution, I added, "A few bucks, maybe?"

"You'll share in the collection plate, just as Charlie and I do."

I folded my arms and sat back against the seat, relaxing for the first time in more than a week. It was great to be employed.

Acquaintances made and a business deal struck, we sped along the highway without any further conversation for five or six minutes. Then Charlie breached the silence, reaching across the seat and slapping my arm. "Play something for us. Can you do "Amazing Grace"?"

I unzipped my guitar case, checked the tuning, then

struck a D chord and began to sing. The two preachers joined in, and we sang all the way to the Kentucky line. I praised the Lord as we descended Jenkins Mountain and turned left in the direction of Whitesburg. I was almost home.

~

WHEN I WAS YOUNG, my mother attended Freewill Baptist church near Neon. That made me, my brother, and two sisters members of that church by default.

Revivalists would often come to our town, especially in the spring or fall when the weather was at its best. Some, not sponsored by any local church, pitched tents and stayed for a month at a time, collecting souls and dollars for service in the army of the Lord. Other itinerant preachers were invited to local churches. They would take over the collection plate for the whole week. I assumed that was the usual length of time God allotted to rescue the sinners in our little southeast Kentucky town. However, it goes without saying, that their efforts were wasted on the hardworking and hard-drinking coal miners who had better use for a pleasant Saturday night. They sinned all the time, revivalists be damned.

Revivals always ended when the flood of collections dwindled to a small trickle. Naturally, the final evening of the revival culminated with one of the church ladies becoming possessed, shouting, and speaking in tongues. When the shouting was over, these women, somehow, regained their sensibilities enough to praise the revivalists and plead for generous donations to help send the preachers on their soul-saving quest to the next little unsuspecting town. And for us few believers, like the few of Sodom and Gomorrah, we knew that when Neon lapsed again into sinning, God would send another revivalist our way. By that reasoning, I assumed that Whitesburg must now be one hell of a sinful place since God was sending Brother Charlie and Brother Jim to save all those lost souls from hell rather than destroying the city by fire.

Most people might think that with such experiences and quasi-expert knowledge, I would have been more wary of the company into which I had just fallen. But I was only nineteen, and like most nineteen-year-olds, I would have sold my soul for a chance at stardom, no matter how fleeting. Even in retrospect, it seems reasonable that I could not bring myself to be suspicious of Charlie and Jim. They were such decent guys. And I was going to be on stage—well sorta—for a whole week. Something I was never able to accomplish at the Bluebird Café in Nashville. So, I discounted all I knew and suspected about itinerant preachers, and I kept on singing "I Saw the Light" until we reached Whitesburg.

Two and a half hours after leaving Abingdon, we were parked in front of the Freewill Baptist Church. Jim got out, yawned, and stretched his arms toward the heavens. Moments later, the front door to the church opened and a fat, balding little man appeared. He made his way down the steps, his hand outstretched as he came. "I'm Pastor Art Caldwell."

"Jim Dickson," Jim said, shaking the pastor's hand vigorously. Pointing at the car, he continued. "And that's Brother Charles Mason, Charlie, and our music man, Jesse Black. Jesse hasn't been with us long but is a dedicated Christian we are proud to have as part of our team. He's from Neon, a local boy who gave up a promising career and sinful life in Nashville to join us on the road, saving souls for Jesus."

"Praise the Lord," said Pastor Caldwell. "Welcome to our humble little church."

After getting acquainted with the preacher and seeing the inside of his small church and activities building, I was ready to head for Neon. But Pastor Caldwell insisted that I go along with him and my two preacher companions to meet Sister Mitzi Malone, a young widow who owned a large home, having lost her contractor husband, twice her age, to a heart attack just two years earlier. Since Sister Mitzi was the church pianist, the pastor was certain she would want to get acquainted with the revivalist guitar player and singer, that being me. And after seeing the thirty-five-year-old with blond hair down to her tailbone, I thought it was a good idea also.

Sister Mitzi allowed as how, since she had three extra guestrooms, there was no reason at all for me to travel to Neon every day and return for evening church services, especially since there was only one car available to the traveling evangelist team. When I heard her slow sugar-sweet dialect that sounded more like she came from south Alabama than southeastern Kentucky, I agreed completely with her incredibly reasonable assessment.

After settling our living arrangements for the week, I borrowed Jim's car and drove to Neon to visit with my family for a couple of hours before returning for the evening services. I was hoping to get a meal of my mother's pinto beans and cornbread, along with a slice of onion and some buttermilk if I was lucky. Of course, I also got the usual inquisition to which mothers always subject their sons who have been away from home for a period longer than a week. She alerted me that she had been contacted by a gentleman from Murfreesboro, Tennessee about a *serious matter*, which, according to my mother, he didn't explain.

"Are you in trouble, Son?"

"Of course not, Mom." I reassured her by adding, "I'm doing God's work now. How can I be in trouble?"

That brought a smile to her face which was still there as I waved goodbye from the preachers' car.

I was back in Whitesburg more than an hour before the revival began, in time to tune my guitar, strike a few chords, and harmonize, just a little, with Sister Mitzi on the piano. When we found the sound almost as good as The Gaithers, we headed for the church, loaded for bear.

WE BEGAN the first night's service with songs Sister Mitzi and I had practiced earlier. First was "Because He Lives," followed by "Blessed Assurance" then "Amazing Grace," done at the request of Reverend Jim Dickson. Brother Charles took to the dais and warmed the congregation, which apparently had already been spiritually awakened by the fine piano and guitar combo and rapturous vocals provided by Sister Mitzi and me. I was feeling gloriously blessed, carried away by the angelic singing of Sister Mitzi followed by the uplifting sermon delivered by Reverend Dickson. By the end of the service, I had almost dismissed my opinion that I was in the company of two well-dressed, handsome scoundrels. And as Sister Mitzi and I launched into "Just As I Am," the congregation flooded the altar, kneeling, speaking in tongues, and praising the name of their redeemer. That night, we collected more than two hundred dollars.

For the next four nights, everything proceeded just as the first, with reverends Mason and Dickson providing alternating sermons. I had been in the presence of some powerful country preaching before, but nothing that came close to what I witnessed that week. I wasn't keeping track but was certain we had done well with the collection plate. By the last night of the revival, word of the miracles taking place at Whitesburg Freewill Baptist Church had spread to nearby towns, including Neon, so I wasn't surprised to see my mother coming through the door for that last service, On her arm was a young girl I recognized as Georgette Gleason, and following behind them was none other than her papa, George, but thankfully, he wasn't carrying his shotgun.

My mother waved a finger in my direction. "Young man," she yelled above the din of the congregation. "You lied to me. This pretty little girl came all the way from Tennessee to find you. She's carrying your baby, and I intend for you to do the right thing." If I had to guess, I would assume my mother's attitude regarding such matters resulted from the fact that she was pregnant with me when my own papa was marched to the altar with a shotgun at his back.

I leaned down and whispered to Sister Mitzi, "Play louder." I strummed hard on my guitar and she banged the piano keys. We harmonized beautifully: "Just as I am without one plea except thy blood is shed for me. Oh, Lamb of God, I come." My guess was that not many people had ever heard such a loud rendition of "Just As I Am." I was determined that no one in the congregation would hear my mother as she made her way toward the altar. At that moment, Reverend Charles stepped forward, raised his arms, and looked toward the heavens, a saintly sight indeed. The congregation broke out in uproarious shouting, and Sister Mitzi and I played and sang louder.

The singing and shouting had a miraculous effect, even with Miss Georgette. Her eyes widened as she ran toward Brother Charles. She began to shout louder than anyone else. The congregation quieted to hear the confessions of the young stranger in their midst. And since Baptists want to hear confessions of sins worse than their own, they all turned toward Georgette as she laid out a scenario of a sordid young life and ended by begging Brother Charles to bless her. I didn't care two damns about her confession except the part where she exonerated me for her current predicament. "I have sinned," she said, pointing at me. "This poor boy is not responsible for my condition. My daddy knows I lied. I hope he will repent just as I have." She looked at me, her hands outstretched, pleading. "Please forgive me, Jesse." Which I did, willingly.

AFTER THE SERVICE, the preachers and I returned to Sister Mitzi's for our last night. We reckoned we had collected more than a thousand dollars and would split our take the next morning. The sister served cold fried chicken she had prepared before the service. She was so sweet and genteel, and the preachers so gracious, I kinda took the fellowship we had around her dining room table as something akin to The

Last Supper. I went to sleep more contented than I had been in days. Despite my misgivings about Reverends Charlie and Jim, I was convinced they were, indeed, doing the Lord's work, and I was grateful to have been a part of it.

Shortly after midnight, I heard a car crank in the driveway. As I made my way to the front door, wiping sleep from my eyes, through the window, I saw the headlights of a car backing onto the street. I opened the door in time to see the taillights of a 1997 Cadillac as it left skid marks on the pavement. I turned back into the house and checked the other guest rooms. There was no sign of Charlie or Jim. I thought about all the times my mother told me, "Son, when you lie down with dogs, you're liable to get fleas."

I went to my room and packed my bag. I thought it might be the right thing to do, stopping by Sister Mitzi's room to explain why I was leaving. I knocked lightly on her door and waited.

"Who's there?" Her voice was that of a southern angel.

"It's Jesse," I said. "I need to talk with you."

She opened the door, and right there before me was the angel I had heard a moment earlier, everything but a halo, which I knew she was earning in the service of the Lord. "Can I help you, Jesse?"

"I don't think so, Sister Mitzi. I don't guess anyone can. Just wanted to let you know that Brother Charles and Brother Jim have skipped out on me."

"Oh my God," she lamented as she opened her door wider and pulled me close to her. "You poor boy."

I stood for several seconds that seemed like minutes, not knowing how to respond. After a few moments, I reciprocated, putting my arms around her waist. She stood on her tiptoes and kissed my cheek. I felt her hand as she reached for mine and led me toward her bed. "You poor boy," she said again.

The next morning, we had breakfast. Not much was said between us. When she began clearing the table, I spoke up. "Guess I should be getting back to Neon."

"Yes," she said, "that might be best. But you'll come back and see me, won't you?"

It was Sunday morning; not much traffic was on the highway. A chill was still in the air. I kept thinking about Sister Mitzi. God knows I wanted to see her again, but I realized what happened between us was a once-in-a-lifetime thing, maybe for both of us. Nothing would ever come of it, and I did not wish to harm her standing in the church she was devoted to. My thoughts were interrupted by the sound of an oncoming truck. It looked familiar, and when I saw cardboard taped to the passenger side window, I had no doubt it was Jake, the Good Samaritan, and I had no doubt God sent him my way. There are no coincidences.

He opened the passenger door. "Get in, boy." And I did.

Holding my guitar between my legs, I shook his hand. "You show up again just when I need you. What in hell are you doing in Whitesburg, Jake?"

"I'm looking for my girl."

"She lives here?"

"No. She lives in Murfreesboro, Tennessee, but I know she was here in Whitesburg last night, and I thought she might still be here."

"Man, you must really love this girl."

"I do," he said, "and she's pregnant with my baby. I done

a lot of bad things in my life and running off and leaving her in Murfreesboro was the worst."

There were many things I wanted to say, but I wasn't about to speak of my narrow escape from the buckshot from Gerald Gleason's shotgun. The best I could happily manage was, "Why'd you change your mind?"

"Well, you know, God tells you what is right. When I got to Abingdon, I found out my whole family got religion. Guess there was a revival, and two preachers—I think their names was Mason and Dickson—saved half our town, including my momma, my daddy, my two sisters, and my youngest brother. And when I heard about that, I got religion too. Changed my whole outlook on life; made me want to do the right thing about Georgette."

"Damn," I said, "They must have been some kinda good preachers."

"Hot dog; they was." He slapped my leg. "Show me the way, Jesse, and I'll drive you home."

As we made our way toward Neon, we said little to each other, but my head was reeling with all kinds of thoughts, from glee to astonishment. When Jake stopped the truck at my front gate, we shook hands. "You know, Jesse," he said, "you should get religion too."

I thought about it for a few moments. "I just might," I said, "especially, if I ever meet up with the reverends Mason and Dickson."

4

MISS JANE'S SACRIFICE

"Why haven't you ever remarried, Miss Jane?" I asked, looking up at the attractive fifty-year-old widow from the top step of her front porch.

"I don't know." Her eyes shifted away from mine. "I suppose it's because there aren't very many men like my husband."

She appeared to ponder her response for a few moments, then asked, "What about you? Why haven't you ever married?"

"Oh, Miss Jane," I said with a hint of a laugh, "that is a story all by itself."

She laughed too, as she got up from the porch swing. "Care to come in for some iced tea, Eric?"

"No, but thank you, sweet lady; I have half a dozen more stops before I'm finished today, and it's already past two."

With that, I picked up my briefcase and walked to my car. Just before sliding into the driver's seat, I raised my voice for her to hear. "See you soon."

I was surprised when she yelled back at me, cupping her hands around her mouth, "Come by this weekend if you can." By then, I was closing the car door, but still heard her unexpected invitation.

I rolled down the window halfway. "Sure. See you Saturday?"

She nodded.

I backed the car onto the dirt and graveled road. She stood on the porch, still looking in my direction as I drove away. We exchanged waves. I watched her in the rearview mirror until she was out of sight, lost in the dust rising from the disappearing road behind me.

I had known Jane Willbanks and her husband, Harmon, all my life. My family's twenty-acre Georgia dirt farm was only three miles from theirs. For years, Harmon Willbanks—like my father—made a meager living—planting peanuts, corn, and potatoes in the infertile red clay that passed for farmland. But as my father had said many times, what the farms in our area yielded most of all was dirt.

When the South Georgia Tractor Works set up an assembly plant five miles outside our town, my father and Harmon Willbanks were the first two employees hired. That was about the time the Willbanks' only son, Trace, was lost at sea, reportedly washed overboard from the deck of a Navy destroyer. The next year, Mr. Willbanks died of cancer, leaving his wife, Jane, to live alone, a widow at forty-six.

After her husband's death, at my mother's insistence, I frequently stopped by to check on Mrs. Willbanks. She had few friends, and as she often said, preferred it that way. Gossip and minding the business of other people were things she assiduously avoided. My regular monthly calls on her commenced when I began working for Serenity Rest Funeral Home, selling and collecting payments for cemetery plots and mausoleum vaults. My mother thought the job would be perfect for me because of my sweet disposition, as she put it, and my gentle heart. But if I, indeed, exhibited these traits, they belied the turmoil and confusion in my heart and mind that I had attempted to understand and resolve since I was thirteen.

At eight, I wanted to play with girls' toys and dress up in my mother's silk nightgowns. Even at that age, I understood these tendencies were not normal and that my parents would be disappointed in me if they knew of my latent urges. I was not like other children, and I knew it. As I approached thirteen, most boys my age had school sweethearts and stole kisses on the playground. I longed to experience special feelings for a girl too, but I couldn't. Instead, I developed a crush on my best friend, David Struthers. When I expressed my feelings, he called me "faggot." Afterward, I avoided close friendships with boys. I would hear the words, "faggot" and "queer" and other abhorrent names many times before my graduation from high school.

My two older brothers, Jess and Will Jr., were typical Georgia boys. Football, pickup trucks, and hunting were their natural obsessions. Beer and girls came later. But none of those things ever interested me. My father enthusiastically supported the achievements of Jess and Will. He took less pride in my prowess at the piano or the still life oil paintings my mother proudly displayed on her kitchen walls. He never uttered an unkind word to me, but I always knew I was a disappointment to him. Not my mother though; she never missed an opportunity to praise my talents or to tell me how special I was.

At fifteen, I concluded I was homosexual, but I never told anyone. I was determined that I would not demean myself by expressing my feelings for a boy. I harbored these secrets, prayed about them. I immersed myself in religion, attending church every Sunday. Our pastor preached against the practices of homosexuality, sodomy, and other sexual abominations. He was emphatic in his assertions that such aberrant behavior was by choice and could be overcome through faith in Jesus Christ. I prayed that God would redeem me and make me normal like other people. Yet, I questioned why God created me—why He cursed me with such imperfections. My frustrations continued, leading me into periods of deep depression. A just God could not have been so cruel. Ultimately, I rejected the church teaching and accepted the fact that I was an atheist as well as a homosexual, and that no God had a part in my creation or confused existence.

For me, there are few fond memories of high school. By attempting to forget the cruel and unhappy experiences of that period, I have sublimated even the pleasantries and successes I might have had. I tried to lose myself in art, music, and literature, but none of these were substitutes for the hunger I had for love and affection. I longed for someone to understand me, to have the same feelings as me. When I discovered that person, my life was even more complicated, for neither of us could freely express our feelings. Our relationship was always platonic because both of us feared venturing into a forbidden sexual abyss from which we could never return.

~

I WAS NOT surprised by Jane Willbanks's invitation, but something was unsettling about her impulsive request. The tone of her voice? The inflection? I wasn't sure. Miss Jane was usually a very deliberate and cautious woman. Maybe it was not impulsive after all. Perhaps she had been thinking about something the entire afternoon and overcame her reluctance to speak of it at the last moment. "Come by this weekend if you can." After I drove away from her, and all week long, I had a recurring suspicion that we would have a conversation about something we had evaded for nearly six years.

"I fixed us some lunch," she said as I walked up the steps to her front porch. I had called an hour earlier to let her know I would be there about noon.

"Just as Mother says, you keep spoiling me," I protested as I put my arms around her and kissed her on the cheek. She opened the screen door, and I followed her into the house.

Two plates were set at the kitchen table. "Not much—sandwiches and a salad. I thought we might take a walk around the place after we eat. I have something I want to talk to you about."

I sat down without looking at her again until she was seated at the table across from me. I knew my face would be giving away my inquisitiveness even though I could not put my thoughts into words. I had an urge to ask her what she wanted to talk about, but before I could ask, she sensed my anxiety and attempted to put me at ease.

"My gosh, Eric, you look as if you just lost your best friend. Something I said bother you?"

"No, Miss Jane. I guess you just took me by surprise."

"Don't worry," she said, "I want to talk business."

"Business?" I laughed. "I thought you wanted to talk about my sex life, and it scared the devil out of me."

"We may get around to that," she said, laughing too, "but I have something much more important on my mind at the moment."

After lunch, she donned a straw hat and headed out the door toward the barn with me following closely behind. We walked along the corridor between stalls that once held Harmon Willbanks's workhorses and an Appaloosa mare, Kitty's Pride. The workhorses had been sold long ago. Kitty's Pride—*too old to ride, t*oo precious to sell, as Miss Jane put it—roamed the open pasture by day and spent nights in one of the stalls. Of all the farm equipment owned by Mr. Willbanks, only a Caterpillar tractor and accessories remained, parked at the end of the corridor. When our tour of the barn was completed, we walked along the wooden fence that stretched for half a mile in front of the property. Most of the enclosed thirty acres were once farmland, but the only evidence of farming now was a small garden spot with a few tomatoes and peas growing on the vines.

As we strolled toward the porch after our walk was completed, Miss Jane took hold of my arm, stopped walking, and looked up at me. "We wanted to leave this little farm to Trace." She hesitated. "But there is no one now."

I could see that the conversation was one she really did not want to have. Embracing her for a moment, I said, "I'm so sorry, Miss Jane."

"It's alright." She patted my shoulder reassuringly. "I have learned to accept things as they are."

"Me too, and, believe me, sometimes it has not been easy." I wanted to tell her much more but thought it best to let the moment pass.

Then she said abruptly, as if she had been poised to reveal a secret as soon as the opportunity presented itself, "I have to change my will. I have put it off so long. Would you believe that it has not been changed since Trace was a teenager? And so much has happened." Her voice trailed. "Harmon was still alive then."

"Can I help you in some way? You know, you probably need a lawyer." "Yes, I'm seeing an attorney next week."

We resumed our slow walk back toward the front porch. Moments after we had seated ourselves, she said, very matter-of-factly with no emotion in her voice, "I'm leaving everything to you."

"No, Miss Jane, I couldn't . . ."

"Yes. It's what I want to do."

"But why?"

"I have my reasons."

I wanted to avoid the next question but saw no way out of asking it. "What reasons?"

"I think you know," she said, "and maybe it's time we talk about it."

I looked at her sadly, feeling as if I should be asking for forgiveness for something I did long ago, or perhaps something I neglected to do. She had reached out to me many times, offering her friendship and understanding, always there when I needed someone to talk to. Yet I had never revealed the dark secrets of my life to her. I thought I had deceived her by concealing the truth and did not feel worthy of the gift she was offering. "I can't accept your generosity."

"You must." She reached across from the swing and patted me gently on the arm. "It's what Trace would have wanted."

"My God, Miss Jane, how do you know that?"

"I have known for a long time."

She got up from the swing. Holding the screen door open, she said, "I have something I want to show you." After disappearing into the house, she returned a few minutes later with an envelope in her hand. She held it out to me, then retracted it as if she suddenly had second thoughts.

"What is it?"

"It's the last letter I received from Trace. I never showed it to anyone, not even his father. I was afraid Harmon would turn his back on Trace."

"Did he want me to see the letter?"

"I don't think so; he probably thought you would be hurt by it. But I think you should know how much Trace cared for you." She handed me the envelope and settled back on the swing as I removed the letter, unfolded it, and began to read.

Dear Mom and Dad,

It is way past the time when I should have written to you. I wanted to call before my ship left Norfolk, but I had so much on my mind, most of which I didn't want to burden the two of you with. But the time has come for me to let you know what is happening in my life. Mother, I know you will understand. I hope you will too, Dad.

You know that I have always looked forward to visiting Europe. Now that I will have the opportunity in a couple of days, I really am no longer eager to get there. The ship is in Gibraltar tonight and leaves tomorrow morning for Naples, Italy. When we arrive, I will face an administrative board investigating my fitness to stay in the Navy. The likely results are that I will receive an Undesirable Discharge and be returned home.

An Undesirable Discharge is usually reserved for someone who has committed moral turpitude, and that is what I have been accused of. I want you to know that I am innocent of that accusation. But I am guilty of something else. I am guilty of being homosexual, something about which I have never had a choice. Can you believe those words were written by me, Mom and Dad? Well, they were, and I am proud that I have finally found the courage to put that admission in writing.

I know this news is a terrible disappointment to both of you, but please don't stop loving me. I need your support more than ever now.

Mother, I have a great favor to ask of you. You have always known how close Eric and I were. When you see him, let him know that I think of him often, and I still consider him the best friend I ever had.

If the board reaches the decision I expect, I will be home by the Fourth of July. I will see you then. Let Eric know that I hope to see him too.

I love you both very much.

Trace

When I finished reading, I looked at her. She was crying quietly. I moved to the swing, sat down, and pulled her close to me.

"He never made it to Naples," she leaned against my shoulder. "That was his goodbye letter."

"I wonder if he planned it that way." I attempted to keep my voice from faltering.

"I don't know. The letter from his captain said that he was lost at sea. I don't want to know any more than that."

"Poor Trace. He must have been terrified."

She clutched my arm tightly.

"I guess he felt as if the whole world was against him," I said.

"It was, wasn't it? It always was. It still is."

I sat quietly, holding the letter, thinking about how Trace's steady handwriting gave no hint of what he must have been considering. After a few moments, I asked, "Why didn't you ever let me know?"

"At first, I was afraid you would think badly of Trace. I would have done anything to prevent that. Later, I could never find the courage, I guess. I didn't show the letter to Harmon. He never knew the truth about his son."

"You must have wondered about Trace and me. You know, we really cared for each other, but nothing ever happened between us."

She was silent again, apparently considering what she wanted to say to me. "Is there any hope for you, Eric? Will you ever know true happiness?"

"What do you mean, Miss Jane?"

"Couldn't you learn to love a woman? Find someone to marry?"

"I could never deceive anyone that way. That's why I've never . . . ."

"Have you ever tried to make love to a woman?"

"I have never made love to anyone."

"Don't you think it is time you did?"

"I wouldn't know where to begin." I offered a pathetic smile, and she responded with a smile of her own.

She got up from the swing and reached for my hand. When I stood, she opened the screen door and tugged at my fingers. "Come on in."

I followed her through the house to the family room. While I watched, she turned on a record player and inserted a cassette tape. She turned to me and moved into my arms. Dulcet tones of Frank Sinatra and other mellow crooners wafted from the speaker and filled the room with forlorn, beautiful love songs. I danced to the music with Jane Willbanks pressed gently against me. When the tape finished, we stepped away from each other, both of us, I think, astonished at what had just transpired. "That wasn't so bad," she said. "Was it?"

"No, it wasn't bad at all."

She left the room for several minutes. While she was gone, I stood by the window, looking out onto the back yard, trying to comprehend the surrealism I was living through. She was attempting to save me from myself, and I was beginning to believe it was possible. Alone in a house with an attractive older woman, whose intentions were predictable, if not obvious. Nothing I would ever experience afterward could be as surprising. Most men my age would have relished their potential seduction by an attractive widow who had not made love in nearly five years. But I was frightened at the thought of her possible success and terrified of my probable failure.

She returned, carrying a tray with a bottle of wine and two glasses.

"Chablis? If you prefer sherry, I have that too."

"No, Chablis is fine."

She poured two glasses half full, handed one to me, then sat down on the couch. I sat beside her while we sipped our wine. We made small talk, both of us, I think, intentionally prolonging the experiment we were preparing ourselves for. After two or three drinks, she started the cassette player again. We danced to words and music of the old standards. When the songs finished, I pulled Miss Jane tightly against me and kissed her softly on the lips.

She held my hand and led me to her bedroom. As dusk descended upon the world outside, we undressed in the deepening shadows of the room and slipped beneath the covers. She turned toward me, and we held each other close. I kissed her breasts and caressed her body. She was warm and willing, responding with sighs of contentment. I wanted desperately to please her, to be worthy of her sacrifice. I moved over her and looked into her face. Tears formed in the corners of her hazel eyes.

I lay down beside her, stroked her hair, and kissed her on the cheek. "Miss Jane," I said, "you can't save me from myself. I am what I am."

"I'm afraid I have made a fool of myself."

"Then you are a kind and wonderful fool."

"Have I destroyed your respect for me, Eric?"

"Of course not. I love you more than ever."

"What would Trace think of me?"

"He would think you're wonderful and unselfish."

"I can only pray that you are right."

We lay quietly for several minutes. I brushed the hair away from her face and kissed her forehead. "If you're okay, I should be going home." I sat up on the side of the bed and reached for my trousers.

"Please don't go yet," she said without lifting her head from her pillow. "Stay with me until I go to sleep."

I lay back down beside her. "I won't, Miss Jane. I won't go yet." I held her close to me, painfully enduring the sounds of her quiet, intermittent crying until she drifted off to sleep.

5

ESCAPE TO THE HEREAFTER

Charlie Green was not a bad guy, but he frequently found himself in untenable situations without even trying. It was as if trouble and mischief came looking for him, and he greeted them with open arms. That may have been why he was expelled from high school and ended up in reform school at the age of sixteen. Incarceration tutored him toward a life of petty crime and eventually earned him a four-year sentence in the Brushy Mountain Tennessee State Penitentiary. Much prayer and a religious conversion into the Prisoner Resurrection Church of Christ were rewarded with a shortened sentence. In return for his promise to do God's work for the remainder of his life, Charlie was released at the age of twenty-four.

When he exited Brushy Mountain, his cousin, Buford, offered him a position in his moonshine enterprise. At first, Charlie resisted the temptation and instead devoted himself to itinerate preaching. Unfortunately, he found the proceeds from the collection plate insufficient to meet his worldly needs. Prodded by his cousin's dogged persistence—made more enticing by liberal samplings of Buford's corn squeezings—the proposed joint venture became more alluring. Charlie was persuaded to forsake the cloth and join the illegal moonshine operation.

All went well for a while. Customers abounded in and around Oneida, Tennessee, and across the Kentucky state line. Soon, Charlie, like his cousin, purchased a new Ford Fairlane and sported a voluptuous young lady in the passenger's seat beside him. But greed was the undoing of the Buford and Charlie Green moonshine business. The distribution network spread far into neighboring Kentucky and evoked rancor from Harlan County moonshiners. During one trip too many, the Kentucky crowd shot the tires off Charlie's new Fairlane. A blazing gun battle ensued, with lots of ineffective shots being fired, but neither side inflicted personal injury. However, there were other indignities—the local sheriff arrived on the scene and arrested Buford and Charlie. During the confusion, the competing Harlan County bootleggers—all relatives of the sheriff—escaped. Buford was convicted and given a suspended sentence. Charlie went back to the state penitentiary for a six-year hitch.

Quickly discovering a religious rebirth, he took up preaching to his fellow inmates. After a few months of propitious piety, he was allowed to officiate the Sunday services when the prison chaplain was unavailable. His sermons were particularly effective, resulting in several prisoner converts. Even the warden's wife, who observed services on occasion, was impressed. She soon intervened on Charlie's behalf. He was given trustee status and assigned as the chaplain's full-time assistant. Following one Sunday service, after ministering to the warden's wife in the chaplain's private quarters, the two of them disappeared. The hunt was on. He was captured and reincarcerated at Brushy Mountain, facing ten years behind bars—this time without a Bible.

"Do you believe in the hereafter?" Charlie asked, lying back on the bottom bunk, his hands behind his head.

"I shor do." Cellmate Luther Grimsley leaned his head over and peered down at Charlie from the top bunk.

"Well, you are looking at a changed man. And hereafter, I am traveling the straight and narrow."

"Me too," Luther said toward the ceiling, as he laid his head back down on his pillow. "Three years in here, and just one more to go." "Yes, sir," mused Charlie—he had not even heard Luther's last comment. "Four more years, and I will be eligible for parole. It's the straight and narrow, just like the Bible says: Straight is the way and narrow is the gate."

"I believe in the hereafter," Luther reiterated.

"Shut the hell up, Luther," Charlie demanded from his bottom bunk. "I wasn't talking to you."

"Well, I'm the only one in here with you—I thought you was talking to me."

Charlie leapt from his bunk and stood upright. "What the hell do you mean you are the only one in here? Don't you know that Jesus Christ is in here with you? Don't you know He promised: "I am with you always?" And that includes your dumb ass, even if you don't know it."

"Christ a mighty! What's eatin' at you?" Luther sat up and swung his legs over the side of his bunk.

"Eight more years, Luther . . . they ain't gonna parole me.

I'll do every damn minute of my sentence. I'll be thirty-nine when I get out of this shit hole."

"Not if you don't fuck up, you won't. Hell, no more 'an four, max five, and you'll be out."

"Don't forget the warden's wife."

"I forgot about that, Charlie. You probably will do all eight more years. I hope that sanctimonious pussy was worth it." Luther fell back on his pillow, laughing.

Charlie reached across the bunk, grasping Luther's scrotum, twisting angrily. Luther sat up, his mouth agape. Charlie held on tightly. "Do you believe in the hereafter, Luther?"

"Yeah," he gasped.

"Well, hereafter you ain't gonna have to worry about the warden's wife 'cause you won't be able to fuck her or anybody else."

Luther fanned the air with both hands, sucking his breath desperately through clenched teeth. Charlie released his grip. "You heartless son of a bitch, Luther. Eight years ain't anything to laugh about." Luther rolled on his side into a fetal position, moaning quietly.

Charlie sat on the edge of his mattress, remorsefully staring at the wall. After a few moments, he looked up at the bottom of Luther's bunk. "I'm sorry, friend; I didn't mean to hurt you. I got carried away."

"It's alright." Still lying in a knotted position on his side, Luther spoke through pain, his voice barely audible.

"Forgive me, friend." "Alright," Luther repeated.

The rattling of the guard's nightstick was simultaneous with the extinguishing of the lights in the cell block. Charlie lay back on his pillow and stared into the semidarkness well into the night. As sleep gradually overtook him, he could hear Luther's labored breathing and intermittent moans. "Hereafter, it's the straight and narrow," Charlie told himself just before falling asleep.

Morning came with a start as he was awakened by the sudden glare of the lights in his cell and the rattling of the guard's nightstick on the steel door. *Eight more years,* he told himself as he slipped his feet into his shoes and got ready for another day that would be lost from his interminable, meaningless life.

LUTHER PREPARED to move from Charlie's cell into the Civil Indoctrination section where he would be groomed for living outside prison walls. He removed his poster of Farrah Fawcett from the wall, rolled it up, and placed it under his arm. "Want this picture, Charlie?"

"No, you take it. It's yours."

"I'm gonna miss you."

"You won't miss me, Luther. You won't miss anything about this place once you get on down the road."

"You'll be goin' too, Charlie, before you know it. Three more years, and you will be up for parole. You been a good con."

"No, there is no way I'm getting out until my sentence is served. That is, unless I can find a way myself."

"Don't try it. You'll just end up with a longer stretch."

"There is a way, and you can help once you are on the outside."

"I don't want no trouble. Straight and narrow, remember?"

"All you got to do is find my cousin and tell him to come to visit me. He lives in Oneida, selling moonshine. Promise me you'll do that."

The door to the cell slid open. The two men embraced.

"I promise, Charlie."

Moments after the cell door slammed shut, Luther disappeared down the steel catwalk, the prison guard following one step behind. With his empty face pressed against the bars, resigned to the probability he would never see or hear from Luther Grimsley again, Charlie watched him until he was out of sight.

It was not Charlie's nature to remain emotionally impotent for very long. His recovery from the depths of despair began the next day when he was introduced to his new cellmate. Noble Collier was a balding man of fifty or so. His crime, forgery, and embezzlement from a Knoxville bank had netted him seven years, of which he had already served three when he made Charlie's acquaintance. His parole hearing was less than three months away. That meant that Noble could be walking around, a free man, within six months.

During his three years of incarceration, Noble had become an expert in ventilation and heating system repairs. He spent his days conducting preventive maintenance on the prison's central system. As he related to Charlie, "I know every crook and cranny of the system and every cell with an exhaust or supply vent opening." This knowledge inspired Charlie to reconsider his plight and devise a plan for shortening his potential stay in the big house.

"They'll be needing a replacement for you when you get out, won't they?" Charlie asked.

"If you want the job, you just have to convince the man that you know something about it."

"Guess that leaves me out. I don't know anything about heating and ventilation."

"I can teach you. Heck, I didn't know anything about it when I started out. So I got some books from the prison library and taught myself. You can do it too. It beats the heck out of firing the boilers or working on the road gang."

"What do I have to do to get your job?"

"I'll take care of it." Noble slapped him reassuringly on the back. A few weeks later, Charlie was assigned as Noble's apprentice.

Armed with system diagrams that Noble had sketched for him and several books from the library, Charlie began his detailed investigation of the prison heating and ventilation systems. Heat from the coal-fired boilers located in the basement was supplied through a main plenum that branched off with ducting up the walls on each end of the building. Horizontal ducts ran through the overheads of the cells at all levels. Smaller vent supply ducts terminated at every other cell just above the floor. During the summer months, fresh air was supplied through the same duct system from huge intake fans mounted on the roof. Charlie's escape route would take him through the cooling fan intakes.

Seven months passed after Luther's release from prison without any word from Buford. In the meantime, Noble's parole came through. His transfer to the Civil Indoctrination section was imminent. In the wake of renewed despair, Charlie prayed for God to become an accessory to one more crime—escape from Brushy Mountain. He had no doubts that he could make his way over the prison wall undetected, but once outside the compound, he would need someone to help him get away from the area before the guards realized he was gone. He thought it might be possible to reach Buford by mail. Charlie wrote a simple letter expressing his desperation addressed to Buford Green, General Delivery, Oneida, Tennessee:

> Dear Cousin Buford,
>
> I am well and hope you are the same. I sure could stand to see a friendly face.I wish one of my relatives would visit me here at Brushy Mountain.
>
> If you see my momma, tell her I love her.
>
> Your Cousin,
>
> Charlie

Many more weeks came and went without any word from Buford. Charlie's optimism was renewed each morning with the expectation that his cousin would contact him; it was crushed each afternoon when he realized there would be no letter for him that day. But he intended to make his break with or without Buford.

Charlie planned his escape for Thanksgiving night when the guards would be working a relaxed schedule. The sun would set early, giving him the cover of darkness soon after his escape. He planned to climb through the ventilation system to the rooftop, then scale the building down the back wall. After cutting through the back fence, he would make his way through the woods north of the prison. Someone would be waiting in a getaway car with camping equipment and a shotgun for hunting. Once he made it across the Kentucky state line, he would disappear into the surrounding woods. Without an accomplice, he would have to hike through the hills in his prison garb with no provisions and no protection from the weather. He would

CHARLIE WORKED his way up through the vertical duct. He never looked back but could hear Frank grunting as he pulled his heavy frame up through the vent. At the rooftop, Charlie squeezed between the large blades of the supply fan. He removed the two remaining bolts from the ventilation screen, which he had loosened and left in place a few days earlier. While Frank continued his labored climb to the roof, Charlie pieced together several lengths of heavy-duty electrical extension cords he had stored in the vent system above his cell along with sheet metal cutters for getting through the reinforced wire fence; he secured one end of the cord around a standpipe and lowered the other end with the cutter attached to the ground. By the time Frank made it through the ventilation fan blades, Charlie was already rappelling himself down the back wall of the prison.

When he reached the ground, he quickly crossed the prison yard to the back fence and commenced cutting away a section of the reinforced wire. As soon as he scrambled through the hole in the fence, he ran headlong for the woods, which lay a hundred yards away. Halfway across, he looked back to see the dark figure of Frank, barely visible against the prison wall. Charlie waited at the edge of the woods until he could see Frank's bent form on the ground, running toward the hole in the fence. Suddenly, lights around the perimeter flashed across the prison yard. Shots rang out from the corner security posts. Frank fell to the ground only a few yards from the fence. The prison siren screamed madly into the dusk. Charlie took off through the woods in the direction of the main road and the railway crossing where he knew Luther would be waiting.

Half an hour later, as Charlie emerged from the edge of the woods near his rendezvous point with Luther, he listened for the hounds which he knew would be set loose soon. At least an hour had elapsed since he climbed into the vent on the wall next to his bunk. By now, the guards would be aware of his escape. He walked hurriedly along the railroad tracks toward the main road. At the meeting point, Luther was nowhere in sight. Charlie thought Luther must have heard the gunshots and siren. He couldn't blame him for getting the hell out of there.

Charlie looked cautiously around; something lying below the railroad right-of-way caught his attention. He scrambled down the embankment to examine a green duffle bag filled with clothing, food, and a sawed-off shotgun. At the bottom of the bag was a flashlight. Luther had not let him down. Charlie's travel on foot would be slowed if he attempted to carry all the supplies. But, at least he could change out of his prison garb, and he would have a gun for hunting once he made it into the woods of the Cumberland Plateau.

He headed north, using the flashlight sparingly for fear

of detection until he reached a steep riverbank. There, he rested at the river's edge. For a few moments, he contemplated the task ahead of him and almost longed for the security of his cell, the only home he had known for more than three years. *That's crazy*, he said to himself, shaking his head at the thought. He shed his prison garb and pulled a pair of jeans, a sweatshirt, and winter raincoat from the duffle bag. After getting dressed, he filled the pockets of his coat with crackers and cans of potted meat. Along with the prison suit, he placed several large rocks from the riverbank into the bag. As the bag sank into the muddy water, Charlie began running along the bank in a northwesterly direction, carrying the shotgun in his right hand.

He ran for an hour before coming to a paved country road, which he followed for about a mile. In the distance, he could see lights coming from a building. As he drew near, he realized it was a church. He moved closer and stood by one of the windows. The congregation was singing a song Charlie had heard many times when he attended church with his mother:

We shall gather at the river, The beautiful, beautiful river...

He removed the shells from the gun and slipped it under his coat, then walked up the steps onto the front porch. As the preacher addressed the congregation, Charlie stepped through the doorway and sat down inconspicuously in the back pew. After a few minutes, the offering baskets were passed down the pews. One of them was passed to Charlie, but he had nothing to give. Two ushers carried the baskets forward and placed them on the altar. While the congregation closed their eyes for the pastor's blessing,

Charlie walked to the front of the church. When the pastor finished his prayer, Charlie was standing directly in front of him. "Do you believe in the hereafter, Preacher?"

"I shor do," the bucolic pastor said with more than a modicum of sanctimony.

"Well then." Charlie pulled back the side of his long raincoat and raised the sawed-off twelve-gauge shotgun level with the preacher's chest. "I'm here after the money—hand it over."

"Shh . . . shh . . . shor," the pastor stammered as he emptied one basket into the other and handed the proceeds to Charlie. "Don't shoot."

Charlie grasped the bills in his free hand and pushed them down into the coat pocket. Continuing to keep the empty gun pointed in the direction of the pastor's heart, he said, "Just don't try to be a hero, Preacher, and I won't hurt you or anyone else."

When he got to the back of the church, Charlie said in his best preacher's style, "You all pray for this poor sinner. I got a long hard road ahead of me." He closed the door behind him, then ran on up the paved road for a few hundred feet before disappearing into the woods.

Charlie knew it wouldn't take long for word of his latest escapade to get to the sheriff. Once he was well into the woods, he headed back north, hoping to reach the river and find a way across before the bloodhounds could get his scent. The thought that rattlesnakes and copperheads might still be crawling sent shivers up his spine, but the possibility of stepping on one of them was not as threatening as the fear of getting caught. He picked his way slowly through underbrush and over fallen trees for several hours. Sometime after midnight, he sat down to rest against a black walnut tree. When he awoke, shreds of sunlight filtered through the overhead forest. He began walking rapidly in a direction he thought would lead him back to the river. Moments later, he heard the first barking of the hounds in the distance and ran breathlessly until he reached the river's edge. He heard nothing more except the occasional ripple of the water along the riverbanks. But he knew that Lady Killer and the rest of the bloodhound pack were systematically sniffing out his trail in silence as they pursued him. He was prepared to jump into the river the moment he heard the howling of the pack again, signifying that they were hot on his trail.

Charlie continued walking briskly, following the river toward its northwest origins. After an hour or more, the river began to narrow. He spotted a cabin in the distance on an elevated bluff across the water. It was almost obscured by the growth of pine and poplar trees that surrounded it. He quickened his pace, looking more desperately for a means of crossing the river. Behind him, he heard the forlorn howling of the bloodhound pack closing in on him. They must have picked up his fresh scent in the afternoon breeze.

A few yards further upstream, he spied a rope and wood swinging bridge. If he could make it to the other side, he might be able to chop the ropes, causing the bridge to fall back into the stream. Halfway across the undulating, swaying bridge, Charlie looked back to see the lead bloodhound sniffing his way along the riverbank, hot on his trail. He knew it would be Lady Killer, far ahead of the pack as usual. Charlie had heard the legendary tales of his tracking abilities. There was no way he could outrun the dog.

When he reached the other side, he opened the breach

and inserted a shell in each of the barrels of his gun. He waited, ready to empty them into the dog if he followed him. Lady Killer approached the swinging bridge, then began to cross it. As the bridge swayed with his motion, the dog moved more cautiously.

Christ, thought Charlie, he's scared shitless. He ran back halfway, jumping wildly. The bridge swayed, rippling dangerously in response to his movements. Lady Killer was now prone on the bridge, inching toward Charlie. When the dog was only a few feet away, Charlie aimed the gun, prepared to end the reign of the pride of Brushy Mountain's bloodhound corps. The dog whimpered softly as he crawled the remaining few feet. Charlie lowered the gun and dropped to one knee. "Come on, boy," he said, extending his hand toward the dog. Lady Killer nestled his head in Charlie's open hand. Together, they crossed the stream and approached the cabin.

He peered through the window from the front porch which was covered with leaves and pine needles, evidence that no one had been there recently. A gravel road led away from the cabin. Charlie knew that a main highway would not be far away. After dark, he and Lady Killer would head down the gravel road and continue his quest to reach the Kentucky state line. With an ax retrieved from the woodpile, he chopped the ropes that secured the swinging bridge to his side of the river. It would not stop the pursuit of the sheriff or the hounds that would soon be baying on the other side, but it would certainly slow their progress.

With one blow of the ax, Charlie dislodged the hasp and lock that secured the back door, gaining entry to the kitchen. Lady Killer followed. Charlie set two logs into the fireplace and lit them. Before long, a fire roared up the chimney. He shared his supper of Spam and beans with Lady Killer and washed the food down with beer from the refrigerator. After supper, he sat in a rocking chair before the fire, sipping wine, while his new companion lay peacefully on a rug near him. He placed the wineglass on a table by the rocker and closed his eyes, hoping for a few moments of sleep that would prepare him for his exhausting trek across the state line and into the Kentucky mountains.

Charlie dozed for several minutes before waking to the barking of dogs outside the cabin. He reached for his shotgun, emptied the shells from the chamber, and laid the gun across his lap as he contemplated his probable capture. Moments later, from behind him, he heard a crash against the door and heard it splinter. He didn't move from his position, but rocked stoically, his hand on Lady Killer's head.

"You enjoying that wine?" the sheriff asked.

"I was before I was interrupted," Charlie said dryly, staring into the fire.

"Well, you better have a few more sips, 'cause they will be your last for a while," the sheriff laughed. By then, three or four deputies and posse members had entered the cabin behind the sheriff.

Charlie picked up the glass, finished his wine, then set the glass back on the table. He still had not looked away from the fire. As he got up from the chair, two shotgun shells fell from his lap onto the floor and rolled to the edge of the hearth. Behind him, the deputies held their guns at the ready. Charlie turned to face the sheriff and raised the sawed-off shotgun, aiming it directly at the sheriff's head.

Three shots splintered the air, striking Charlie in the

chest. He fell to his knees and crumpled forward into the hereafter. Lady Killer whimpered, then lay beside his fallen friend.

One of the deputies picked up Charlie's gun. He broke open the breach. "Goddamn! It's empty; guess the poor son of a bitch wanted to die."

"You ain't ever been in prison, Morgan; you don't know what it's like—Charlie Green did," the sheriff said, turning toward the door. He reached for his handkerchief and wiped at the moisture filling his eyes. "C'mon, Lady Killer," he commanded.

Outside, the sheriff closed his eyes for a few moments. He opened them, looking skyward as the sun began to slip behind the trees, "Have mercy on him, Lord. Guess he wasn't all bad. At least he must have loved dogs."

6

A ROSE FOR DOLLY

"Did she mean so little to you?" I asked Carl, believing I already knew the answer. "Aren't you even going to the funeral?"

He kept his eyes closed, not speaking. He just sat at the kitchen table with his open palms against his face, rubbing his eyes with the tips of his fingers.

I thought for a moment he was wiping away tears. But, in my heart of hearts, I knew better. *Not Carl, no, not Carl,* I reminded myself. I had become convinced he was no longer capable of being hurt or crying. Even in such circumstances as these, Carl Daniels was a remarkably unemotional man.

But inside my head, I could hear Dolly saying, Don't be so hard on him, Hank. He really is a good guy.

I bent over with my palms on the table just in front of him. "I think she would have wanted you there, don't you?"

Carl still didn't speak.

"You son of a bitch."

He looked at me. For the first time, I saw hurt in his face.

"You might wait until you have all the facts before you drop the guillotine." He got up and walked to the kitchen door, peering aimlessly across the backyard. If his purpose was to deflect the anger I was feeling, he failed.

"Then let's hear your side of things," I said. Carl continued to stand with the door ajar staring into space.

Disgusted with the futility of a one-sided conversation, I walked into my room to finish getting dressed. As I took one last look at my hair in the mirror, Carl leaned into the room and stood against the doorframe. His scraggly beard and gaunt appearance told me he was wrestling with the events of the past three days, still searching for the courage he needed to face his culpability in Dolly's death.

"Damn," he said, "Hank, I just can't bring myself to go see her like that. She was so beautiful and..."

"You love her, Carl?"

He didn't answer but looked at me as if he was pondering my question.

"Well, you sure as hell made her think you did."

"Wasn't my fault. I tried to tell her it wasn't going to work, but you know how women are." He spoke, not in a callous way, but as if he expected me to understand that women are too naïve for their own good.

I had the urge to hit him squarely between the eyes as I walked past him toward the front door. "Fuck you," I said looking back over my shoulder.

The ten-mile trip from Gretna to Avondale would give me time to get my thoughts together and to prepare to look at Dolly, lying in her rose-colored casket. It would allow me time to wonder if I could have stopped her before she fell so madly in love with Carl. Maybe I should have told her he would never love anyone else after Janice, but that would have been only a guess. Besides, it probably would have made her more determined to win his love. Carl was a good-looking guy—blond hair, blue eyes, square-cut chin, and a smile that attracted girls like a magnet. At six feet tall, he cut a handsome figure in his Navy Lieutenant's uniform. During the two years we shared an apartment, Carl was never in want of female companionship, and it was not unusual for him to bring home an extra for me. On those occasions, I happily entertained his second choice, while he made love to the first in the adjacent bedroom. There were nights too, when I lay alone in my bed listening to the enviable sounds of Carl's lovemaking to a girl he had seduced for the first time. But his promiscuity—and mine—ended when Dolly came into our lives. That first night when he brought her home with him, was still fresh in my mind. My sleep was disrupted by muffled voices and laughter. I rolled over to look at the clock—two a.m. Shortly afterward, I heard the familiar sound of Carl's bedroom door closing. *Another conquest,* I thought as I drifted out of consciousness again. The next morning, I was awakened by the smell of strong coffee coming from the kitchen. I rubbed the sleep out of my eyes and yawned my way toward the aroma.

She didn't get up when I entered but smiled at me through the whitest teeth I had ever seen. Her ebony eyes almost matched the color of the hair that framed her face and fell onto her shoulders.

"How's the coffee?" I asked, delighted and awe-stricken by the Creole beauty seated at the table. There was something about her that made me know she was different from all the other women Carl had brought home.

"Fine. Want some?" She didn't wait for my response but got up and poured a cup for me.

I pulled a chair back and sat across the table from her, all the while not taking my eyes off her face.

"You're Hank," she said as if she needed no confirmation.

"The one and only." I smiled. "And you?"

"Dolly Miller." She extended a hand, still holding her coffee in the other.

"Miller?" It was not the Creole name I expected.

She smiled again. "Delia Peres. Everyone calls me Dolly. I married Miller." She lifted the cup to her mouth with both hands and sipped. "But I don't want to talk about that. ... Tell me about Carl."

"He's everything you think he is."

"We only met last week, so..."

"Then he's everything you hope he is." "Seriously," she said with a little pout.

"Seriously, he's the greatest guy in the world. You are one lucky girl, Dolly Miller." I was only half kidding.

I pushed back the chair and stood. "Gotta get dressed. I have to run in to the base this morning to check on my people." As the security officer at the Navy base in Algiers, I had to make certain my Sunday watch personnel were all posted and sober. She stood too. "Guess I'll have to find out for myself about Mr. Daniels, huh?"

"I hope you stay around long enough to do that." Maybe it was envy that prompted those words, or perhaps I was just trying to warn her not to fall too hard for Carl. A look of disappointment crossed her face.

I wanted to compensate for my thoughtless statement

but was lost for words. We just looked at each other for several seconds, neither of us speaking. Then I touched her face as gently as I could. "If anyone can catch him, you can."

She was smiling when I closed my bedroom door.

Although we shared an apartment and leaned on each other as friends do, Carl always remained somewhat of a mystery to me. He seemed to guard his feelings carefully, refusing to allow me or anyone else to know him well. However, when we both had too many drinks, he was sometimes compelled to talk about his former fiancée, Janice, who eloped with his intended best man. By then, he could find humor in his betrayal by the two most trusted people in his life, but the hurt he still felt more than a year later lay just below his stoical veneer. I think he had become afraid of falling in love, and each time he dumped a new girl, he was just getting even with Janice. But it was easy to see he cared about Dolly in a very special way. Dolly filled an emotional void, not only in Carl's life but in mine. For the first time since I had known him, he seemed truly happy. He no longer grazed the pastures of Lagoon Bleu, our favorite nightclub, for free-ranging females. Instead, he chose staying at home with Dolly while I occasionally made the club scene alone. Nights on the town often included the three of us, with her alternating between Carl and me on the dance floor. It was during the sensual sounds of Sarah Vaughn singing "Misty," while I held Dolly close that I realized I was in love with her.

As summer approached, Carl and I anticipated orders, sending us off to Navy ships somewhere on the East Coast.

Carl was scheduled to go first, then me a few months later. I expected that he would make plans to take Dolly with him as his wife. Instead, he found ways to distance himself from her. He began to frequent Lagoon Bleu and his other old haunts alone and to avoid Dolly's calls, while I made excuses for his failure to answer the phone.

I understood Carl's fear of commitment probably more than anyone else. Janice's betrayal had sown the seeds for distrusting all women, even Dolly. Still, I believed their feelings for each other would bring them back together. They did, but not in the way I anticipated.

It was almost nine p.m. when Dolly called with some important news for Carl. I was alone in the apartment. I told her she could find him at Lagoon Bleu, where he had gone almost every evening that week. I had just finished watching an episode of *All in the Family* when I heard Carl's key turn in the lock. "Hey," I said, "Dolly find you?"

He walked past me into his room without speaking.

I got up and rapped on the door. "Hey, asshole."

"Get the fuck away, Hank."

I cracked open the door and stuck my head in. Carl was lying across the bed with the lights out. "Want to tell me about it, buddy?" I asked.

"Fucking women."

"You mean Dolly?"

"Her too. ... Fucking women in general."

"What the hell is wrong with you? She is the best thing that has ever happened to you."

He sat up. "It's not Dolly. It's every damn thing." He reached into his back pocket and pulled out a letter. He shuffled through it and handed me the last page. “What the hell am I going to do about this?”

I opened the door further for better lighting then read through the three or four paragraphs on the page. The last few lines of the letter made me understand why Carl had avoided Dolly for the past several days.

> My marriage to Brad was a terrible mistake. I hope you can forgive me for all the hurt I have caused you. And if you can read between these lines, you know how much I still love you.
>
> Always,
>
> Janice

When I finished, I threw the page on the bed beside him. “Want my advice?”

He didn’t answer.

“Tell her to get fucked.”

“That’s easy for you to say.”

“What about Dolly?”

“I don’t know. I just don’t know. I don’t want to hurt her.”

“You’re going to break her heart. You know that?”

"For God’s sake, Hank, what do you expect me to do?”

“Marry her, Carl. She’s good for you.”

“I can’t do that.”

“Why not?”

“I just can’t,” he said. “Ask her if you want to know why.”

I went back to the living room and changed the TV

channel for some mindless viewing. A few minutes later, there was a knock on the door.

It was Dolly. "Carl here?"

"Yeah." I pointed toward his room. She knocked lightly as she cracked the door open. "Carl, can I come in?"

I turned up the volume on "Ironside" to drown out the voices coming from the other room. After a while, I dozed, and when I awoke, their talking had ceased. I took a quick shower and went to bed.

Dolly awoke me sometime around midnight, standing in my doorway. I sat up, "What's wrong, honey?"

She didn't answer, but I could hear her crying. With the translucent light from the living room outlining her face, she looked like an angel.

"Come here." I motioned, and she moved next to my bed. I put my arm around her waist. "Why are you crying?"

"He doesn't want me anymore." She sobbed, placing her hand on my shoulder.

I looked up at her. "He's just all mixed up right now. Give him a little time."

"No, it's over." She sat on the edge of the bed. "I don't want to go home. Can I stay with you a little while?"

"Sure you can." I moved over to make room for her.

She lay on the bed beside me. After a few moments, she turned her face toward mine and kissed me. The warm taste of tears on my lips told me it was a kiss of gratitude and not passion. "Dear, sweet Hank," she said. "I am going to miss you."

"We'll see each other, Dolly. Don't worry about that." I put the cover over her and held her close to me.

"Do you love me, Hank?"

"You know I do."

"Do you want to make love to me?"

"I can't do that." I brushed her hair away from her face.

"Why?"

"Because you would never forgive me, and I would never get over it."

"Then just hold me, Hank I need to be held."

She turned her back and moved close to me.

After a moment, she said in a whisper that I barely heard, "I'm pregnant."

"Damn. ... Carl?"

"Yes."

"What'd he say?"

"I didn't tell him."

"You have to."

"No, don't tell him."

"I think he should know."

"Promise you won't tell him."

I stroked her hair. "All right, I won't if you don't want me to."

She lay in my arms, crying quietly until she fell asleep. I kissed her cheek. then lay back on my pillow. Staring into the shadows of the room, I swore I would find a way to help her. I would make Carl see what a fool he was. Sometime later, I closed my eyes. When I awoke that morning, she was gone.

I TOOK the Avondale exit from the Westbank Expressway then drove along River Road to Rue Fontaine. It led me deeper into Bayou Country. I would never have found my way if I had not made the trip once before with Dolly. Carl didn't come with us that day for reasons of his own, but she insisted that I see where she lived.

As we had driven along the low-maintenance road shrouded by moss-laden live oaks, she pointed out to me the places where her ancestors once lived and worked. "Slave quarters used to be right over there." She flicked her finger in the direction of an overgrown thicket covered with moss. "My father's great-grandfather bought all this land for fifty dollars during the depression. He was a fisherman, and so was my papa, mon pere." She smiled.

On the other side of the road was an oak-lined roadway leading to a large antebellum-style home with columns rising from ground level to the top of the second-floor veranda. The house was in need of repair, but its past grandeur was obvious.

"This where you live?"

"Yes," she said, waving her hand at a spot next to the road where she wanted me to park.

I brought the car to a stop. We sat looking up the road toward the house. I waited, expecting her to tell me to drive on, but I think she was having second thoughts about our visit. After a moment, she sighed as if she had just made a momentous decision. "I wanted you to see it. Maybe you can tell Carl what it's like. We can go now."

Two weeks later, Dolly walked out of our lives, and we never heard from her again until the phone call came. "Hank Denham?"

"Yes, this is he."

"I'm Marie Peres, Dolly's mother."

The somber sound of her voice prefaced words I did not

wish to hear, but I couldn't avoid asking the inevitable question, "Has something happened?"

"Cher, I have bad news." She paused. "Dolly passed."

"Passed?" In disbelief, I choked back tears. "You mean she died?"

"Yes, Cher, this morning. She would have wanted me to call you."

Her voice was filled with a solemn dignity, but I heard it break as she spoke, "Can you tell me what happened?"

"She went to a priestess about the baby. Something went wrong. It didn't turn out well."

"Abortion?"

I remembered her saying "yes," but little else. After expressing condolences, I went to my room and fell onto my bed. I wanted to pray, but the words wouldn't come. At that moment, I had nothing but loathing for Carl.

Now, as I drove the final yards toward the house, I saw to my right, in a garden of aged gray tombstones, a freshly dug grave. A sense of foreboding came over me. It was Dolly, beautiful Dolly that would be placed in that piece of ground then covered with dirt and cement. Now I understood Carl's reluctance to be here. I didn't want to see her, lying lifeless and still. That was not the way I wanted to remember her, but unlike Carl, I couldn't stay away.

By the steps leading to the front porch, a brass band formed with trombone, horn, saxophone, and drums. A hundred or more people gathered behind a tuxedoed man holding a black umbrella. I had prepared myself for a decorous and plaintive ceremony, one that would leave me impotent and empty. But now I understood that a celebration of death as a part of life would unfold shortly.

The thought gave me confidence that something wonderful awaits all of us on the other side and that Dolly had found it. I watched curiously as I made my way onto the porch and into a large foyer. Ahead of me were two open double doors, through which I could see a rose-colored coffin against a far wall. As I neared the coffin, I was met by Dolly's mother and father. I accepted the hand of Mrs. Peres as I expressed my deep hurt and love for her daughter. Mr. Peres clasped my shoulder and thanked me for coming.

I held the hand of Marie Peres as we made our way to the coffin surrounded by floral arrangements and lighted candles. I smiled sadly as I remembered the dark eyes that now were closed forever. A small bouquet of scarlet roses rested in Dolly's hands. At first, I didn't notice the upright card among the roses, but something made me look more closely. My eyes welled with tears as I read the words: I will love you always.

"I knew you could catch him, honey," I whispered to her as I bent over to read the signature on the card, signed: Carl. Now my mind was spinning, attempting to understand why he didn't marry her. Across the room, sitting alone, was a disfigured young man in a wheelchair. As I turned to leave, Mrs. Peres took hold of my hand and led me toward him.

"Gabriel," she said, "this is a friend of Dolly's. He came to see her."

The wheelchair-bound man didn't speak. There was no movement except for an involuntary jerk of his head.

"Hank, this is Gabriel Miller, Dolly's husband." She placed her hand lovingly on his immobile arm.

"I'm sorry about your wife," I stammered as I backed away, my eyes turning toward the door.

I walked quickly onto the porch. My mind was swirling with disconnected thoughts as the brass band began playing "Nearer My God To Thee." Moments later, the pallbearers carried the casket outside and set it on the lawn while the procession formed behind. To the slow rhythm of a sorrowful dirge, they marched toward the newly dug grave. I wanted to stay until the end, to hear the tumultuous and joyous sounds of "When the Saints Go Marching In," as the band returned to the house. But I could hear Dolly saying, "Go to him, Hank. He needs you now." Carl was home alone, mourning for her in a way that only she and I could understand. I needed to comfort my friend, to put my arm around his shoulder and say to him, "You really are a good guy, Carl. Dolly told me so."

7

THE PURPLE MOHAWK

I picked the wrong day to have my hair cut into a Mohawk and dye it purple. But at the time, I had no inkling that someone else with nefarious plans was having his Mohawk dyed purple about the time I was tipping my hairdresser. Like most things I do, the coiffure was a spur of the moment decision, and I had no time to consider whether someone else would emulate my good taste in hairstyle. Besides, what are the odds that two people would end up with purple Mohawks in the little town of Crabtree, Alabama?

I am homosexual—gay. I don't say that with any particular motive or purpose, but only to put everything into proper context. I don't hide it. I don't flaunt it. That's how it is—God's choice for me, not mine. And I have learned to live with His choice.

No one can accuse me of being a bully or brute. I suppose I might even be considered effeminate—blame that on God too. I do have my violent moments of outrage, directed mostly at ignorant assholes and the everyday mishaps that other people stoically endure but I cannot abide. These violent outbursts are usually terminated by my little sister punching me in the nose. That always brings me back to my serenity and good senses.

But on with my story.

With my new hairdo, I took my usual seat at the bar of Jay and Fancy's Leisure Lounge, surrounded by my good friends and drinking companions. We are bound, not by sexual orientation, but by our tastes in music, philosophy, and art, and by our distaste for modern politics. Naturally, our conversations took a bent toward Rene Descartes and Jean-Paul Sartre--it happens in every quiet little drinking lounge—the more booze, the more Sartre. Having read his writings extensively and professing existentialism, I hold my own in these conversations. And that is what I was doing when the attention of my listeners was drawn away toward the front door of the bar.

He was tall, crew cut, with ears that needed to be compensated for by a full head of hair, Crabtree's newest man in blue, police rookie, Josh Jackson. His uniform cap was tucked under his arm, military style.

"Hey, you."

Each of us at the bar, swiveling our heads back and forth to see who he was addressing, pointed our fingers at our chests and resounded, almost in unison, "Who, me?"

"No, not you, that guy in the Mohawk." He pointed in my direction.

I slid off my bar stool. "Me?" I pointed my thumb at my chest.

"Yeah, you. Come with me, sir."

"Me?" I wanted to give him an opportunity to undo his mistake before he made it.

"Yeah."

But Officer Jackson was undaunted. He continued up the sidewalk with me at his hip.

By then, people were taking notice. They stepped aside and gawked. It could have been my Mohawk, but I didn't want to believe the hairdo would attract that much attention. Whatever the attraction, I was relishing it. If I couldn't have fame, at least I might enjoy notoriety, no matter how fleeting. I was beginning to understand Baby Face Nelson or Machine Gun Kelly—relishing my moment in the spotlight.

As we turned down the next street, another policeman, followed by a man and woman, walked in our direction.

"Is this the man?" Officer Jackson directed his inquiry at the couple.

"No," the woman said. "You kidding?"

The man sneered. "You think I would let this little queer take my wife's purse?"

"You son of a bitch," I said, my manhood insulted. "I am perfectly capable of snatching a purse if I were so inclined. I took the damn purse, and you know it."

"In a pig's ass," the man shouted back. "If you tried, I would kick your ass right up between your shoulders."

By now, the two cops were in the middle of the squabble. Officer Jackson spoke to the woman. "You sure this isn't the man?"

Her husband spoke up. "Hell, no."

"Shut up!" the other cop said.

"He definitely isn't the man," the woman reassured Officer Jackson. "He was much bigger, and not so ... so... so ..."

"Effeminate?" I wanted to be helpful.

Moments later, a police car stopped at the curb. An officer got out, walked around to our side of the car and opened the back door. That was when I saw the usurper of my hair style, a brute of a man with a twisted nose.

"This the man?" The officer asked, looking back and forth between the brute and the woman who had apparently been robbed.

"Yes, that's him."

"It's him," the man said.

"Why didn't you kick his ass up between his shoulders?" I wanted to know.

Officer Jackson pointed toward my friends who were gleefully watching me as my chance for infamy was quickly fading. "You're free to go, sir."

"All right, Officer, but I would like to ask that man in the car a question."

"Well, I guess I owe you that much. I hope there are no hard feelings."

"Of course not." By then, I had taken a liking to Josh Jackson and almost wished I had been guilty of a crime he could take credit for solving. I was ready to confess to enhance his career, but now he would have to make it without my assistance. I felt, under the circumstances, that I was justified in asking the man under arrest one question.

I walked over to the police car and peered in. "Pardon me, sir, but who does your hair?"

8

OLD MEN CRY TOO EASILY

Jacob Monroe bent over the table to blow out seventy-eight candles. He smiled wistfully as his family sang "Happy Birthday." While he lingered over the minuscule flames, memories engulfed his mind. Enmeshed and entwined, thoughts of loves, children, old friends, successes and failures ebbed and flowed. He reached to touch them, to make sense of them, but they faded before he could grasp their essence or purpose. Bewildered, he looked around the table at faces he knew well, but whose names now floated away on confusing gossamers. Tears seeped from the corners of his eyes, leaving small trails down the sides of his face. As he moved away from the table, he fumbled at his back pocket for a handkerchief to wipe them away. "Why are you crying, Grandpa?" His great-grandson of seven tugged at his fingers. He placed his big hand on top of the boy's head and gently pulled him to his side. "I don't know, Vincie. I guess old men just cry too easily." He rejoiced silently at a moment of lucidity that helped him remember the boy's name.

"Boys cry too, Grandpa," Vincie assured him.

The old man blessed the boy with a gentle hand, held to the side of his face. "I know, Son, but they stop crying when they become young men. ... I guess old men cry because they will never be boys again."

"Vincie bothering you, Papa?" Jacob's oldest daughter, Janie, looked up from cutting the cake. She held up a slice on a paper plate and motioned, knife in hand, for Vincie to come to the table.

"No, Sis, of course not." Jacob recognized his daughter, but her name quickly floated into the ether. "He's reminding me that I have lived too long."

As Vincie ran to get his cake, Jacob moved slowly toward his favorite chair and sat. He became aware of a piece of cake being placed on the table beside him and of his thank you to his son, Edward, whom he recognized for a moment. He heard the cheerful noises from the dining room—the clanking of spoons in coffee cups and unintelligible simultaneous conversations. He did not remember turning on the TV or taking note of Emma as she sat down on the arm of his chair and put her arm about his shoulder.

"Happy birthday, Jacob." She held his hand and gently kissed it.

"Emma. I couldn't forget you, Emma; others maybe, but not you."

"Fifty-two years, Jacob. Neither of us could forget after that much time."

"I suppose so, but something isn't right, Emma. It's all slipping away from me, all of them, everyone but you."

She brought his hand to her face and held the open palm against the warmth of her skin. "I've loved you a long time, Jacob Monroe. I won't stop now."

"You are wonderful, Emma. ... After all I have done, you will love me to the end."

"What have you ever done that would make me stop loving you?"

"Sylvia? You have forgotten about me and Sylvia Webb?"

"I never forgot, Jacob. I just chose not to remember."

He shifted his body in the chair and gently caressed Emma's arm. "And it doesn't ever bother you that I was unfaithful?"

"That was nearly forty years ago, Jacob. I had too much living to do to ever remember it."

"Then why does your indiscretion with Bill Morrison still prey on my mind?"

"Does it?"

"That seems to be all I can think of lately."

"I wish you wouldn't, Jacob. There wasn't anything to that rumor." She bent and kissed his lips then stood erect as she backed away from his chair.

"Emma." He reached out his arms toward her, but she disappeared into the midst of others who laughed and made small talk around the dining room table. *If only I could believe that,* he said to himself.

"You want something, Dad?" Edward approached from the dining room.

"No, Son."

He gently scolded the old man. "You haven't touched your cake."

"I was talking to your mother."

Edward patted his shoulder. "I know, Dad."

Jacob picked up the control and pointed it toward the television. He flicked at several buttons but failed to change the channel.

"You never did understand technology, Jacob." The voice spoke from behind his shoulder. The words were followed by a hardy laugh.

Startled, Jacob turned and leaned over the arm of the chair as his eyes searched for the source. "That you, Wendell?"

"Yes ... happy birthday, Jake."

"I am surprised you remembered."

"I always remember, Jake. We were partners for thirty years. How could I forget?"

"We would have been partners even longer if you had not been so damn stubborn."

"You've forgotten what actually happened. You were the stubborn one. I went to Indonesia to cut a deal, and you threw one of your temper tantrums. Do you remember that?"

"I remember that our company was going broke, and you wanted to wine and dine a bunch of Indonesian Army officers."

"If you had backed me, we could have signed that contract."

Jacob stood and turned to face the voice. "Damn it, Wendell. You would never admit when you were wrong. We could have been manufacturing in Mexico with the cheapest labor in the world and a ready-made market right here at home. But you wouldn't listen."

"Truth was, Jake, you didn't want me to take Millie to Indonesia."

"Why would that have bothered me?"

"Because you know you had your eye on my secretary."

"Damn you, Wendell! Millie had nothing to do with my disagreement with you."

"Yeah, Jake, just keep telling yourself that."

There was silence now as Jacob stared toward the wall behind his chair.

"We've got to get this straight between us, Wendell. Don't go—not before we talk."

Tears began to flow again and once more his fingers felt for the handkerchief in his back pocket. "Don't go, Wendell ... please. I should have told you a long time ago it was my fault. I was wrong. I was jealous of you and Millie. And I wanted to be the one who put the big deal together. I wanted to be the one to save the company. We could have made it work in Jakarta if I had been more supportive."

"Dad, you okay?" Edward placed his arm around his father's shoulders.

Jacob nodded as he wiped at the tears, but he couldn't recall why he had been crying. Perplexed, he sank back into the chair and closed his eyes. After a moment, he started to doze. "You feel like opening your presents?" He thought it was Janie's voice, but there was something different about it. He heard the voice again: Are you ready to open your presents?

"Vanessa?"

He was twenty. His khaki uniform jacket was across the back of the kitchen chair. He reached for the girl with the long auburn hair and pulled her into his arms. "I love you, Nessie."

She turned her face up to kiss him. "You want to see what I got you?"

"I wish you hadn't ..."

"Oh be quiet, Jake. You only have one birthday each year."

"But I know how tight your money is. You shouldn't be spending it on me."

"Why not?"

"Because I'll be leaving next month for Korea, and you will need every penny once I am gone."

"I'll be okay, Jake. And I'll wait for you. You know I will."

"What about Andy? What will you do when he comes back home?"

"It's over between us, Jake. I swear it's over." She was smiling unconvincingly while tears welled up in the corners of her eyes.

She walked across the studio apartment, then bent and opened a bureau drawer. She held up two packages wrapped in birthday paper.

Jacob smiled as he opened the first package. He removed a pair of black trousers and held them at his waist. "Thank you, honey." He kissed her cheek.

"The shirt matches," she said, reaching to help him unwrap the other gift. "You are right, Nessie," he said, holding the still-folded shirt to his chest.

She took the shirt from him, unfolded it and held it up for him to see. Her dark eyes glistened with delight. "Go try them on."

He left the room and after a few minutes returned wearing the shirt and trousers. "How do I look?"

"Handsome ... handsome." Vanessa rushed to embrace him. Jake's arms enclosed her as they fell together across the bed. "Got you where I want you," she said before kissing his face again and again.

"You are playing with fire, woman."

They laughed.

"Are you going to take your new clothes off before you make love to me?"

"No. I'm just going to hold you like this for a while. I don't want to ever forget this moment."

She kissed him again. "I love you, Jacob Monroe."

"I love you, Nessie." He stroked her hair as she pressed her body against his. With the subtle fragrance of her perfume filling his nostrils, he fell asleep.

Jacob was awakened by a light knock on the door. He opened his eyes to see the white cap of the nurse as she leaned over the wheelchair being pushed into his room. "That you,Nessie?"

She laughed. "Sorry, Jacob, but you're stuck with Nurse Agnes this evening."

The old man rose unsteadily to his feet. He searched the room through vacant eyes. "Was Emma here?"

"No," the nurse said as she helped Jacob into the chair. "You been seeing people again?"

He didn't answer but held tightly to the TV control as Agnes turned the chair and pushed it into the hall.

"Where we going?"

"Downstairs to the dining room, Jacob. We are going to celebrate your birthday."

"My birthday?" He tilted his head upward to see the nurse's face.

She leaned forward to speak to him. "Yes, sir. It's your seventy-eighth birthday today. I think that is worth celebrating. Don't you?"

He brought his hands to his face to hide the tears filling his eyes.

The nurse stopped the chair and knelt before her patient. She adjusted the small blanket that lay across his knees. "Don't cry, Mr. Monroe. Let's enjoy your birthday party. Your family is waiting for you downstairs."

"Emma too?"

"I'm afraid not, dear."

He dropped his hands to his lap. Grasping the TV control, he stared straight ahead as Nurse Agnes pushed the chair toward the elevator.

9

DISCOVERING MAY

"When you goin' to marry me, Joe?" May stood on the ground, her head tilted upward toward the gangly young man standing above her.

He leaned against the front porch post, looking much older than twenty. His week-old stubble added years to his face, making him handsome in a rugged sort of way.

She fingered the ends of the porch floor planks at her chest level. After more than twenty years of Georgia winter rain and withering summer sun, the porch, like the rest of the unpainted four-room shack, was showing its age. She mindlessly plucked small pieces of white, rotted wood as she anticipated Joe's response. It occurred to her that the porch was in need of a scrubbing to wash away the mud and grime, tracked from the barren front yard by her six younger siblings.

"Pssht," he said derisively, rolling his eyes, "I ain't ever goin' to marry you, May. Nobody is." He walked to the swing and sat, his long legs extending almost the width of the porch.

An old mongrel dog lay sleeping near the end of the swing, just out of reach of the afternoon sun. He raised his head suddenly and scratched at his ear with his back foot.

Joe kicked at the dog, barely missing his head. "Git, you sumbitch, Clyde."

Clyde yelped, then slunk to the end of the porch, as far away from Joe as he could get.

May raised her voice. "Don't kick my dog."

"Sumbitch's got fleas. "She traced her bare foot in a sandy circle on the ground, avoiding his eyes. "Why do you say nobody will marry me, Joe?" May was afraid she might cry, and she didn't want him to see her face if she did. He had told her too often no man would ever want her for a wife, and each time she heard his words, they hurt more than the last. But she kept asking, always hoping to hear something different. "You know why, May." He cocked his head and made a sucking noise through his teeth.

"Why?" Her voice held a plea, begging Joe not to hurt her, but she was ready for whatever he might say.

"Damn it!" He gave a disgusted jerk on one of the chains holding the swing, making a clinking sound.

She knew that she had angered him but pressed for an answer. "No, Joe. You tell me why."

"Okay ... okay, May. 'Cause you screwed half the boys in this county. That's why."

She waited, fixated on the sand art she had created with her toe. After a moment, she looked toward the swing. "That just ain't true, Joe, and you know it."

He said nothing but dragged the heel of his boot across

the wood floor, creating a scraping sound and a low thump, thump, thump as the swing moved back and forth.

Clyde seemed to understand when it was safe to be near Joe again. He moved out of the sun and resumed his position near the swing.

Joe reached down and patted the old dog's head.

Clyde licked Joe's hand.

May looked at Joe now, but he avoided her eyes. "You break my heart. You know that?"

She moved toward the steps leading up to the porch.

He continued to swing, gazing out over the yard past May.

But she could read his face; in it was a sliver of kindness that, once in a while, managed to slip through his unmerited arrogance. After a few moments, she walked up the steps, onto the porch, and sat down beside him.

He put his arm around her and pulled her close to his shoulder. His boot dug against the porch floor, propelling the swing faster. They sat in silence as the motion of the swing dampened, then stopped altogether.

May tilted her head to look into his eyes. "I feel just like that old dog, Joe. You know what I mean?"

"Hell, no."

"I mean, you kick us both and we just come back for more."

A weak smile played at Joe's lips. He began pushing the swing again with his foot against the floor, seeming to relish the power he held over both May and the old yellow dog. May resented the way he took her for granted, but she would be content for the moment, until she was alone again. Then Joe's words would haunt her. He did not offer much, but his was the only affection she had known since she was fourteen. If what he gave was love, it sometimes hurt too much to desire or accept. But she needed that small fragment from him. She would endure his cruelties, settling for whatever occasional kindness he had the capacity to give. Her thoughts and the afternoon stillness were ruptured by the noisy approach of children in the distance. Soon, the forms of May's siblings began to emerge above the crest of the hill as they walked along the dirt road toward the house, first, sixteen-year-old Carl then Denver, twelve. The girls, ranging from six to fourteen, straggled behind.

"It's almost suppertime," May said. "Daddy will be home soon. You stayin'?"

"No, I ain't stayin.'"

"You're welcome, you know."

"That old man don't like me hangin' 'round."

"Oh, he don't mind, Joe; honest, he don't." She got up from the swing and smoothed her dress with both hands. She turned and looked at Joe, still sitting in the swing, his legs sprawled across the porch. May shook her blond hair, feeling it settle across her shoulders and halfway down her back.

He stood and touched her hair with his open palm. "You shor are purty, May. Guess that's what keeps me comin' back."

"Be careful, Joe," she said, looking up through her soft, blue eyes, "One of these days, you're goin' to come around, and I won't be here."

"That ain't very likely, May." He scoffed. Then, as if suddenly comprehending the possibility of her going, he reached for her. "You wouldn't leave, May, not even if you could."

She stepped back. "I might, Joe."

"Where would you go?"

"I don't know ...anywhere, that's where." Her eyes sparkled at the thought. It was the first time she had been happy all day.

The children streamed across the front yard, cluttered with empty cans, broken toys, and the rusted hulks of several old cars. Carl and Denver, followed by the four girls, Ivy, April, Jenny, and Beatrice, poured onto the porch. Moments later, the house was bursting at its corners with discordant sounds of too many children with too few comforts.

May watched as Joe straddled his old yellow Suzuki, cranked it, and rolled out of the front yard without looking back.

A mother hen, with a half dozen chicks chirping after her, clucked angrily as she scurried to get her brood out of Joe's way.

A cloud of orange dust trailed after the bike as it crested the hill. By the time the dust settled back to earth, the bike and rider had disappeared. With the rev of the engine in the distance, she knew that Joe was heading down the main highway. May leaned against the front porch post, fighting back tears. She wiped at her eyes with the hem of her dress. The clamor from the living room reminded her that her brothers and sisters needed her much more than Joe did. She turned toward the door and the chores that awaited her. Tonight would be no different from a thousand nights before —she would be alone, thinking of Joe and wishing for someone else, anyone who would love her and make her feel special.

After the supper dishes were done, May sat on the front porch swing. She closed her eyes and listened to the sounds of crickets and tree frogs in the scrub pines, poplars, and oaks as darkness settled over the woods. She was vaguely aware of Clyde's occasional deep breathing as he slept beneath the window at the other end of the porch. Sporadic laughter from the living room, where her family watched reruns of *The Dukes of Hazzard,* brought an occasional smile to her face.

"You are purtier than Daisy Duke. You are the purtiest sister in the world." Denver often told her. "You are as purty as Momma." There was sadness in his voice. He was only eight when his mother disappeared from his life, but his eyes still came alive when he spoke of her.

There were times when May resented the sacrifices she had made because of her mother's flight to freedom. But she understood why her young mother slipped out of their lives that early morning four years ago. The scene that occurred that morning, just a few feet from where May now sat, came alive in her mind, replaying itself as it had many times in the past. "Where are you goin', Momma?" May held open the screen door and looked out. She had been awakened by unfamiliar sounds at three a.m.

"Shhh." Her mother flicked a cigarette onto the front yard and placed her forefinger against her lip. "Don't wake your daddy."

"Where you goin', Momma?" She ran to her mother and threw her arms around her waist. "Don't go," May continued before Mildred could respond. "Don't go, Momma." Tears streamed down May's face.

"I have to go, honey."

"Why?"

"'Cause I'll die if I stay here."

Mildred looked toward the road as if she was expecting someone to come driving down the hill. Soon, the headlights of a car flared in the distance. The car came to a stop at the top of the hill. Moments later, the headlights flashed down the dirt road. Mildred put her arms around May's shoulders and kissed her on the forehead. "You be good, May."

"Where are you goin', Momma?'

"I don't know, honey, but I will let you know when I get there."

May watched as her mother walked down the steps, across the yard, and up the road toward the car that now displayed only its parking lights. She wanted to scream and awaken her father, do something to stop her mother from leaving. But the only thing she could do was to sob into the darkness.

"I love you, Momma," May half shouted and half whispered. But she was sure that her mother never heard.

Shortly, the car headlights flashed, then drifted behind the hill, leaving only a faint glow above the crest of the road. After a few moments, the light disappeared.

As the horizon turned black, she sobbed into her hands, "Momma ... Momma ... Momma."

That morning seemed a lifetime ago. The faded woman she saw herself becoming bore little resemblance to the ebullient, inquisitive high school freshman of four years earlier. That young girl had evaporated into the night like the mysterious car that took her mother away. May's hopes and dreams had evaporated too. She no longer allowed herself to think of leaving Hamlin, going to Columbus, Macon, or even Atlanta. Her ambitions had been reduced to only the possible, with little room for improbable dreams. If Joe refused to marry her, she would die a spinster in that little four-room shack at the end of Cahill Road.

May heard the screen door open.

Jerome Cahill walked onto the porch and seated himself beside his daughter. After a moment, he took a Camel from the pack in his shirt pocket and lit it. He kicked the swing into motion. The house was quiet now. The only sounds were the interminable noise of the crickets and frogs and the squeaking of the chains as the swing glided back and forth. Cigarette smoke wafted from his nose and mouth as he spoke.

"You okay, May?"

"Yes, Daddy."

"Whyn't Joe stick around tonight?"

"He thinks you don't like him."

"Somethin' I said?"

"No. He just gets a feelin'."

"Truth be known..."

"I know, Daddy."

"Truth be known, May, he ain't nearly good enough for you."

She thought for a moment, then looked into her father's eyes. "Truth be known, Daddy, he's all I got."

"He ain't all you deserve."

May smiled. "I don't hold out much hope for someone

better, Daddy. Ain't no one goin' to come up that road lookin' for me."

He flipped the butt of his cigarette into the darkness. It fell to the ground, glowed for a moment then burned out. "I ain't a fool, May. I know you ain't happy."

"I'm happy enough,.."

"No, May, I can see a restlessness in you. It's the same as I saw in your momma 'fore she left."

"I ain't goin'. I could never leave the little ones. Except for you, I'm all they got."

"Just promise me that if you get too restless, you'll let me know."

"I promise." She kissed her father's cheek then got up and walked into the house. When she looked back through the screen door, he was standing at the edge of the porch, smoking another cigarette. He was staring up the road, where she had watched her mother disappear into the early morning darkness.

Momma ain't comin' back, Daddy. She always knew that was true, but she realized her father was still tortured by her mother's leaving. He had never given up hope and was still waiting for his Mildred to come walking down the dirt road toward home.

That night, May lay awake, staring at the black ceiling. Beside her, Beatrice and Jenny slept peacefully. May remembered a time when she was about ten, standing by the kitchen stove as she watched her mother cook chocolate fudge. She anticipated licking the spoon and scraping the last morsel of warm chocolate from the pan. Her mother was twenty-six and still beautiful after five children. May thought of the garden that grew out back and the horses and cows that grazed the pasture, a green front yard with flowers growing along the fence. She remembered how her father managed all his chores after a hard day's work at the paper mill forty miles away, and how he never complained.

But something went wrong in their lives. The love and tenderness her parents once showed each other faded. May was aware of an estrangement, beginning when her mother was pregnant with Jenny. It lingered and became more evident just before the birth of Beatrice. By the time Mildred slipped away that early morning, she and Jerome scarcely spoke to each other.

If Jenny and Beatrice hadn't been born, maybe things would be different. May was almost instantly ashamed of her thought. She gently touched each of the sisters sleeping next to her and tucked the covers under their chins. She loved them just as she loved all her siblings but sometimes longed to be far away from them, away from all their demands, stealing her youth. In a moment of empathy, she realized these must have been her mother's thoughts on sleepless nights as she agonized over her decision to leave. May envied the freedom Mildred must have found but hated her for it. *Why didn't you think of me, Momma? Why didn't you think of us?*

She cried into her pillow until her anger subsided, leaving only feelings of desperation and a longing to be comforted. She needed to be loved, to be blissfully carried away from reality for just a little while. She thought of Joe and how tender he could be when he made love to her. She would willingly accept his hurtful words after the fact if he could only hold her now. A momentary escape from it all—he could give her that if nothing more.

The words of her father came back. *He ain't nearly good enough for you, May.*

She thought about the way Joe used her, how charming he could be in one moment and cruel in the next. She was that old dog, sleeping just outside the window. She saw herself slinking away after being kicked, returning to the swing to lie at his feet and lick his hand. He would never give her more than the kind of life she was already living, more children, more drudgery, and more derision. How clearly she could see things now. She fell asleep, devoid of emotion, and contented in her belief that she no longer wanted Joe.

MAY AWOKE with an unsteady resolve to change her life. The conclusions she had reached in the calm of the night seemed less certain as light streamed in through her window. She went through all the motions required to get her father off to work and the children on the way to catch the school bus. Throughout the day, she found comfort in the mindless performance of household chores, seldom having time to think of Joe. But he occasionally found his way into her thoughts, making her recall their intimate moments, blinding her to his faults. All afternoon, she wavered, unsure of what she would say to Joe that evening. Her thoughts turned to her siblings. Carl would be graduating from school next year, then Ivy two years later. May would watch Denver and April grow up and leave home. Afterward, she would still be sitting in the front porch swing each afternoon, waiting for Jenny and Beatrice to come home from school. Maybe Joe would come around, but only if she was still pretty. It didn't seem fair that she was the only one without a dream to pursue, doomed to become the spinster she feared.

Why can't I go back to school?

The improbable thought came from a long-suppressed desire which May had pondered occasionally for four years but had never given voice to. *Why not me? If Carl and Ivy and Denver help with the chores, if they do their part, I can go back to school. I can graduate in three more years.*

The longer she considered it, the more realistic and reasonable the idea sounded to her. *I'll be in the same grade as Ivy. But I don't mind.* She laughed, almost giddy with impatience to tell someone of her idea.

It was nearly four p.m. when Joe's bike appeared on the down slope of the road. He stopped near the porch and swung his foot across the seat, dropping the kickstand in an uninterrupted motion. He removed his helmet and pushed back his hair with both hands. His good looks almost took May's breath away, momentarily clouding her determination to break free of his hold over her. But somehow, she masked her emotions. "Don't come up the steps with your dirty boots. I just scrubbed the porch."

He stood by the Suzuki, looking perplexed, apparently amused at May's stern warning.

"Well, ain't we perky today? Talked with your pa, I bet."

"Talked with myself, Joe."

He laughed. "Then I know damn well you didn't learn nothin', May."

"You might be surprised."

"'Bout what?"

"What I learned 'bout myself, that's what."

"And what was that?" He leaned his elbows onto the porch and smiled coyly as he nestled his face in his hands.

May had fallen victim to Joe's flirtations too many times but was now determined to remain as detached as possible. "I ain't sayin' right now."

"Then it's bullshit, May."

"You think so?"

"Yeah, pure B.S."

May got up from the swing and walked to the edge of the porch where she stood above Joe. As she looked into his upturned face, she thought about how handsome he was and how cruel he could be with his words. Yet, she believed there was an innate goodness inside his hard shell and a vulnerability he desperately tried to hide. She hoped her words would not hurt him, but she had to say them.

"I ain't goin' to see you no more."

He scoffed as he stepped back from the porch. "Now I know it's bullshit."

"No, Joe. I'm goin' back to school with the kids."

He threw back his head and laughed. "You're too damn old to go back to school. Ever body will laugh at you."

"They laugh at me now, Joe—you do."

"But you know I love you, May."

"Then tell me you want me to go back to school."

"That don't make no sense. Yesterday, you was beggin' me to marry you."

"I was scared yesterday, Joe. I ain't scared no more."

He looked away but didn't speak. His fingers found the edge of the porch floor planks, and he began to pull at the white, rotted strings of wood, still wet from May's earlier scrubbing.

She watched in silence, feeling as if she towered above him. For the first time since they met, he had no power over her. After a moment, she walked away and sat down in the swing. Joe turned defiantly toward the Suzuki. He picked up the helmet and tossed it across the yard. It landed with a thud against an old car hulk, then bounced askew in another direction. He chased down the helmet then returned to the bike. He threw his leg across the seat and climbed on. With his foot poised to kick the starter, he looked across the porch at May. "When I leave, I ain't comin' back."

"I know, Joe."

The bike screamed as the tire skidded across the yard before gaining traction. Moments later, orange dust trailed the rider until he disappeared over the crest of the hill.

May closed her eyes, fighting back the tears that moistened her face.

The old yellow dog moved from his favorite spot under the window and lay at her feet near the swing. He whimpered as he curled his body against her legs.

"I know you're there, boy," she said as she started the swing into a slow undulation.

The voices and laughter of children in the distance told her that her brothers and sisters were coming up the road and that the house would soon be teeming with their noises.

10

THE BEST HAMBURGER I EVER ATE

My favorite food in the whole world is an old-fashioned hamburger. I'll tell you why.

A few weeks ago, my ten-year-old son and I each ordered a hamburger, fries, and a Coke at a drive-in. I unwrapped my burger and began eating ravenously before my son had even taken the wrapper off his food. I noticed he meticulously laid his burger and fries on an open napkin placed upon his lap. I stopped eating and watched as he picked up the hamburger and savored his first bite.

"Ummmmm," he said through a mouth filled with food. "This is the best hamburger I ever ate. Don't you think so, Dad?"

"It's good," I admitted, "but I'll have to think about whether it is the best I've ever had."

Long after the burgers and fries had been washed down with Coke and we turned our car toward home, I pondered my son's proposition. I am certain he didn't give the matter a second thought and never expected me to consider it for another moment. I could have answered him right away, but it would not have been enough to simply tell him about the best hamburger—where and when I ate it, how it tasted. There is much more to the story.

There were five of us in the old Dodge sedan. Our mother, who was thirty-six, and my older brother rode in the front. My two younger sisters and I were relegated to the back seat, jammed between pillowcases filled with clothing, pots and pans, and a few other personal belongings. That morning, we left behind the only home we had ever known in a little southeastern Kentucky coal town. All our possessions were on our backs, in the pillowcases on which we sat, or in duffle bags and beat-up suitcases in the trunk of the car.

We were on our way to find my father who had left us penniless after the Black Star Coal Company closed the local mine. When Mother learned Dad was living in Baltimore, she made plans to find him. So, we set out on that five-hundred-mile journey.

In preparation for our trip, Mother sold everything we possessed except our clothing and the few items we packed into the car. We said goodbye to our friends and headed out on highways Mother had never before driven.

"We'll be all right with God's help," she said, "and if we watch our money."

We understood that meant we would have to tighten our belts for the trip, and nothing would be bought that we did not need. It also meant we would eat bologna sandwiches two or three times a day and drink only water.

My mother was not a very experienced driver. She had never been outside the county where she was born. It was up to my fifteen-year-old brother to read the map and keep her headed in the right direction. Several wrong turns and double backs impeded our progress, but we still made it to Roanoke before dark that first day. Mother found a filling station where we were allowed to park for the night. The next morning, we ate our last bologna and bread before continuing.

When Mother attempted to start the car, it wouldn't crank. The starter was broken. We waited until early afternoon while the station attendant got a rebuilt starter and installed it. It cost nearly all of our dwindling funds, leaving us just enough money to buy gas for the remainder of the trip.

"With God's help, we'll be all right," my mother said. I watched tears well up in her eyes. She set her jaw, started the car, and drove onto the main road.

That day, we made it to a small town a few miles inside Maryland. None of us had eaten anything since breakfast except a piece of bread. Mother stopped at a filling station just before dark. The attendant filled the tank half full and gave us permission to park for the night.

"That's enough gas to get us to Baltimore." Mother counted her change. "You kids stay here. I'm going to the store down the street to get something for us to eat."

Across the street from the filling station was a silver diner with an obnoxious yellow and purple sign that flashed every few seconds: Hot Dogs and Burgers... Hot Dogs and Burgers... Hot Dogs and Burgers.

"I would sure love a hamburger, Mother." I pointed at the sign.

"Me, too," my brother and sisters chimed, one after the other.

"I don't have enough money, sweethearts." Mother opened her purse and stirred the contents. "But I'll see what I can do."

After twenty minutes, she returned carrying a small brown bag and two RC Colas. "You'll have to share the drinks." She took four hamburgers out of the bag and handed one to each of us.

The best hamburger I ever ate? That was the one. I held the wrapped burger, feeling the pleasant warmth of it against my hand, savoring the aroma of onions, tomato, mustard, and pickles all blended together. Even the texture of the lightly waxed paper wrapper remains unforgettable. I unwrapped the hamburger reverently as if it were a sacrificial offering, aware it might be a long time before I ever tasted anything like it again. I lifted the sandwich to my mouth and bit through the bun, mustard, lettuce, tomato, onion, pickle and patty. "Ummmmm," I muttered, "Ummmmm," as I began to chew slowly.

After swallowing my first bite, I stopped eating long enough to look at my mother's face. She sat quietly in the driver's seat with her eyes closed. She had nothing to eat.

"Where is your hamburger, Mother?"

"I didn't get one for me."

"You want some of mine?"

"No, honey," she said, "you eat it. I'm not hungry."

11

WHAT BECAME OF BOBBY BLEDSOE?

Bobby Bledsoe was the kind of child who was destined to be a turd when he grew up. Mothers all thought him wonderful. Guys just wanted to punch his lights out. He was a pudgy little goodie-goodie, the boy on the front row who always raised his hand to answer teacher's questions or to squeal on the class mischief-maker. It was no wonder he got his ass kicked at least once a week.

"Tommy Turner, if you hit me with that ball, I am going to tell your mother." Fourteen-year-old Bobby had dropped the bat and placed his hands on his hips. He stood over the cardboard home plate defying me, the Sandy Koufax of the neighborhood.

"It's just a tennis ball, you big cry-baby." I caught the ball thrown back to me by the catcher, Pete Kowalski.

"Come on, fat ass." Obviously, Kowalski didn't give two shits about being politically correct.

Bobby took his Babe Ruth stance at the plate, bat in hand, almost begging me to hit him with my next pitch.

"Hum boy; hum babe." Pete held his glove high and inside on the batter.

As I wound up and let go of the ball, my inner demon whispered, *hit the turd.* And so I did, right square on the side of his noggin, and Bobby fell to the ground motionless. We all rushed the plate, the batters and fielders. Someone yelled, "You killed him, Tommy. You killed Bobby."

We gathered in a circle looking down on Bobby's rotund belly. His short little arms lay deathly still at his side.

"Someone do something." I think it was Ron Skinner. His voice was changing back then, and he kind of squeaked out the words.

I removed my glove and scratched my rear end. "Anybody knows how to do mouth-to-mouth insemination?"

Kowalski was bent over laughing, but everyone else looked on helplessly. Finally, Bruce Bigelow pushed his way through the ring of gawkers and knelt next to Bobby. "I do," he said with obvious professional pride. He pinched Bobby's nose and began to blow into his mouth. Bruce raised his head each time to count 1 ... 2 ... 3 and noisily suck in air before ceremoniously blowing again.

By then, someone had alerted the girls playing on the other side of the park that Bobby had been conked in the head and was probably dying if not already dead. I became aware of the female concerns when his sister, Betty, began pounding me on the back. "Killer, killer, killer."

In spite of Bruce's grandiose efforts, Bobby still lay on the ground looking like a dead man.

With Betty clinging to my back, I pushed Bruce away from his prone patient and knelt beside Bobby. By then, Betty was beating me relentlessly on the top of my head. I put my mouth against Bobby's ear and yelled at full decibel level, "Get up, you phony turd, or I will kick your fat ass." Bobby didn't budge.

I looked up, surveying the concerned faces, all of which glowered at me with adolescent indignation. "It's okay. I have everything under control here. I'm just going to do a little CPR."

Betty stopped her attack and pleaded with me to save her brother. "Please save him, Tommy. I will do anything."

"Anything?" I winked at the budding beauty.

"Anything." She slowly blinked her eyes.

I had never noticed the bulges beneath her blouse until then. *Damn, I gotta save Bobby.*

I placed my left hand just below his sternum and pushed hard with my right hand. After a couple of exertions, I caught a glimpse of Bobby's fluttering eyelids.

"He's alive. He's alive!" Judy Jones screamed. The girls all grabbed hands and danced up and down in a circle.

I bent close to Bobby with my ear against his chest, checking for a heartbeat. I felt two grubby little hands pull my head toward his face. He chomped down on my left ear and held on until I punched his gut. "You fat fucker. I knew you were faking." I would have punched him again if not for the thought of Betty's bountiful bosom, which had only recently come to my attention.

Bobby got up, dusted off the seat of his britches, and trotted triumphantly to first base. With a thumb in each ear, he stuck out his tongue and made a gross farting sound. I thought about beaning him again with an errant throw to first but noticed that Betty was watching me. So, I gave her brother a thumbs-up and whizzed the ball by the next three batters. I was no longer interested in the game or Bobby, but rather, whether I could get to first base with burgeoning Betty.

Our tenth-grade homeroom teacher, Christine Cook, was a short, dark-haired girl of twenty-three with brilliant blue eyes. Our class was her first since graduating from the University of Tennessee a year earlier. She wore short skirts and smelled as sweet as honeysuckle. It was her habit to sit on the edge of her desk while reading from a textbook entitled *Kentucky Founders.* All male eyes were glued to her as she occasionally crossed and uncrossed her legs. After getting a glimpse of her black and green garters, I developed a terrible case of myopia and was forced to move to a desk on the front row. Bobby Bledsoe put up one hell of a fuss about exchanging seats with me. I might have empathized with him, but I figured having Bobby that close to Miss Cook was a real wasted opportunity for the male species.

You tell me what red-blooded fifteen (about to turn sixteen) year-old American boy wouldn't want to get a close-up glimpse of Christine's garters. But by the next afternoon, rumors of my obvious voyeurism were making their way across the length and breadth of Sycamore High campus. I learned of my notoriety when Betty pointed her finger at my nose and called me a teenage lecher and swore she never wanted to see me again. Big boobs and all, she turned in a huff and walked away. More intimidating though was Pete Kowalski when he gave me a shadowy nod and a jerk of his head beckoning me to follow him into the boys' bathroom.

Standing astride the urinal adjacent to mine, Pete whispered out the side of his mouth, kinda like a mafia hit man, "I hear Mr. Wilson's looking for you."

"What for?" I couldn't imagine what I had done to warrant a visit to the principal's office; still, my legs grew weak at the thought of facing the six-foot-four snarling grizzly bear.

Pete rolled his eyes. "Miss Cook—Christ, why you gotta be so damned obvious?"

Principal Wilson appeared uncertain as to the best way to approach the delicate subject of Christine Cook's garters. He started by describing how things were when he was a boy. Women dressed less seductively; they wore longer dresses, and boys were less easily distracted from their studies. He continued by telling me of his disappointment in my uncharacteristic behavior. He finished by threatening a three-day suspension. "But you know we have the big game with Carlyle this weekend. I wouldn't want to punish the whole team for something one player has done. They might need their star quarterback."

"Thank you, Mr. Wilson. I really appreciate that, and I apologize if I offended you or Miss Cook. I'm really sorry."

"Still, I've instructed Miss Cook to move you to the back of the room."

"Geez, if you think so, Mr. Wilson. I just hope I can see the blackboard from there."

"Oh, I think you'll manage to see everything you need to, Tommy." He chuckled and growled at the same time while slapping me on the shoulder. "Let's just keep this stuff about the big game between the two of us, okay?" He extended a bear claw in my direction.

The next day, I moved to a seat near the back of the room and Bobby moved to the front row. Before I sat down, he turned to look directly at me, stuck his fingers in his ears and made a less obvious farting sound. I gritted my teeth and muttered, "You little fat fucker." The urge to kick his ass dissipated when my eyes met those of Miss Cook. There was a coquettish twinkle in her baby blues that told me she was not too affronted by my uncharacteristic behavior.

It was at that moment I realized the genius of Bobby Bledsoe. There he was on the front row, sniffing honeysuckle, and slyly sneaking peaks at Miss Cook's garters while I took my seat behind Rosie Radcliff, a potential goalie for the Detroit Red Wings. Worst of all, I might never get a chance to see what was inside Betty's double-D bra.

THE FACES in our small town never seemed to change, and chances were that you would graduate from high school with the same kids you met in the first grade. So, the final semester found the old gang mostly intact. Pete was still the class clown, Bruce the ultimate professional, and Bobby the star student and potential class valedictorian—though word around the school was that he was a fag. No doubt about my manhood though. I was the super jock, lettering three years in three sports and still crazy about Betty Bledsoe, who was only a junior, but sexier than ever. She had forgiven my lusting after Miss Cook, but not my annoyance with her big brother.

The war was raging in Vietnam three years after President Kennedy sent the first group of military advisors and nearly two years after Lee Harvey Oswald splattered JFK's brains on a Dallas city street. Still, that Far-Eastern conflict was the farthest thing from the minds of the jubilant graduates of Sycamore High on that early June afternoon in 1965. We had our visions, hopes, and dreams stretching before us. At least, that's what Bobby said in his speech from behind the lectern in the school auditorium.

By the end of summer, we had all gone our separate ways. I was off to the University of Kentucky on a baseball scholarship, clinging to hope of making the team while on academic probation. Pete Kowalski and Ron Skinner joined the Army on a dare. Ron never came home, but managed to get his name on a black marble wall in Washington, D.C. Bruce Bigelow went off to Detroit to work on a Chevrolet assembly line. Bobby Bledsoe was accepted into the NROTC program at Notre Dame. I heard he graduated in less than three years to become a Second Lieutenant in the Marine Corps. Hard to imagine. I lost track of him after that and never heard anything about him until he came home to Sycamore for the last time a few years later.

And Betty? She dropped out of school during her senior year after getting knocked up by a football jock by the name of Craig Childers. I guess he was my backup in more ways than one. Later, I heard Betty was living with an aunt in Cincinnati.

After that, my life at the university became a blur, lost in hazy smoke, red pills, and white powder. At the end of my sophomore year, I was back in Sycamore, stocking shelves for the only grocery market in our town. My memories of that period are marked by events whirling past, occasionally slowing enough to remind me of my insignificance. I would never make a difference in this world. None of us would. Not Pete Kowalski, not Ron Skinner, not Bruce Bigelow, and certainly not Bobby Bledsoe.

Martin Luther King Jr. was shot dead on his motel balcony in Memphis, Tennessee by a nonentity named James Earl Ray. Robert Kennedy met his death at the hands of a misguided Palestinian who lay in wait in a Los Angeles hotel kitchen. I watched their funerals on television, watched RFK's funeral train make its way through the Pennsylvania countryside, the tracks lined by mourners, the pictures made poignant by the angelic voice of Art Garfunkel singing "Bridge Over Troubled Water." A year later, Ted Kennedy drowned Mary Jo Kopechne at Chappaquiddick. President Nixon was bombing Cambodia, and our boys were still coming home in body bags, even to the small town of Sycamore.

I GOT off work early and would have been at the graveside on time, but my routine visit to the methadone clinic took more time than usual that Saturday morning. I arrived just as the final strains of "Amazing Grace" swept gently across the cemetery. I fell in with the crowd, attempting to be as inconspicuous as possible. I looked around, recognizing the faces of many of my childhood friends and fellow graduates of Sycamore High. Some nodded and smiled. Most stood quietly, appearing respectful, successful, dignified, and hopeful in spite of the sadness of the occasion. I dropped my eyes, looking mindlessly at my unpolished shoes. I wondered if they all had heard about me, about what a failure I had become.

My thoughts were ruptured by a volley of seven rifles pointed into the air, one more volley, then a third, punctuating the end of the twenty-one-gun salute. A major in full-dress uniform bent before Bobby's mother and presented her a tri-folded flag. As mourners filed past the casket one last time, I got behind Pete Kowalski. A photograph of Marine Captain Robert M. Bledsoe, straight and tall, grim-faced, and determined, the Medal of Honor about his neck, sat at the head of the casket. Pete stopped, stood stiffly, and saluted with his one good arm—the other had been left in a swamp somewhere in the Mekong Delta.

It is strange, the things that come to mind at moments like that. I couldn't help but think of the day I beaned Bobby with the tennis ball. The thought made me smile as I wiped tears from my cheeks. *Get up, you fat turd. I know you're faking. Get up, Bobby. Get up.*

12

JULIUS THE TALKING DOG

This is a true story. Only my name has been changed to protect my identity. Julius, my two-year-old Lhasa Apso, tugged annoyingly at my trouser leg, urging me to get up from the easy chair by the fireplace. I hobbled down the hallway with his teeth firmly clinched on my trouser cuff. When we were out of my wife's earshot, he began to chastise me.

"Darn it, Cornelius, I told you I would never speak a word in the presence of anyone but you."

"But I only told Momma."

He raised one side of his mustache in a half sneer. "Momma my little brown butt! I heard you bragging to Frank next door about how you taught me to speak—good thing he thought you were bullshitting him."

Julius only used foul language when he was really upset, and of course, he apologized almost immediately, as I knew he would.

"Pardon my French, Cornelius, but the deal was that my

talking would remain a secret between you and me—just you and me. Remember?"

Of course I did, but there was no way I could keep such a thing from Penelope any longer. I thought Julius would understand. However, it was apparent he had let his ability to talk go to his head and was prepared to play hardball with me. He continued his inquisition, obviously venting lingering pent-up frustrations one would never anticipate in a playful little Lhasa Apso.

"How many others have you told?" He shook his head from side to side in a display of frustration with his blabbermouth *ma*ster.

"I haven't told anyone else, Julius." I raised my right hand. "Scout's honor."

"You want Janice Dean or Laura Ingraham knocking on our door, microphone in hand, followed by three cameramen? That what you want, Cornelius?"

That sounded like a pretty good idea, but I decided then and there that I had allowed Julius to watch too much television. And although I enjoyed our daily exchanges about current events, the Middle East crisis, getting Joe Biden out of office, crime in our streets, and the latest goings-on in Great Britain, I realized Julius was becoming a little too informed. Still, my instincts told me I should appease the canine sophisticate. "Okay, okay, Julius, tell you what I will do."

"Yeah, I'm all ears." He smiled at his own cleverness.

Julius was approaching his second birthday when he uttered his first words in English. Prior to that, I interpreted his unintelligible utterances as a process of developing a menacing growl, apropos to his breeding as a Tibetan Monastery Sentinel Dog. However, I soon learned that he had been uttering a Buddhist chant while in deep meditation. "I don't think I can eat this crap again tonight, Cornelius." Julius sat back on his haunches and gave me a defiant look. While my mouth was agape and I sat in stunned silence, he continued. "How about a little chunk of that steak you're eating?"

"Wha ... Wha ... What did you say?"

He stood and wagged his tail.

I looked at him suspiciously through the corner of my eye as I began cutting on the two-inch-thick T-bone. "Penelope's been gone too long," I said aloud before forking another bite of steak into my mouth. "I am beginning to hear things."

Julius dropped into a sitting position and set up an ear-piercing howl.

I jumped off the counter stool. "What the hell?"

"You like that better, Cornelius? That sound more doggy?"

"Damn, Julius, you really can talk!"

"Yeah. So what?"

"Don't you know how unique you are?"

"How so?"

"Dogs can't talk human. That makes you one in a billion, in ten billion, the only one in the world. You and I will be famous. We will make millions. We'll be wealthy."

"Where do you get this we stuff? You got a Chinaman in your pocket?"

"No. I mean we can get on television, in the movies. We'll be rich."

"Sorry, Cornelius, but that is against my religion."

"Religion? Dog religion?" I laughed and slapped my knee.

Julius gave me a pitiable look. "How about a little credit? I'm Buddhist. I am vowed to a life of poverty."

"You may be, but I'm not. I guess you can't tell that from my lifestyle, though."

"Don't be so hard on yourself, Cornelius. From the looks of that paunch, you haven't missed too many meals. On the other hand, I get nothing but ALPO."

"You want some steak?" I lowered my plate so he could get a gander at the medium-rare delicacy. I thought perhaps the situation required a little diplomacy—after all, I have learned a few tricks from fifteen years of marriage.

"If you don't mind. And cut it into bite-sized pieces. I would do it myself, but you have probably noticed I have no opposing thumbs."

I set the plate on the floor and stepped back to watch him devour it.

Just before he took his first bite, he looked up at me, obviously anticipating all the gourmet meals I would prepare for him in the future. "I appreciate the steak, Cornelius, but please try to be a little less condescending. It is an affront to my intelligence. Could I have a napkin please?"

I watched as he methodically chewed, uttering an ahhh after each bite. By the time the steak was consumed, I concluded that life with a talking dog was not going to be easy.

~

After dinner, I sat down to watch the evening news. Julius took his spot on a throw rug near my chair, wagged his tail a couple of times, then fell asleep. My mind was spinning ninety miles an hour, thinking about how I might capitalize on my dog's talent. I thought I might persuade him by comparing him to some dog heroes. I mused aloud about man and his dog. I spoke of Lassie and Old Yeller. I sang a few lines from the song, "Old Shep," and concluded by likening my canine companion to Rin Tin Tin. Tears were in my eyes, but Julius appeared unaffected.

"It's all right, Julius. You don't have to talk in the presence of others if you don't want to," I said with syrupy insincerity.

He sat up. "I thought we could have some meaningful conversations—be good friends without you thinking of ways to make money off me."

"We can, Julius, if that is what you want. But it wouldn't hurt for you to say a few words in front of others, maybe on the Greg Gutfeld Show or something. How about that, buddy?"

"Not a word, Cornelius, not a word, and that's final."

"OK, but just tell me your secret. How is it you can talk and other dogs can't? Is it reincarnation or something?"

"Reincarnation? Cornelius, sometimes you are a real simpleton. There is no such thing as reincarnation."

"But you said you were Buddhist."

"That's right, but we don't believe in reincarnation. There is a deeper concept called transference or *rebirth.* That's what we believe. Ever read the book, *The Tibetan Book of the Dead*?"

"No, should I?"

Julius shook his head in frustration. "Probably not. More than likely you wouldn't understand. Take me for example. I was born a dog; I will die a dog. But I have the soul of Waldo Khan."

"Waldo Khan?"

"Yes, a distant cousin of Kubla Khan, and I will transfer his thoughts to some other being during my dying process."

"What about now? Can't you do a little transference on the Jimmy Kimmel show?"

Julius jumped to his feet, barked, then bit my hand. "Asshole."

I THINK I did quite well keeping my dog's secret talent hidden from my wife when we talked on the phone. However, when I met her at baggage claim, I could scarcely keep from blurting out, "Julius can talk." And on our forty-five-minute drive from the airport the urge was nearly overwhelming. However, I knew the little chatterbox was pretending to sleep on the back seat while listening to everything I said.

I decided to strike up a conversation to divert Julius's attention and lull him to sleep. "So how was your mother?"

Penelope responded by asking the same question she

always asked after being away for a few days. "Fine. Did the dog mess up the house while I was gone?"

"Of course not. He's been a perfect dog." I thought perhaps such a placebo would please Julius and assure him of my loyalty.

When I finally heard contented breathing from behind me, I touched Penelope's arm and mouthed the words, *Julius can talk.*

She gave me a puzzled look.

I mouthed with more exaggeration, while pointing with my thumb to the dog in the back seat, *The dog can talk,* Penelope blurted out, "For God's sake, Cornelius, what are you trying to tell me with those horrible faces you're making?"

Julius growled.

"What's wrong with him?" Penelope turned to look at the dog.

"Nothing," I said. "Julius has had an upset stomach for a couple of days."

She clutched my hand. "Don't tell me he pooped in the house."

"No. He always runs to the door and barks."

Julius growled again and broke wind.

Penelope frantically waved the odor of dog fart away from her nose. "Puwee."

I rolled down the driver side window. "Sorry, honey, but what can you expect from a dumb dog?"

"Mon Dieu!" Julius said as he covered his ears with his front paws.

I cleared my throat and quickly turned the conversation back to Penelope's mother.

THAT NIGHT, as Penelope and I cuddled in bed, preparing for missed you sex. I realized I had to tell her about Julius. I rose up on my elbow to look into her face. "Honey, I've got something on my mind."

She smiled and tweaked my cheek. "I hope so, sweetheart, I've been gone for two weeks, you know."

"That too, baby, but there's something else."

Her eyes widened. I think she anticipated a new sex technique I had read about while she was gone. "What else?" she asked in a sultry voice.

"Julius can talk."

"And pigs can fly." She rolled over and pushed my hand away from her breast. "Is that your idea of dirty talk?"

"No, honey, no, he really can talk."

"Go to sleep, Cornelius. I'm tired."

Penelope refused to speak to me for the next three days. I waited for the weekend, lit a log in the fireplace and popped the cork on a nice Australian white wine. After each of us had a couple of drinks, I could see little red hearts floating right out of her eyes. The situation was ripe for makeup sex and just right for clarifying the Julius thing.

"Honey, I'm really sorry about the other night. But let me explain." I lowered my voice to a whisper. "Julius talked to me while you were gone."

Julius growled and clamped his teeth onto my trouser cuff.

There I was in the hallway, defending myself from the ire of a little beige and white fuzzball. That was when I realized I needed to change tactics. Julius would be great doing simple dog tricks. We could go on the Greg Gutfeld Show, do a few stupid pet tricks, maybe a little rudimentary verbalizing—nothing fancy or intellectual.

"You know that T-bone you had last week—medium rare?"

Julius nodded, looking interested.

"There's more where that came from—all you can eat."

"And what do I have to do?"

That's when I explained the Greg Gutfeld bit. "I don't know, Cornelius. These things have a way of snowballing."

"You have my word—nothing more than basic stuff. How about it, buddy?"

"Okay, I'll do it for you." He stuck out his front paw, and we shook hand and paw. "I hope I don't live to regret this moment."

In New York, rehearsals went well. I saved the talking part of the act for the televised show, explaining to Greg and his producer that spontaneity was essential to Julius's talking performance.

When our turn came, Greg made the introduction: "Ladies and gentlemen: Cornelius Cooper and his talking dog, Julius."

We bounded onto the stage, drumroll and all. Julius sat, wagged his tail, and waited for my commands.

"Okay, Julius, stand on one leg."

He raised himself up from the floor on one leg and hopped all around the stage, returning to sit by my side. The audience broke out in raucous applause.

"Now, Julius, do a handstand."

Julius stood on his front paws and walked across the stage and back to my side. The crowd was clapping wildly.

"Okay, Julius, one last trick. Do a somersault."

Julius jumped ten feet into the air, did a triple somersault, then landed with a four-leg split. The audience went crazy. I raised my hands to quiet them down.

"Ladies and gentlemen, now the most amazing part of our act. Julius will talk for you."

"Julius, what does Rin Tin Tin say?"

"Roof, roof, roof."

The audience broke out in laughter and wild applause.

"Now, Julius, tell me what do houses have on top of them."

"Roof, roof, roof."

Polite applause and occasional laughter.

I had set the audience up for a grand finale. "Julius, tell me who was the greatest baseball player who ever lived."

"Roof, roof, roof."

The audience booed. "Fake, fake. Make him talk. Make the dog talk."

Julius pushed me aside and stood with his front paws on the microphone stand. "Ladies and gentlemen, I apologize for this corny bit. I told Cornelius the Babe Ruth joke was older than dirt and would not go over well with this sophisticated audience. Besides, everyone knows Hank Aaron broke most of the Babe's records."

After the audience hooted and hollered with deafening applause, Julius disappeared behind the curtain and refused to come to me when I called his name. I attempted to see him the following day but was informed that Julius had disappeared somewhere in the building. For two days, riding the elevator from floor to floor searching for him, I decided he was capable of making his own decisions. So, I prepared to head back home without my talking dog

~

On my drive back to Patch Wood, Nebraska, I thought about Julius and wondered how he would do in New York on his own. His wellbeing was much more important to me than my sadness at losing the best little pal a man ever had. For the next few days, I was too disconsolate to work, regretting that I had ever attempted to exploit his ability to talk. My wife set me up with a psychiatrist. When I attempted to explain the bit about a talking dog, she just scoffed.

"You do need help, and I'm afraid this case is beyond my level of expertise. You really think your dog talked, don't you?

"Yeah, we were on Greg Gutfeld."

She gave me a prescription for paranoia and sent me home to get plenty of rest.

Three days later, I received a phone call from a Fox Network executive. "I don't know what kind of fraud you have pulled on us, Mr. Cooper, but this damned dog has not spoken a word since you left him with us. I think you hoodwinked us with some kind of ventriloquism."

I saw a chance to get Julius back home where he belonged. "It was all part of my act. You have to admit it was pretty good."

"Not good enough," he said. "Come and get your damned dog, or we will send him to a shelter."

I hopped into my car and drove into the Fox parking

garage in New York at 2 a.m. the next morning. Julius was waiting for me in a cage in the green room.

When we were in my car and headed west, Julius finally spoke up. "Sorry, Cornelius, I just missed you too much, especially those grilled steaks you fixed when Penelope was gone."

"There'll be more of those, Julius, I promise."

"Thanks, Cornelius. You're the best."

I patted his head. He was quiet for the remainder of the trip. When we reached Omaha, he said, "It's great to be home again."

"Yeah, we're almost there, buddy."

He sighed and rested his head on the seat beside me. He has never spoken another word since that day. I don't know what will happen to his duty to transfer his soul to another being.

It could be the end of the road for the soul of Waldo Kahn, and I really do feel terrible about that.

13

AN ADMIRABLE WOMAN

Claudia Peters considered herself a sophisticated and admirable woman. She assuaged her guilt for any minor sins she might commit by tithing to her church and giving to the unfortunate.

She lived on Bolton Street in one of the well-to-do sections of Baltimore. Her husband, an Army Colonel, was stationed at nearby Fort Holabird. At the time, he was in London on extended temporary duty. Their daughter, Cecelia, attended Hofstra College. Mrs. Peters kept busy by participating in activities suitable to her social station. Her schedule was controlled by a desk calendar on which were written such events as: Monday, Tea with General's Wife; Tuesday, Wives' Luncheon; Wednesday, Golf; Thursday, Tennis Lesson; Friday, Hairdresser; Sunday, Mass. Saturday was notably blank, which did not necessarily indicate that Claudia Peters had nothing planned for that day of the week.

The boy was in awe as he approached her gleaming white-stone apartment building. It contrasted starkly with the roach-infested, red brick tenement in which his family of six lived a few city blocks away. Massive oak doors guarded the front of the building. He rested two grocery bags on the wrought iron railing, rang the bell, and waited for the buzzer that unlocked the doors. With a bag cradled in each arm, he entered the hallway and ascended the winding stairway to the second floor. At the top, he made one last adjustment to the positions of the bags. With his next step, one of the bags split, emptying its contents down the length of the stairs. At the bottom, a milk carton split open, spilling its contents across the highly polished hardwood floor.

He set the bags on the landing and ran quickly down the stairs, removing his store apron as he descended. He began wiping the floor with the apron. From the top of the stairs, a woman screamed. He looked up to see an irate, attractive lady, whom he assumed to be Mrs. Peters. With her arms outstretched, lifting her hands in incredulity, she scolded him. "My God, boy, what have you done?"

Terrified and embarrassed, he stood to address the lady at the top of the stairs. "I'm sorry, ma'am, but the bag busted."

"The bag burst?" she asked angrily. "The bag burst?"

"Yes, ma'am, that is what I meant to say, the bag burst. I really do know better."

"What do you mean?" she demanded.

"I mean I know that it isn't proper to say *busted*."

She frowned, attempting to hide her amusement and the smile that played at her lips. It was her nature to vanquish a wounded prey, but the innocence of the handsome young man had disarmed her. And although her outrageous anger had dissipated, she did not wish to give that impression. She walked, slowly, deliberately, halfway down the stairs, shaking her head in disbelief. "That isn't why I was chastising you," she said. "You have made one hell of a mess, and I'm not going to clean it up, so you will have to."

"I sure will, ma'am. If you will give me a bucket and some rags, I'll be glad to do it." The boy had no idea that his ingratiating demeanor had already mitigated the severity of his blunder and that, by then, Mrs. Peters considered the matter an unavoidable accident.

She folded her arms and watched imperiously from the stairs as he wiped the floor. He dared not look in her direction until he was confident that no evidence of spilled milk remained. With a final wipe, he stood, looking up at her. Having maintained stern control of the situation, she could now show her merciful side. She smiled and gave a nod of approval. The boy retrieved the spilled items from the stairs. He carried the groceries into the apartment, following behind the kindly Mrs. Peters.

"And here's a dollar for you," she said after the boy had handed her change for a twenty-dollar bill.

"No, I couldn't."

She pressed the bill into his hand and folded her fingers about his. "You must."

They stood, silently looking into each other's eyes. After a moment, remembering who she was, Mrs. Peters chastised herself for her near lapse of judgment as she removed her hand from the boy's. "All right, young man, I have things I must do." She opened the door for his exit. The boy descended without looking back. She watched from the top of the stairs. Just before he opened the large oak door, she called to him. "What is your name, young man?"

"Bradley," he replied. "Brad."

"You must come again, Brad."

At *Tea with General's Wife*, the story of a clumsy eighteen-year-old delivery boy was told with amusement and a scintilla of derision. It was retold at the Wives' Luncheon, enhanced by recounting the boldness of a delivery boy who held her hand a little too long when she attempted to tip him. There was no opportunity to introduce the matter during a round of golf or while exchanging flirtatious repartees with her tennis instructor. But an appointment with her friend and confidant, Maureen, proprietor of Styles by Maureen, provided the perfect venue for relating her amusing encounter. By then, as told by Claudia Peters, the boy had attempted to kiss her on the cheek as he graciously accepted her two-dollar tip. "He was much too forward for my tastes, but he was ever so cute." At Sunday confession, she failed to mention her infatuation with a young man. However, she did admit her flirtation with her tennis professional.

The events of that afternoon did not fade quickly from the mind of the delivery boy. Bradley relived the nightmare of the spilled milk often during the next week, and he berated himself for his carelessness. A less understanding person than Mrs. Peters might have called the store and complained. But the touch of her hand against his had reinforced her forgiveness and reassured him of future opportunities to make amends. He saw no reason to report the incident to his manager, and he kept silent, except for the casual mention of Claudia Peters to his Saturday night date. They laughed together at his clumsiness and his description of the terror the lady evoked in him as she perched above him on the stairway. "But she was really a very nice lady."

It could not be said with any sense of proportion that Claudia Peters was a selfish woman. Indeed, her numerous charitable activities attested to her generosity and good works. Most postal requests or donations were answered promptly, usually with a sizable check enclosed. Several hours each week were devoted to preparing pamphlets in support of causes for unwed mothers. Every Saturday afternoon was set aside to read to residents of the local nursing home. Most Saturday evenings, she dined with a male companion, an old friend of the colonel. Certainly, nothing occurred on those evenings that merited a mention during her Sunday confessionals.

By all reasonable measures, Mrs. Peters was a stalwart of the community, admired by those who knew her. And she saw herself in this light. She took pride in her self-control—in particular, her ability to remain sexually abstinent during prolonged separations from her husband—except for a few meaningless dalliances over the years. Now, she was inexplicably enthralled with a delivery boy half her age. Her desire to see him again overwhelmed her. She convinced herself that there was no sexual component to this desire, only a maternal need to be kind to a boy who was much less fortunate than she. She dialed the store and requested that Bradley deliver several grocery items to her apartment.

When the boy arrived, he apologized effusively for his earlier blunder. She happily assured him that no harm had been done and that such an accident could have befallen anyone. In his naiveté, he presumed that the lady's behavior was nothing more than common courtesy. If he had known how impatiently she waited for his arrival, or how her heart raced at the sound of the front doorbell, he might have understood the opportunities before him. But she dared not let him know. How could she explain to him or anyone else, when she could not even comprehend that she had used a pretext to bring him to her that late afternoon? And even as she invited him to stay with her for a while longer, she was in denial of an enveloping desire to seduce him.

The hour they spent together was innocent enough: talk of family, friends, school, the colonel's accomplishments, and her own charitable activities. The daughter, whose portrait smiled at them from across the room, was discussed only briefly. Mrs. Peters's plans for Cecilia did not include a possible encounter with a delivery boy from the slums--a charming boy, of course, but with limited possibilities. This sobering thought prompted her to bid the boy good evening and to acknowledge that her actions concerning him were outside the bounds of acceptable behavior. But despite this realization, she unobtrusively touched his arm and lightly kissed his cheek before opening the door for him to leave.

At Monday's Tea with General's Wife, no mention was made of the boy. During Tuesday's Wives' Luncheon, she smiled demurely and feigned total disinterest when the subject was broached by one of the other wives. She cancelled Wednesday's golf outing because of a splitting headache, which disappeared when the boy delivered a package of pain reliever to her apartment. But by Thursday morning, the headache had returned, requiring the cancellation of her tennis lesson. She called the store but learned that Bradley was off for the evening. A few glasses of Riesling failed to provide the relief she sought. She called her husband's friend and invited him to her apartment. They shared a few more glasses of wine, a few embraces, and passionate kisses. The friend turned the colonel's picture face down to avoid his stare, but it was a wasted effort. Mrs. Peters came to her senses when the colonel's friend removed his trousers and stood in his knee-length boxer shorts. The fantasy of the boy, his young, firm body, unclothed, could not be displaced by the image of a middle-aged, paunchy lothario. She bid him goodnight and cancelled dinner, which had been a foregone agreement for Saturday night. She would call the next morning, invite the boy over, and tell him she wanted him to make love to her. Consequences? She had not considered anything beyond the fulfillment of her irrational carnal desire.

Following a fitful night of sleep, Mrs. Peters awoke and reflected upon her decision of the previous evening. Some doubts crept into her psyche, which might have been altered with rational contemplation. But she had abandoned rationality to an unfamiliar force which was driving her to fulfillment or destruction. Relying entirely on emotional notions, she was prepared to accept the consequences of either. Later that morning, she dialed the store, placed an order for several frivolous items, then waited for the front doorbell to ring.

By the time Mrs. Peters made her fateful decision, the boy had already awakened to the possibility that she was excessively fond of him. He had taken notice of the frequency of her calls to the store and her obvious ruses to gain his attention. Too often for coincidence, she had touched his arm, kissed his cheek, or held his hand. He was not surprised when she called for an early afternoon delivery. Less than two weeks earlier, he considered Claudia Peters far above his class. Now, he sensed that opportunities lay before him, which he could, heretofore, only have imagined.

She pressed the buzzer then watched from the top of the stairs as the boy emerged from between the oak doors. She waited as he climbed the stairs toward her. Inside the apartment, she took the package he had delivered from his hand and dropped it to the floor. She stood facing him, wanting him to take her into his arms. Sensing his youthful uncertainty, she pressed her body against him and kissed his lips. They embraced as they moved together toward the sofa. He pushed her dress above her waist and hastily removed her panties. As she lay looking up at him, he asked, "Mrs. Peters, are you sure you want to do this?"

"Yes, Brad, do whatever you want with me."

Nature—and perhaps God—has a way of protecting us from ourselves when we are most vulnerable. Or maybe each of us, even the undeserving ones among us, has a guardian angel. As Claudia Peters anticipated the physical sexual experience of her recent life, her guardian angel stepped in. Unfortunately, the boy's protector and benefactor fled the scene, leaving the consequences entirely to nature. For at the point of consummation, with passions at their height, the boy prematurely terminated his arousal. He fell upon Mrs. Peters, holding her tightly, writhing in ecstasy.

"What happened?" she gasped as he continued to nestle his head contentedly against her shoulder.

"I couldn't wait," he said. "I'm sorry."

Mrs. Peters lay frustrated and perplexed, with all sexual desire dissipated. As she stared at the ceiling, the extent of her foolishness slowly washed over her. After a few moments, she extricated herself from beneath the limp body of her lover and slid onto the floor. She stood, straightened her clothing then left the room for a few moments. Upon returning, she paid the boy for the items he had delivered. "I owe you an apology, young man." He never looked back as he descended the stairs and walked out the door. On the hardwood floor, where milk was spilled several days earlier, a large area near the stairs had lost its gloss—odd that her fastidious eye had not noticed it before.

Tea with General's Wife the following Monday was uneventful. At the Tuesday Wives' Luncheon, plans were made for the ladies to travel to the state capital in Annapolis to meet with the governor. Mrs. Peters was happy to be back on the golf links on Wednesday after a two-week absence. The banter and harmless flirtations with her tennis instructor on Thursday were a welcome relief from the self-imposed stress she had experienced recently. Friday's appointment with her hairdresser provided an opportunity to discuss the details of her narrow escape from the clutches of "that impetuous delivery boy--I shan't be ordering from that market again." Even so, the confidential disclosure provided comic relief for the salon patrons. By Saturday evening, Mrs. Peters desired the companionship of the colonel's old friend. And before morning, she admired the figure he cut in his knee-length boxer shorts. At Sunday confession, she failed to mention the friend or her aborted attempt at seducing a young delivery boy. However, she did admit her flirtation with her tennis professional.

14

LAP DANCE

Charlie Grimsley had passed Buddy's Gentlemen's Club a thousand times before Millie's death and never once thought of going inside. But something about the gaudy neon sign was unusually enticing that Friday evening. He found himself sitting behind the wheel of his Chevrolet Malibu parked less than twenty feet from the club entrance. From above the sign, a dapper man in a tuxedo and top hat smiled down and beckoned with a crooked finger. A burly bouncer with a sardonic grin held the door open as if offering him a personal invitation. Charlie's palms sweated as he grasped the wheel and pondered his Baptist misgivings. But the seductive advertisement, alternately flashing from orange to blue to yellow, had its way with him. He got out of his car and walked toward the brute now standing in the doorway.

"Good evening, sir. Welcome to Buddy's," the bouncer said with the obvious enthusiasm and pride of a Waldorf Astoria doorman.

Shielding his face with an unobtrusive wave of his hand, Charlie slid past the hulk and took a table in the darkest corner of the club. He shifted his buttocks nervously on the chair as his eyes adjusted to shadowy silhouettes seated around a dimly lit oval stage. Multicolored diva lights reflected off stainless steel dance poles, sending occasional accusatory flickers his way. The suggestive sounds of *Analyze This* paralyzed his brain while Mona the Magnificent made love to a ten-foot metal phallus beneath pulsating lavender strobe lights. Charlie ordered bourbon—the only drink he knew—and wondered if Millie was watching from somewhere above. He closed his eyes and massaged them with the tips of his fingers as he thoughtfully apologized to his late wife.

Mildred—Millie, he called her—had never been a sexual woman, always willing but never eager. *Maybe it was my fault. I wasn't the greatest lover in the world; just an average working slob.* He picked up his glass and pensively turned it around and around between his palms, occasionally lifting it to his mouth. *I'm lonely, Millie.*

Twenty years as the financial manager for a used car dealership provided a good living for the two of them. They never wanted much, a small home of their own, a reliable car, and children. Their hopes for the latter ended with two devastating miscarriages. "Too dangerous," the doctor advised. So Charlie curbed his sexual appetite and Millie withdrew into a shell. They shared their reclusive lives only with each other except for Sunday morning church fraternization. She read inveterately, tended her summer garden, crocheted, and withered away. He savored his stamp collection, studied great games of the chess masters, and listened to *Prairie Home Companion.* Intimacy was limited to holding hands while watching the evening news, NPR, *Nova,* or the History Channel. The implication of sex rarely reared its ugly head.

Charlie was pulled from his moment of contemplation by the pulsating sounds of a bass guitar. Sexy Simone took to the stage and mounted a pole. She moved to the beat of *Pump It Up,* while close-up patrons whistled, applauded, and waved money above their heads. Simone was joined on stage by Beautiful Brittany and Desirable Desiree, each straddling a pole. Their bodies moved in unison to hypnotic raunchy rhythms.

Charlie stood and slowly made his way to a table closer to the stage. Thoughts of Millie remained in the darkened corner where he first sat. He downed his drink and ordered a second. The pulchritudinous trio simulated lovemaking right before his eyes, and his long-suppressed libido rose to the occasion. The girls closed their act by doffing their tops and writhing bare breasted, to the edge of the stage—tempting serpents from the Garden of Eden. Charlie watched enviously as men in business suits clamored to be the first to slip money into the dancers' thongs. He uttered a sigh, his guilt somewhat assuaged by the voyeuristic acts of his apparent respectable compatriots. He reached for a handkerchief and wiped his brow.

Each dancer climbed down from the stage and mounted the lap of a front-row patron. They began grinding to *Baby Got Back.* He gulped down his drink and for a fleeting moment, considered ordering another. But thoughts of Millie found their way from the darkened corner to his table near the stage and intervened.

Charlie chastised himself for being a fool and got up to leave. He was nearly to the door when a song from the past echoed from the walls of the club. *Earth Angel, Earth Angel, will you be mine.* He stopped and listened to the next line. *My darling dear, love you all the time.* Years ago, that had been his song for Millie. The DJ's voice boomed above the music: Gentlemen, for your vicarious pleasure, our feature presentation, Miss Angel Anderson. Charlie turned and walked back toward the pulsating strobe lights.

A girl in white glided gracefully across the stage, golden hair streaming down her back. *I'm just a fool, a fool in love with you.* The lure of the siren song tugged at him, pulling him closer to the rocks of ruin he had carefully avoided all his life. Charlie sidled tentatively toward the stage. He sat, mesmerized, as the dancer let her white chiffon drape fall near his hand. He picked it up, holding it to his face to inhale her perfume. His eyes never left the ethereal beauty as she caressed the glittering pole. Down to a halter and lacy white panties, she was dancing for him and no one else. Her eyes met his as she dropped the halter to the floor. He gasped at the beauty of her small, erect breasts.

The waitress broke his trance. "Would you like a drink, sir?"

"Yes, please, another bourbon."

Charlie paid the waitress, then, with uncharacteristic boldness brought on by the effects of two alcoholic drinks, touched her arm. "Pardon me, but is Miss Anderson allowed to sit with customers?"

"You mean a lap dance with Angel?"

Charlie nodded.

"She doesn't do lap dances. Would you be interested in keeping her company in one of our champagne rooms?"

He nodded again. "How much is that?"

"Two hundred dollars for half an hour plus drinks."

He pursed his lips. The doubt on his face told the waitress he could not afford such an indulgence.

"We take credit cards." She wiped his table and waited while Charlie twisted in the wind.

I'm just a fool, a fool in love with you. The music trailed off as Angel disappeared through the curtains behind the stage. Charlie sat, desolated. *I have to see her again.* He looked up at the waitress. His words were barely audible. "OK, just this once."

Charlie was shown to a small room behind the stage. Moments later, the girl who called herself Angel entered. She placed a CD into a small player on a corner table. He anticipated the thump of a bass guitar to rumble across the floor, up his legs, and into his ears. Instead, the soothing sounds of *Clair de Lune* filled the room.

She came toward him, smiling, swaying to the piano artistry of Yiruma. "I just love Debussy; don't you?"

"Yes." He gave no indication that he not only didn't recognize the music, but he didn't know the name of the composer.

She was older than she appeared on stage, perhaps thirty, still twenty years his junior. Her eyes were gray, not blue, and her teeth not quite perfect. But there was something about her—compelling, sad, and seductive. She was nothing like the other girls out there lap dancing under pulsating lights.

She sat beside him on the loveseat and poured two glasses of champagne from a half bottle. She touched her glass to his and kissed his cheek. "Here's to a beautiful friendship."

He pulled back and put his hand to the spot of the kiss, savoring her unexpected show of affection. "I . . . I'm Charlie."

With a slight nod, she raised her glass and sipped. "Glad to know ya, Charlie. I'm Angel." She leaned toward him, allowing the white silk dressing gown to open.

Charlie's eyes fell upon her inviting breasts, inches away from his lips. He thought of Millie and what a beautiful young girl she had been. Tears formed in the corners of his eyes. "I'm an old fool, Angel. What would you possibly see in someone like me?"

She reached for his hand. "You're married, I bet."

"No, my wife died a year ago."

"Oh, I'm so sorry." She set down her glass and held his hand between hers. "This your first time with another woman?"

He nodded. "And I . . . it isn't you . . . I'm not sure why I'm doing this."

"You poor man." She lay back against the arm of the couch and tugged at his hand until his head rested on her bosom. Oblivious to the world, he lay quiet while she stroked his thinning hair.

A River Flows in You began to play. Charlie closed his eyes, content with his lips close to her warm flesh. He kissed her soft breast. She gently pushed his head away and looked into his eyes. "Not yet, Charlie. Let's get to know each other better."

He sat up. "Why do you do this?"

"Dance, you mean?"

"Yes, dance ... and other things." He couldn't bring himself to describe the salacious acts he envisioned taking place in other champagne rooms. But he knew instinctively his angel could not be like the other girls of Buddy's Gentlemen's Club.

"I need the money."

"Surely, you could do other things."

"It isn't easy when you have a sick child."

"A child? How old?"

"Nearly seven. His name is Elijah. It's biblical you know."

"Yes, I know. Where is he now?"

"With my mother in New Jersey. He needs a heart operation. That's why I do this." She motioned with both hands taking in the room.

Charlie touched her arm. "I'm sorry. Maybe I can help a little."

She stood, her voice rising in anger. "Do you think that is why I told you about him? I wouldn't hear of taking money from you."

Any doubts he might have had fell away. Girl with the Flaxen Hair caressed his ears. He got up from the couch and put his arms about Angel. "You're too wonderful for this."

She sighed contentedly as she pressed herself against him. He could feel her warm moist breath on his neck. He quietly reveled in the moment, certain that fate had brought him to Buddy's that evening.

"You are such a gentleman, Charlie," she whispered.

His mind floated into sublime oblivion as she nestled closer.

A knock at the door and the voice of another dancer brought him back to sudden reality. "You're on in five, Angel."

A LIGHT MIST fell as Charlie made his way to the blue Malibu. He drove slowly, the effects of four alcoholic drinks still muddling his mind. He touched his face and thought of Angel's kiss and savored the lingering warmth of her soft breast against his cheek. The windshield wipers oscillated across his field of vision as he turned the car onto the freeway. As their rhythmic whispers dispelled water from side to side, they spoke her name, *An-gel, An-gel, An-gel*. He wondered how many other men she beguiled. *No, she isn't like that.* He told himself there was something special between Angel and him. It was true that she entertained other men, but they meant nothing to her. He believed in fate, and fate had brought them together.

The headlights raked across a familiar three-foot hedgerow as Charlie turned into his driveway. To the left was Millie's rose garden where she spent her summer hours. Charlie could almost see her, wide-brimmed straw hat, chambray apron, small garden spade in hand. He looked away and sat for a moment waiting for the garage door to open. An involuntary sigh slipped from his lips; he was relieved to be home safely. Rain was falling heavier now. The wipers stuttered for a moment then resumed their constant motion. Their chant had changed into a monotonic dirge, *you're a fool, you're a fool, you're a fool.*

The car crept forward and stopped inside the garage. The overhead door closed and the automatic light flicked off. An overpowering presence of his departed wife greeted him as he stepped through the kitchen doorway. He pulled back a chair from the table and sat with his face buried in his hands. "I'm sorry, Millie. I'm sorry."

It was almost 8 a.m. when Charlie pushed back the covers and sat up on the side of his bed. The events of the previous evening slowly waxed through his mind. He puzzled over his unsavory behavior and promised himself he would never go back to Buddy's.

After a breakfast of toast and coffee, he dutifully paid penance to Millie by vacuuming the carpets just as he had done for twenty years. He hoped she would take note and forgive him for his indiscretion. In the late afternoon, he mowed the lawn. When the supper dishes were done, he opened a coin album and examined a few of his favorites before returning the album to its shelf. At eight, he turned on the television and surfed the channels, but nothing interested him. By nine-thirty, his car entered the freeway toward Buddy's Gentlemen's Club. A half hour later, the tuxedoed man atop the neon sign was tipping his hat to Charlie. Like many lonely men, Charlie basked in the subtle effects of flattery from a young woman. And whether the inevitable point of no return occurred on the tenth, twelfth, or twentieth visit to Buddy's is irrelevant. It was only a matter of time when, during the mesmerizing musical movements of *Destiny of Love,* tears would roll down Angel's angelic face. And when they did, he would allow her to cry softly into his shoulder.

"Now, now." He stroked her hair. "It can't be all that bad."

"Yes, it is, and I don't know what to do." Her shoulders shook with each sob." I told you I would help."

"No, no. I wouldn't hear of it."

"You know I would do anything for you." He tilted her chin upward, forcing her to look into his eyes. Yiruma's piano filled the room with the lilting sounds of *Kiss the Rain.* Angel took his hand and led him to the loveseat. "I have something special for you."

She allowed her robe to slip from her shoulders as she straddled his lap. Her warm breath caressed his ear. "You are the only one I would do this for."

"I know." He placed his palm tenderly on the side of her face. She grasped his hand and moved it to her naked breast. He lay back against the love seat as the dancer writhed slowly onto her knees in front of him. She unzipped his trousers.

"I'll get you the money, whatever you need." Charlie closed his eyes and listened to Yiruma's hypnotic notes while Angel's caresses carried him to a place he had never been. And now that he had experienced it, he would travel there night after night as long as his creative accounting methods at Eureka Used Cars helped him afford the fares

~

Charlie parked his car in his regular spot beneath the flashing neon sign. He looked up at the man in the top hat, and touching two fingers to his eyebrow, gave the gentlemen a salute. He wanted to share his good fortune with someone, and the man atop the sign was the closest thing to a personal friend he had ever had. Surely, the debonair bon vivant deserved to be the first to know that this was the night Charlie planned to ask Angel to be his wife.

He took his usual table and ordered bourbon. Mona the Magnificent, Desirable Desiree, Beautiful Brittany, and Sexy Simone plied their trade above the appreciative applauding voyeurs. Charlie ordered another bourbon then another as he waited to hear *Earth Angel, Earth Angel,* but the music never played.

He raised his empty glass toward the waitress. When she set a new drink on his table, he touched her arm. "Where is Angel tonight?"

"I thought you knew. She isn't working here any longer."

"Since when?"

"This afternoon. She came in and said she was heading back to New Jersey."

Charlie got up from the table and staggered to the door. The bouncer helped him to his car. "Maybe I should call a cab, Mr. Grimsley. I don't think you should be driving."

"I'm fine, Clint. I'll be careful. Everybody knows old Charlie is always careful." He gave a derisive laugh as he closed the car door. The man in the top hat laughed too as Charlie frantically dialed Angel's unresponsive cell phone number. The man was still laughing when the taillights of the Malibu disappeared among many other lights heading for the freeway.

Charlie was too unsteady to chance driving into the garage. He left the car parked where it had rolled to a stop in the driveway. After fumbling with the key, he stumbled into the living room and fell half on, half off the sofa. He lay that way until the relentless ringing of the phone brought him out of his drunken stupor sometime after nine a.m. *Angel. She's calling to explain.*

"Angel?" He rubbed the stubble on his face and realized he would be terribly late for work again, but he needed to hear her voice. "Mr. Grimsley?"

"Yeah." Charlie's heart fell to the floor at the sound of a man's voice.

"Bill Presley at First National. You got a minute?"

Charlie's hands shook from the effects of two much bourbon. They trembled more in anticipation of what Bill Presley was about to say. "Yeah, go ahead." His words were barely audible.

"You're overdrawn."

"Transfer five thousand from savings."

"You only have two thousand. That may cover your current overdrafts, but there won't be anything left in any of your accounts."

"What about my CDs?"

"You didn't roll them over last month. Don't you remember? You took out more than eighty thousand."

Later, Charlie was unsteady as he stood before the mirror, attempting to shave. He thought of Angel and all he had done to help her and her son. His entire savings and Millie's insurance money were gone. It would be only a matter of time before his deceptive bookkeeping entries at Eureka would be discovered.

He stepped into the bedroom and picked up Millie's picture. He kissed her lips through the glass, then held the frame against his heart. Tears blinded him as he made his way to the car in the driveway. He slid into the seat behind the wheel and turned the key. The engine growled then settled into an almost imperceptible rumble as it rolled reverently into the garage. In the rearview mirror, he could see the hedgerow he and Millie so carefully maintained.

Three hundred miles away, Norma Jean McGraw rested on the back seat of a Mercedes S-600, making its way along Interstate 40 toward Little Rock. Her husband, Greg, slipped a disk into the CD player. *Clair de Lune* wafted through the high-fidelity speakers.

She opened her eyes and held up her hands to examine her nails. "What is the name of the club in Little Rock, honey?" Greg kept his eyes on the road ahead. "The Cypress Club . . . I hear it is a classy joint with lots of high fliers. We should do well there."

"I think I should change my persona. Don't you?"

Greg glanced over the back seat. "Why? I kinda like that whole angel thing."

"I think I'll do Heavenly Heather or maybe Luscious Lola—you know that old song, *Whatever Lola Wants?*" She was quiet for a moment. "Nah, I suppose I'll stick with Angel Anderson, at least for this gig. Charlie Grimsley sure believed I was an angel."

Greg laughed. "For a while, I thought you were really falling for the old guy."

She closed her eyes and listened to *Yiruma* as the skyline of Memphis disappeared from the rearview mirror. "Maybe I was."

Charlie pressed the garage remote. The door lowered, slowly shutting out his view of the hedge and the last remnant of early morning light. He closed his eyes and clutched Millie's picture to his chest. He waited for unconsciousness as an earth angel in a wide-brimmed straw hat beckoned him.

15

THE JIGSAW PUZZLE

The door was closed. But it was early yet, not quite 8 a.m., and Laura's appointment with her radiologist wasn't until 8:30.

I brought the car to a stop in front of the clinic and waited. A few moments later, an attendant unlocked the glass door and waved to us. I wanted to end the conversation we had been having on a positive note. "We just have to have faith, honey."

"That's easy for you to say." My wife's pained expression told me that I didn't understand the mental anguish she was enduring. "I'm the one with breast cancer."

"I know," I said, feeling a little alienated by her subtle rebuff, "but we are in this together." We leaned toward each other for the perfunctory exchange of kisses just before she opened the passenger door and got out.

She stepped inside the vestibule and waited while I parked the car.

I could see her through the glass enclosure as I walked

from the parking lot. At fifty-five, she was still a beautiful woman. I was sure no one could guess she had undergone a mastectomy seven weeks earlier. I entered the vestibule and embraced her. "I love you, sweetheart; I always will no matter what happens."

She smiled and gently touched my face with her gloved hand, almost apologetically. "I know, honey. I know."

It was December and snowing—just in time to give us a white Christmas.

The smell of the live Christmas tree with its bright multicolored lights and decorative ornaments belied the suffering of the patients who would soon fill the waiting room. At least the tree offered a reminder that as long as we have life, we can have hope.

After a week of Laura's daily radiation treatments, we had fallen into a routine. I took a seat in the waiting room while she signed in as the first patient of the morning. A few minutes later, she joined me and opened up a month-old copy of *Southern Homes*. We sat in silence now, keeping our fears quiet as other patients began to fill the room.

They came—some on walkers, some leaning on a husband or wife, a few in wheelchairs, others alone, seemingly unscathed by their cancer ordeals. They were all part of our little fraternity, brought low by a common malady that made us brothers and sisters without social class or distinction. We were bound together for a few days or weeks by fear for our own lives or the life of someone each of us loved. Initiation of new patients into our fraternity began with a simple hello that echoed around the room, with each veteran acknowledging the newest member.

Those of us occupying the waiting room while Laura

and other patients underwent treatment exchanged bits and pieces about our lives. We spoke in near whispers and muted voices, I suppose out of reverence for something we did not understand and feared. A few people opted out of the familiarity, choosing instead to watch four songbirds flitting about in a glass enclosure in the middle of the room. One man sat far away from the group, shielding his face with a *Newsweek* magazine. Another busied himself at a long table that sat against a wall.

Out of curiosity, I walked over to see what he was working at so assiduously. On the table were the makings of a large jigsaw puzzle, the border and a few interior pieces already assembled. He selected a tile from the box, eyed it for a moment, then set it down on the table.

As he pushed several similar pieces with his finger and pressed each into place, I said over his left shoulder, "Looks hard."

He looked up at me for just a moment, then his eyes went back to the puzzle. "It is," he said, "too much white."

I glanced at my watch as I returned to my seat. *Hmm, forty-five minutes ... Laura should be finished with her treatment by now.*

My thoughts were interrupted by the man seated next to me. We had become somewhat acquainted during the week as we talked about the news of the day, weather, and politics. I knew his last name to be Simpson because of the announcements, calling his wife to the treatment room.

"How's the wife doing?" he asked.

"Okay. She's handling it okay. Yours?"

"Radiation is burning the heck out of her skin." He pursed his mouth then slowly pinched his lower lip between his thumb and forefinger. "It's the chemo that is really getting to her, though."

"Laura isn't taking chemo. The lymph nodes were clear, so only radiation and Tamoxifen."

"Ruby has a hard time keeping her food down." There was an unspoken resignation in his voice as if he realized all her suffering through radiation and chemotherapy might accomplish nothing. "She's been at this for over two years, and she's tired, very tired."

I was about to say something that might comfort him, but he resumed talking. "My wife is lucky compared to many of these folks. Some of them have no chance of surviving." He indicated with his head toward the man seated at the other end of the waiting room. "Name's Maynard; lost half his tongue and jawbone."

"God!" I said, putting my hand to the side of my face while trying to imagine the man's agony.

"Might have three months at the most."

I stared at the floor as I attempted to maintain control of my emotions. I realized that Laura's prognosis was good. *Full recovery* was her doctor's verdict, *no more risk than anyone who has never had cancer.* However, if that were true, why was she undergoing the ordeal of radiation treatments? Although I had never voiced these concerns to Laura, they were always present, lying just below my optimism. Now I realized I should thank God for her doctor's proclamation and rejoice that she was not facing a survival expectancy of three months or less.

Simpson continued talking in hushed tones, as if commiserating about the woes of others might somehow diminish his own. He briefly pointed a finger in the direction of the man working on the puzzle. "Ben has no one."

"Ben? The man with the puzzle?" I whispered.

"Yeah."

"Where does he live?"

"Homeless shelter when he isn't here."

I turned in my seat to look directly at Simpson. "What do you mean, when he isn't here?"

Simpson got up and walked into the vestibule. I followed, knowing that he wanted to talk freely about the man seated at the table.

"You say he stays at the homeless shelter?" I asked even before Simpson turned around to face me.

"Yeah. He rides the center bus in the morning, and they pick him up every evening."

"Damn," I said. "What kind of cancer does he have?"

"Every kind there is, I guess—lung, bone; it's gone into his spine."

"How about his radiation and chemo? How's that coming?"

"I understand he completed all his treatments more than a month ago. There's nothing more they can do for him."

"Then why does he keep coming back?"

"Because the folks at this clinic are the only ones who care about him."

"What about the people at the shelter?"

"I guess they will be happy to give his bed to someone else after he's gone."

"Poor sonofabitch."

"You see that puzzle he's working on?"

I nodded.

"Fourth or fifth time he's put it together. He'll finish it by the end of this week, scramble the pieces, then start all over again."

"Jesus Christ! Why?"

"Keeps his mind off dying, I guess."

Simpson walked back into the waiting room, and I followed. A few minutes later, Laura appeared. As I helped her into her coat, I glanced at Ben, still leaning over the table, moving puzzle tiles into place.

As WE DROVE HOME, Laura and I were both silent for a long time. After several minutes, she asked, "What's on your mind?"

"What do you mean?"

"I mean, you haven't even asked how my treatment went or what Dr. Dillon said."

"Honey, I'm sorry. How'd it go?"

"Fine. Doctor says I'm holding up well." She smiled as she reached across the console and patted my hand. "Now tell me what you are so deep in thought about."

"You know the old guy at the table?"

"The one working on the puzzle all the time?"

"Yes. Can you believe he is living at a homeless shelter?"

"You're kidding." Laura raised the pitch of her voice. "A homeless shelter?"

"Yeah."

"I guess we don't know how fortunate we are, do we?"

"No, not until we see what troubles other people have."

We fell into silence again. I couldn't get Ben off my

mind, and I surmised that Laura was thinking about him too. I turned off the city bypass onto Highway 64, the final leg of our trip back to our home in the foothills of the Smokies. I looked at Laura and started to say something, but she spoke before I could get words out of my mouth.

"So, what do you want to do about that man—Ben?"

"How did you know?"

"After twenty-five years?" She laughed.

"Well, I was thinking, day after tomorrow is Christmas, and the clinic won't be open again until Monday. It might be nice to invite Ben to our house for Christmas."

"I knew it. I knew you had something like that in mind."

"What do you think? Would it be okay?"

"Isn't that what Christmas is all about, honey?"

I reached for her hand and held it for a moment. "All right then; I'll ask him tomorrow."

Laura's appointment was at nine, but we arrived several minutes early, as was our habit. Upon entering the waiting room, we were greeted by the faces of people we had become accustomed to seeing. A few nodded. A few greeted us with hello. Mr. and Mrs. Simpson sat in their usual places. Maynard was seated alone at the far end of the room. The chair by the jigsaw puzzle was empty and pushed against the table. We took our seats beside the Simpsons.

"Ben not here yet?" I asked Simpson as Laura handed me her coat and gloves.

"No one has heard anything this morning."

"You think he's okay?"

"I don't know."

Perhaps two years of anguish and uncertainty about his wife's condition had prepared Simpson to accept the demise of others without question. Thankfully, I had not yet reached that stage of despair.

I stood. "Has anyone checked with the shelter?"

He shook his head.

I walked over to the reception desk and knocked on the glass. The girl stood and slid the window open."Do you know what has happened to Ben?"

"You mean Mr. Moyer?"

I turned my head and nodded toward the empty chair at the table. "I guess. Have you heard anything?"

"Wait a minute." She left the office and walked in the direction of the treatment area. After a few moments, she returned. "The doctor says it will be okay to tell you.."

"Yes?" I felt as if I owed Ben one last Christmas, the warmth of our home, and the shared enjoyment of a special meal prepared by Laura's loving hands.

"The people at the center said that he was taken to the emergency room last night."

"Anybody call to check on him?"

By now, Laura was standing by my side. "Calm down, Wade. Everyone is looking."

"I don't care. I just want to know if he's okay."

I turned back to the girl. "What hospital?"

"Baptist Memorial. If you give me a minute, I will call to see how he is." She pushed the buttons on the phone and waited, turning her head away from me as she spoke. "This is Dr. Dillon's office. I'm calling to check on our patient Ben Moyer."

She appeared to listen, then spoke again. "He was admitted to emergency last night, terminal cancer."

Laura took hold of my hand as we both waited to learn something more.

"Thank you," the receptionist said before looking at me.

"He didn't make it. ... died early this morning."

Laura pressed her face against my chest. "I know you wanted to help, honey. But there's nothing you can do." Her eyes filled with tears as she pulled away from me and sat down to await her turn for treatment.

I was drained of emotion when I took my seat next to Simpson. "Ben died this morning."

Simpson placed his arm around my shoulder. "'I'm sorry," he said. "But don't become too invested in the patients you meet here, regardless of how big your heart is. Most of them won't survive."

I sat staring at Ben's empty chair as I heard Laura's name being called. Without thinking about it, I got up and walked to the table where the jigsaw puzzle was partially assembled. I pulled out the chair and began pushing pieces around and pressing them into place.

I thought about all the times Ben must have completed the puzzle, broken it down, and started putting it back together. It was like his life, like Laura's life and the lives of other patients coming to and going from the clinic waiting room. All of them, in some measure, had been torn into pieces then reassembled. For some, the mosaic had been made whole again, but not for Ben For him, the pieces still lay in disarray on the table, waiting to be put back together.

I began to work feverishly, finding the right fit for almost every tile I picked up, as if Ben's hand was guiding mine. I was lost in my task when I felt Laura's hand on the back of my neck.

"How's it going?"

"Pretty good." I pushed back the chair. "Guess I'll finish it Monday."

She bent to kiss my cheek then whispered, "Looks hard."

"It is," I said, "too much white."

16

EXTRA! EXTRA! READ ALL ABOUT IT

An article in the local *Ypsilanti Clarion* announced today that it will now publish only three days each week. This brought home the realization that newspapers all over this country, supplanted by the internet, are closing or reducing distribution for lack of readership and advertisers. I am somewhat distressed by this trend. Newspapers have been such an essential part of my life, commencing when I started delivering the *Knoxville News Journal* at the age of twelve. I, like many people, have relied on the daily press for "all the news that's fit to print," as well as legal notices, obituaries, arrests, weather, crime reports, astrological readings, marriages, and divorces, to name a few. No doubt, newspapers have saved countless lives—perhaps, the life of someone near and dear to you. In fact, one timely published edition of that very same *Ypsilanti Clarion* is the reason a close friend of mine is alive and well today.

My friend, whom we shall call Alfred, is no angel but is not and never has been a bad guy. Circumstances may suggest that he was deserving of the fate then about to befall him. Even so, he remains grateful to this day that an opportune issue of *The Ypsilanti Clarion* saved him from an untimely end—a last minute reprieve from almost certain castration.

Pamela, his secretary, had legs that went all the way up. And she showed them off by wearing skirts that did little more than cover the turn of her rotund derriere. Alfred—subject to temptation like many men—was frequently distracted by panty shots, revealing her brilliantly colored briefs which bore the names of the applicable day of the week. On Mondays she wore yellow, Tuesdays green, Wednesdays orange, Thursdays blue, and on Fridays, always red. Alfred never got to see Saturdays; only her live-in boyfriend, Wayne, was so lucky. However, on one occasion, Alfred was privileged to a close-up view of Friday.

Prior to that consequential evening, his exposure to the leggy blonde's panty flashes was limited to the maximum allowable daily dosage. His inclination to risk higher exposure was kept in check by visions of his cute little wife, Suzie, bifurcated tail, horns protruding from her forehead, guarding the door to his office. However, this imaginary caricature of his wife did not entirely prevent his eyes from occasionally lingering too long on the little pie-shaped piece of nylon peering from under Pamela's skirt. After all, he sometimes needed a reliable means to verify the day of the week.

Alfred was well aware of Pamela's pending marriage to Wayne Wiggins, local TV weatherman and live-in boyfriend. A picture of the toothful prognosticator, holding a Wolverine-emblazoned umbrella, sat on the corner of her desk, reminding all salivating suitors that she was taken. Alfred was kept at bay, not only by this constant reminder but also by daily threats by Suzie to raise his vocal range if he ever strayed. These threats, although not altogether effective, did dampen his longing to check the spelling of the days of the week, embroidered across his secretary's briefs. To limit any potential opportunities, Suzie often called during the day to ensure that both Pamela and Alfred were still on the clock.

The impediments strewn in Alfred's path kept his sexual urges for Pamela in check most of the time. However, a farewell party at Gary's Glowworm Beef and Ale Bistro for a departing fellow employee set the scene for his undoing. As the evening unfolded and empty glasses covered the table, Pamela's reticence evaporated, and she got closer and closer to whisper into Alfred's ear. "Bet you can't guess the color of my panties."

"Sweetheart, I don't have to guess. It's Friday, isn't it?"

She giggled. "You've been peeking, Al."

"Maybe." He laughed and winked.

She moved closer. "You're putting me on."

"No, honey, I'm not putting you on. I'll bet you're wearing red."

She slapped his shoulder. "You dirty old man."

"Well, am I right?"

"I guess you're just going to have to find out for yourself."

A light mist fell onto the two revelers as they leaned against each other on their way across the parking lot. At Pamela's Ford Escort, they embraced, casting caution aside in the afterglow of too much pale ale.

Alfred held open the driver side door. "Are you going to be all right driving home?"

"I don't know. Maybe I need a few minutes to sober up a little." She motioned her head to the seat beside her. "Get in, boss, and let's talk a while."

Alfred glided around the rear of the car and opened the passenger door. "You sure this is okay?"

"Why not? We've known each other for nearly two years, and nothing has happened yet . Get in."

ON THE WAY HOME, Alfred reached for his handkerchief and pulled out a pair of red Victoria Secret thongs. His car screeched to a halt in the parking lot of Lucky Luke's Lube Shop where he dispatched his dangerous cargo into a BFI dumpster. It was nearly midnight when he finally fumbled with his keys at the front door lock. Fortunately, Suzie had fallen asleep on the sofa, lawn shears in hand. He tiptoed his way past his slumbering wife, carefully closed the bedroom door, and slipped under the covers, leaving Suzie to guess what time he arrived home.

At Pamela's apartment, Wayne Wiggins waited anxiously, gravely concerned that his sweetheart would be on the highway, driving long after dark in the rain—forecasted in his 8 p.m. weather report. The relief he felt at her safe arrival was short lived when he discovered her red Friday panties were missing. Reluctantly, he accepted her barely plausible explanation that in her inebriated state, she must have left them in a restroom. However, the next morning, she had no explanation for bare footprints on the

Escort's windshield and passenger window, and tearfully confessed she had been raped by her boss.

Alfred was jarred from his slumber by the ringing of the bedside phone. He turned over and waited for Suzie to answer on the living room extension. He had almost sunk back into oblivion when Suzie burst through the bedroom doorway, little red devils with pitchforks glowering in her eyes. "You bastard."

He sat up and squirmed to the side of the bed furthest away from this irrational, irate little woman. Unsure of what Suzie might know about the previous evening, his survival instincts kicked in. "What the hell's wrong with you?"

"Don't play innocent with me; you know what you've done."

His mind raced to the company parking lot. *She couldn't know. She's just guessing.* He was not about to confess to anything. "What've I done?"

"You know what you've done, you bastard."

Innocence, undeserved persecution, and a plea for understanding rolled off his tongue. "For God's sake, honey, tell me what you think I did."

"You raped your secretary."

That false accusation gave Alfred the vindication he needed for a convincing defense. "What? Whatever gave you that idea?"

Suzie shook her head in disbelief. "You're disgusting."

"Did Pamela just call?"

"No."

"Who?"

"It was a man." Suzie sat on the edge of the bed, her arms wrapped around the bedpost, her face leaning forlornly against her hands. After a moment, she sighed, smiling sardonically. "You'll probably go to jail."

A vision of an effete weatherman with an asinine smile peering at him from the corner of Pamela's desk flashed into Alfred's brain. *I'll squeeze his nuts—if he has any—until he pukes.*

"I hope they come and arrest you."

He winced at the glee in his wife's voice.

She continued, "Do you remember John and Lorena Bobbitt?"

His hands moved automatically to protect his crotch. "You're not going to believe some crackpot making a prank call."

"Prank call, my ass! How did he know your secretary's name?"

"It could have been some weirdo from work who knows both of us, somebody I pissed off . . . people are always getting prank phone calls."

"Bull!" Suzie left the bedroom in a huff. A few minutes later, she returned, holding the lawn shears. "If I were you, Al, I wouldn't sleep too soundly tonight."

DETERMINED to get to the bottom of the accusations, Alfred jumped into his car and sped out of the driveway, heading for Pamela's duplex apartment. He bristled at the thought of the asshole, Wayne Wiggins. *If that smiling little weasel is there, I'll break his damn neck.*

Pamela cracked open the door and peeped through the opening. Alfred stood on his tiptoes, his eyes searching the sliver of room visible through the doorway. "Where's the goddamn worm you live with? "

"What do you want?"

"Tell Wayne to bring his ass out here so I can kick it."

"If I were you, I wouldn't mess with him, Al. He's a black belt in Tae Kwon Do."

Alfred motioned with both hands. "Bring it on. Tell him to get his ass out here, or I'm coming in after him." At that moment, Wayne, looking formidable in his Bermuda shorts and University of Michigan T-shirt, opened the door wide. "You looking for trouble, puke?"

Taking his best Marquis of Queensbury stance, Alfred motioned with his jabbing hand. "Come on out, you little weasel. I am going to kick your ass for you."

With a loud yelp, Wayne bounded out the door, his body contorted in a flying, spinning kick. He followed that with a back flip and came up with arms flailing and an ear-splitting "yeeehaa!" Alfred backed away, keeping his guard up, his hands prepared to land a punch at the first opportunity. Demonstrating his versatility and precise execution of Tae Kwon Do, Wayne attempted several back spins and flying kicks, all of which penetrated the air, but failed to inflict any damage on the amused rapist. After several minutes, an exhausted Wayne Wiggins flopped onto his back on the front lawn. Alfred jumped astride the prone man and sat on his chest. "Why did you call my wife?"

"Why did you rape my fiancé?" Wayne made a half-hearted attempt to extricate himself, but Alfred's one hundred eighty pounds kept the weather warrior pinned to the ground.

Alfred began choking the forecaster. As Wayne gargled

and gasped for air, Pamela beseeched her boss. "Don't hurt him, Al."

He held tighter to Wayne's throat. "Tell this retarded bastard I didn't rape you."

"You have to admit you took advantage of me while I was drunk."

"I think you had something to do with that."

Color drained from Wayne's face as he spit and sputtered.

"You're killing him; you're killing him, Al."

"You bet your ass I am unless you tell him the truth."

Pamela bent down, almost whispering in Wayne's ear. "Can you hear me, sweetheart?"

Wayne almost nodded.

"He didn't rape me, honey. It was partly my fault. Do you forgive me?"

Wayne almost nodded again.

"Do you still love me, honey?"

If Wayne nodded, it was imperceptible to the naked eye.

"Let him go, Al, please, please."

"I will on one condition."

"What's that?"

"What day is it?"

"Saturday. Why?"

"What color are your panties?"

Wayne squirmed, making muffled sounds of "you sonofabitch."

Pamela smiled and tugged at the waistband on her exercise shorts. She pulled at the elastic band of her nylon panties, revealing a sliver of brilliant heliotrope.

Alfred shook his head, releasing his hold on the storm soothsayer. "You are one lucky bastard, Wayne."

On the drive home, he whistled "Everything's Coming up Roses," belying the dread he felt at the thought of facing Suzie and the lawn shears. He envisioned Lorena Bobbitt holding up the severed appendage of her husband, John, for the entire world to see. He realized he would have to sleep in the basement, behind a barred door, next to the water heater for several nights, maybe for the remainder of the month. Perhaps by then, his wife would finally accept his explanation that an obscene phone call was responsible for his unfortunate banishment from her bedroom.

He parked the car in the driveway and tarried for a moment, dreading the renewal of the tirade he had faced that morning. Lying on the stoop was the Saturday issue of *The Ypsilanti Clarion.* He picked it up and carried it under his arm to the kitchen. As he unfolded the paper and placed it on the table, his eyes shone with rejuvenation at the sight of the bold headline: **YPSI Area Plauged by Prank Phone Calls**

God bless our newspapers. Computers can never adequately replace them.

17

TOO EARLY FOR MAGGIE AND THE DOG

It is too early these summer mornings for Maggie and the dog. I usually awaken by six a.m. The dog sleeps until eight, Maggie 'til nine.

I will have her tea waiting when she slips quietly into the kitchen. Then it will be two cups with sugar and cream and a half hour of solitude as she sits, looking from the front porch across a wide green valley into the far hills. She has earned these serene moments as she reflects upon memories and secrets locked safely inside her heart and head. I can only imagine her thoughts as she ponders a life she sees tending toward its end. Cancer has a way of making a person do that.

The doctor can cut away the malignant tumor, and, in time, declare the patient cancer-free. But the knowledge that the body has been invaded, that it remains vulnerable to recurring attacks, lingers long after the operation, chemotherapy, and radiation are over. There is an ever-present fear the amorphous rapist still lurks in the shadows, waiting for an opportune moment in which to strike again. Cancer can be severed from the flesh but not from the mind. And that is how it must be with Maggie.

I once believed I knew her every emotion and could anticipate her words before they were spoken. That ability, whether actual or imagined, has been lost to her quiet introspection. Our laughs together are infrequent, and smiles must be coaxed to her lips. She frowns at frivolities in which she could once find unbridled humor. Stoicism has replaced vulnerability. Her life has taken its serious turn much too early for my liking. I yearn for the Maggie I have known and loved for so long; I yearn for the Maggie of my youth.

"Do you know what next week is?"

She tightened her fingers around mine as we walked along a rock-strewn path below our house. It leads down to a small rippling stream. We go there often in the quiet of the evening just before sunset. We often reminisce together, reminding each other of a bond that has endured between us as friends and lovers for nearly half a century. Toby runs in front of us, sniffing out the trail ahead.

Maggie's question came as the sun settled just above the distant ridge, turning the horizon crimson. Our hands clasp more tightly in an unspoken celebration of three years of cancer freedom for her.

"Red sky at night." I attempted to evade a discussion I feared would diminish our contentment. She tugged at my hand, causing me to stop talking and face her.

"Well, do you remember?"

"Sure. Do I ever forget?"

"The question is, do you think about it often?"

"Three years, cancer-free."

She smiled. "More important than that."

"Our anniversary, how could I not remember?"

"Not our wedding anniversary. I know you never forget that." She looked up at me through the eyes of a dreamer, a romantic who had crashed to earth many times but still held out hope for perfect love. A glimmer of gold shone in her eyes. She smiled sweetly. "I mean the anniversary of our first date, July twenty-second."

"Nearly fifty years; hard to believe."

"Yes, fifty years." A feigned pout crossed her face. "But we weren't always together during that time."

"I always loved you even when you weren't with me." I kissed her cheek then took her hand in mine again as we walked along the stream. "I think we should celebrate that as our real anniversary, don't you?"

"If that is what you would like." I led her around a large boulder lying across the path.

We continued down the trail. My thoughts wandered to our first walk together a long time ago—seven blocks from our tenement apartments to the Rialto Theater on North Avenue. I held her hand that day, but we had little to say to each other. In the seclusion of the darkened theater, we became acquainted. I had no memory of the film, the heroes, or the villains, only the realization that the prettiest fifteen-year-old girl in Baltimore was beside me, and I wanted to kiss her.

The kiss came later as we said goodnight on the white marble steps below her family's apartment. I was oblivious to the usual neighborhood noises, the rattling of bicycles up and down the dimly lighted sidewalk, children at play, shouting above the din of the evening street traffic and automobile horns. I turned my face toward hers and our lips touched. It was an innocent kiss, over almost before it began. But something special had happened between us that would endure through all our happiness and disappointments yet to come. I was sixteen and in love.

I WAS PREPARED to hang up if a man answered. It wasn't the first time I had begun to dial Maggie's number, hoping to hear her voice. But in the past, I never completed the calls, always stopping short before the phone rang. Now, as a light rain hissed against the sides of the phone booth, I waited, uncertain how she would react to my call. Then, she spoke.

"Hello."

I savored the sound of her voice, as youthful as when I first kissed her. After a moment, I asked, "Mrs. Fallon?"

"Yes, this is she."

"Maggie?"

"Josh, is that you?"

"How are you, Maggie?"

"I'm fine. It's been a long time. I guess I'm lost for words."

"Twelve years, but some things never change."

I waited for her to speak again. When she didn't, I said, "Twelve years, and I've never stopped loving you."

"I've thought of you often and wondered if I ever crossed your mind."

"Only a million times."

"Then I'm glad I wasn't a fool."

"What do you mean?"

"I would be a fool, feeling the way I do if you never thought of me."

We met the next day just before noon. I stopped the car alongside the curb and reached across the passenger seat to open the door. She got in, and I sped away before we looked at each other or spoke.

At the light, I turned to her. "You're still beautiful."

My compliment brought a smile to her face. She blushed, as demure as ever.

"I'm just a housewife," she said. "My dreams have all been put behind me."

We drove on.

"Surely you still have something to look forward to." "I have my children."

"Your husband?"

"Bill's a good man."

"But?"

She stared out the passenger window. "I have always been a dreamer. You know, wanting everything to be perfect. Marriage isn't like that—at least mine isn't. But, like I said, I have my children ... and Bill loves me."

"Why isn't that enough?"

"I feel as if life is passing me by. I just exist without hope for something better."

"We all feel that way sometimes."

"Perhaps," she said, "but I always do lately."

"Any place you would like to go?" I reached across the console and touched her hand, attempting to divert her from her pensive mood.

"Let's just drive and talk," she said. "I think I would like that."

We drove around the city that afternoon, visiting our old haunts and noting all the changes that had taken place. The theater where I first found the courage to tell her I loved her was closed. The adjacent delicatessen was out of business. And the drugstore where I used to buy her chocolate sundaes was barred and shuttered. So many changes had taken place in twelve years, but nothing had happened that caused me to stop loving her.

Just before three p.m., she looked at her watch. "I have to go soon. My boys will be getting off the school bus at 4:30, and I need to be there."

I understood that whatever I might wish for Maggie and me, her children would always come first. I took her hand in mine. "I will get you back in plenty of time."

"The Music of Our Lives" played on the radio as we made our way across town. We smiled at songs we had shared. As Eddie Arnold sang the lyrics, "I had you right on the tips of my fingers but I let you slip right through my hands," tears came to our eyes.

I reached for her hand. "I need to kiss you, Maggie—before I let you go."

"I know," she said.

I drove past her house into a cul-de-sac lined with elms and oaks. Under the shade of the trees, I leaned across the console and placed my hand tenderly on her cheek. She responded, turning her face upward toward mine. I kissed her closed eyes, then her lips with all the gentle passion I possessed. My soul reached into hers. I felt Maggie's hand on the side of my face as she returned the emotion and passion of my kiss. For a few moments, she was mine again. When it was over, we moved apart and sat in silence. Moments passed before I found the words to speak. "Twelve years is a long time between kisses."

"I have never been kissed like that before," she said, "How am I ever supposed to get over it?"

"You will, Maggie, but I'm not sure I can."

She opened the door and got out. I watched as she walked away without looking back.

MAGGIE DESCRIBES herself as an evening person. She reads late into the night and, sometimes, early morning. I, on the other hand, am an early riser, a morning person. By the time she is stirring her tea, I will have already watered the lawn and taken Toby for his morning walk. As she reminisces, cigarette in hand, cup at her fingertips, the dog and I will be returning from the trail. For more than ten years, our routines have been predictable, and Maggie and I have each grown accustomed to the other's idiosyncrasies.

"We will be lucky to have ten good years," Maggie had said as we drove away from the wedding chapel.

I remember thinking her words curious, considering how eagerly we both had approached our long-delayed wedding day. "Why do you say that?"

"Because I am too happy. I know it can't last."

"It will, Maggie. I promise."

That reassurance might have sounded hollow, considering that Bill died prematurely at fifty from cancer. And perhaps my two divorces added to Maggie's uncertainty about the longevity of our marriage.

Maggie and I are devoted to each other, considerate and caring. Passion has waned as it does in most marriages and with couples our age. But we both speak of the kiss under the oaks and elms. I think she looks back on it with some sense of betrayal of her wedding vows but with a conflicted desire to experience that same passion and romance again and again. I wish there had been many more days together and many more kisses. However, I am a realist, believing that such a moment occurs only once in a lifetime. We have had our ten good years, and I have kept my promise to Maggie. I pray for ten more years, but I am not blind to the dim prospects of my prayers being answered. I keep such thoughts to myself, sharing them only with the dog during our morning walks.

Shortly, I will smile at Maggie, kiss her forehead, and inquire, "Did you sleep well?"

"Yes, I had a good night," she will say just before she sips her tea.

18

BREAKS OF THE GAME

He fell to one knee then pitched forward less than a second after my roundhouse right landed flush on the side of his face.

I skipped backward to a neutral corner, my hands raised joyously above my head. I knew in an instant that he would not get off the canvas. By then the referee's count was at four and barely audible under the roar of the crowd.

Sweet Sammy Sloan's body relaxed and flattened like a roadkill opossum as the referee counted down: five... six,...

Sammy's legs twitched.

I felt good, dancing while I pounded my gloves together. *Got your ass this time, Sammy. Got your ass good.*

Seven... eight... nine. The count continued to the inevitable end: ten. Like a caped magician performing a feat of levitation, the referee waved his hands over the prone, motionless boxer. But Sammy didn't levitate.

I danced to the center of the ring, hands still raised while

I basked in the knowledge that the championship was mine at last.

The referee took hold of my arm and held it in the air, signifying victory.

My seconds rushed toward me. They surrounded me, jubilantly slapping my back. One of them placed a faux-gold encrusted leather belt into my hands. As I held it against my waist, my manager draped a sea-green robe about my shoulders. *"Champ, Champ, Champ!" my seconds* shouted, raising their fists into the air.

A microphone was lowered from above the ring into the hands of the announcer. His deep bass voice bellowed across the arena, "After two minutes and fifteen seconds of the third round, the winner by knockout and the new ABC Middleweight Champion of the world, Mike Malloy." It was his turn to raise my arm.

"Champ, Champ, Champ," my manager and trainer chanted as they led me toward a television camera and microphone where George Simon, the Sports Channel premier personality, waited to interview the new, unlikely champion.

"How do you feel, Champ?" the announcer asked. A week earlier, he wouldn't have given me the time of day or a chance in hell of beating Sweet Sammy.

"Great.... I feel great, George." I wanted folks to believe George Simon and I were best of friends." When did you know you had him, Champ?" He put his arm about my shoulder, urging me toward the mike.

"When his face hit the canvas." I smiled. "I knew right then he wasn't going to get up."

"Did he hurt you at any time, Champ?"

"No, no, he never did hurt me. He got a couple good licks in, but he never did hurt me."

"The last time you fought Sammy, he beat you up pretty good. You lasted just five rounds. What did you do different this time, Champ?"

I laughed. "I knocked him out, George. You saw it. He didn't hit me, and I hit him. That made the difference. Got him pretty good."

"Will there be a return match?"

"If he wants it, George. I think he deserves a chance."

"Thanks, Champ." He pulled away the mike and began a monologue to his viewers.

Sweet Sammy Sloan still lay motionless on the canvas. By then, his seconds had turned him onto his back and removed his mouthpiece. They cut the wrist bandages and took off his gloves while the ring doctor squatted next to him. The doctor pulled open Sammy's eyelids one at a time as he shined a small flashlight into them.

I shook loose from my supporters and made my way to the corner where I had dropped Sammy to the canvas. 'You OK, pal?" I spoke into his expressionless face.

The doctor leaned over the top rope and spoke to two medical technicians standing below him near the ring. They bolted the steps carrying a Stokes stretcher which they untied and unrolled on the canvas next to Sammy. Moments later, they lifted his limp body onto the stretcher. With the assistance of his handlers, the technicians fed the stretcher through the ring ropes to the floor of the stadium and an awaiting gurney.

Muffled sounds of disconcerted patrons rumbled above the filled arena. Fight fans stood, many of them still not believing their champion had been felled by the likes of Mike Malloy, a boxing has-been and undercard punching bag. They attempted to get a look at their fallen warrior, who was being unceremoniously carried off the battlefield on his shield.

I climbed through the ropes held open by my trainer and walked down four steps to the red carpet leading back to the dressing room. My manager led the way through the crowd that now had spilled into the aisle. Some of the fight fans stretched their arms toward me to give me a congratulatory slap on my shoulder. A few voiced their approval of my handiwork or recalled less glorious nights in my boxing career." Way to go, Champ." "Good work, Champ." "You're still a bum, Malloy."

Back in the dressing room, I doffed my robe and crawled face up onto a massage table. Staring at the ceiling, I began to see Sammy Sloan's blank face as he lay on the floor of the fight ring. Traces of blood still oozed from his nose. It had been wiped away but reappeared as I looked down at him. All the jubilation was gone from my victory. Would Sammy ever fight again? Had he saved any of the money he made the past five years as champion? What about his wife and children? Would they be OK?

"Find out about Sammy, Jerry," I said to my manager who had begun to massage my arm and leg muscles.

"We called already, Mike."

"How is he?"

"Died on the way to the hospital."

No one in the dressing room spoke. The only sound was my tortured breathing as I fought back an urge to scream.

"Ain't your fault, Champ," Jerry said after several seconds. "You just did your job."

"You ever kill anyone, Jerry?"

"No, but I had another boxer..."

"You ever kill anyone, damn it?" I sat up.

"No, I never did, Champ. I never did." Jerry squatted down by the table and began untying my shoes.

There was a knock at the door. My trainer got up and cracked it open. He shut it quickly and clicked the deadbolt. He turned to look back at Jerry. "The goddamn hallway is full of reporters."

"Goddamn, Maggot." When he was irritated, Jerry always called Carlos that. "Tell them vultures my boy is hurting. He ain't in no condition to talk to nobody right now."

Carlos placed his hand on the deadbolt to unlock the door.

"Wait a minute. I think maybe I ought to speak to them," I said. "I'll have to face them sooner or later. It might as well be now."

I slid off the table, picked up my robe, and threw it around my shoulders.

Jerry followed me to the door, opened it, and I stepped out into the hall.

"One at a time, fellas; one at a time." I held up my hands to quiet the news lizards.

"You hear that Sammy Sloan died?" One of the reporters yelled from the back of the pack.

"Yes," I said. "I heard. I'm very sorry."

"Does Sammy's death taint your victory?" A woman reporter, fighting for dressing room equality, yelled above the baritone babble.

I raised my head to direct my voice toward her. "No, ma'am, I don't think so. We were both doing our jobs, both of us taking the same risks."

I thought about my earlier fight with Sweet Sammy when he pounded me into oblivion, leaving me bloodied and beaten on the canvas. I never heard an apology from him, never a call to the hospital to find out my condition. It had taken me four years of beatings and occasional upsets of my opponents to get another shot at Sweet Sammy. I had intended to not waste the opportunity. It could be me next time, carried out on a stretcher half dead, never again to regain consciousness. My next fight might be my last.

"How does it feel to kill someone?" A reporter yelled from the other side of the hall.

The title was mine. The fighters who wanted to beat my brains out would come gunning for me. That is how the fight racket works. No champion lasts forever. Sweet Sammy Sloan didn't, and neither would I. I might not ever win another fight, but as long as I was destined to keep the title, I would hold my head high. I would act like a champion.

"Breaks of the game, fellas; breaks of the game." I smiled coldly.

A disquieting silence fell over the hall.

"That's all, boys," Jerry said. "That's all he's got to say."

As he held the door open, and I walked back into the dressing room, I heard the low rumble of incredulity as the reporters continued to hurl questions in my direction.

Jerry closed and locked the door.

Trembling, I fell to my knees with a prayer on my lips for Sweet Sammy Sloan and the new champion, Killer Mike Malloy.

19

BUCKY LEE'S IN LOVE

William Lee (Buck) Buckhorn subsisted comfortably on a substantial medical retirement from the United States Marine Corps and a thirty-year sinecure with the United States Postal Service. He had accumulated a considerable stock portfolio and bank account. Divorced for more than fifteen years, he was free of all emotional entanglements except for his bitch dog, Jezebel, a ferocious-looking rottweiler, and his best friend, Jerry (J-Rat) Ratcliff. Buck was a loner. And from all outward appearances, he was completely happy.

Buck earned his medical retirement because of a convenient case of post-traumatic stress disorder, resulting from a four-month tour in the jungles of Vietnam. His disabled veteran status provided the entrée to his life of ease at the main post office servicing Elizabethtown. Buck often admitted that the most demanding part of his job was his drive to and from the post office each day.

J-Rat, a former Navy Lieutenant, survived a Vietcong

mortar attack that sent shrapnel through his lower body, destroying his colon and both hips, but leaving his libido too much intact. He perambulated on two stainless steel hips and dumped his partially digested waste into a colostomy bag. Their somewhat similar military experiences brought Bucky Lee and J-Rat together. Their love for riding Harley Hogs, playing golf, and accumulating wealth fueled their camaraderie, making the two men steadfast friends.

A large portion of Buck's wealth was embodied in his collection of antique military weapons and artifacts, stored safely in his basement and guarded by Jezebel. Thus, she was more than a companion. Her tenacious loyalty to Buck—and his to her—was intricately woven into the fabric of the friendship between Buck and J-Rat. For her stalwart vigilance, she was given unencumbered reign of Buck's three-bedroom bungalow. With Jezebel on guard, he was free to make weekend trips to out-of-town golf courses accompanied by J-Rat. In Buck's absence, Jezebel frequently urinated on the kitchen floor, leaving an enduring pungent smell of ammonia that could not be scrubbed away. This indulgence to Jezebel was a source of irritation between the two men but was insufficient to cause any permanent damage to the friendship.

"Jesus Christ, Buck, when are you going to put that bitch outside?" J-Rat rubbed his eyes and held his breath as he entered the vestibule. He craned his neck, directing his words down the hall toward Buck's bedroom. "That goddamn smell is worse than tear gas."

"I'm going to replace the kitchen tile. That's the problem." Buck yelled back.

"What good will that do, Bucky? She'll piss all over the

new tile too." J-Rat made his way back to the front door, opened it, and breathed in fresh air.

"She only pisses when I am gone for more than a day." Buck defended his canine companion with all the fervor of a United States Marine—Semper Fi.

"You must be spending a lot of time away from home, Bucky ... Christ that stuff is potent!"

Carrying his golf bag, Buck lumbered down the hall past J-Rat and out the door. "You want to go golfing or do you want to piss and moan about my dog?"

J-Rat put his arm on Buck's shoulder as they made their way to the Mercedes parked at the curb. Buck threw his golf bag into the trunk, crawled into the passenger seat, and shut the door, thereby cutting off the world from whatever he might have said to J-Rat as they headed across town toward the Village Greens Golf Course.

J-Rat was twice divorced. He was rumored to have driven his first wife mad due to his peculiar pecuniary propensities—he only enjoyed sex if she allowed him to pay her ten dollars per episode, a habit he had acquired in Vietnam. Disillusioned when he reduced the amount to five dollars per session, and searching for true love, she ran away with a college exchange student from Zimbabwe. His second wife, a former beauty queen and go-go dancer, caught J-Rat in a compromising situation with a female meter reader from the gas and electric company. The divorce decree provided his wife with ample compensation for her emotional pain and suffering and added greatly to the pain and suffering of

J-Rat. He consoled himself by surfing internet pornographic and singles websites. There—in addition to finding the impetus for self-gratification—he made the acquaintances of some very eligible, very successful, and very attractive prospects for quasi-permanent relationships.

From all appearances, nothing was missing from the lives of these two friends. However, even for contented men such as Buck, loneliness and lust sometimes creep into their psyches, blighting their rational thought processes, inexplicably wiping away all memories of soured relationships with the opposite sex. Friendships no longer filled voids. The company of a faithful dog, while comforting to the soul, does nothing to relieve the revitalized urges lodged in a man's groins. There is only one thing that can do that: the proximity of a willing woman's vagina.

As most of us know, macho men such as Buck are reluctant to discuss their innermost feelings. Thankfully, there are others—J-Rat for example—who are sensitive and possess innate abilities to detect when things are amiss in a friend's affairs. J-Rat prided himself on being such a man. He knew that something was wrong in Buck's life. The situation required intervention by a kindred spirit, and no amount of protestation and denial by Buck could divert J-Rat from his quest to make things right for his feckless friend.

J-Rat decided to divulge his newly found secrets for happiness to Buck. He picked an opportune time and place—on the second tee just as Buck prepared to strike the ball. J-Rat's disclosure not only provided information vital to his friend's sexual and mental well-being but also served to divert Buck's concentration from his drive on the par five hole. He sliced the MaxFly-1 deep into the woods, allowing

J-Rat to make up for his disastrous hook on the first fairway and to possibly even the score.

"Fuck, fuck, fuck." Buck banged the head of his driver into the ground. "Why did you bring that shit up during my backswing?"

"Jesus Christ, Bucky, I thought you were taking a practice swing."

"Practice my ass. You knew I was just about ready to kick your crotch on this hole too."

"Do you want to know about pussy, or do you want to complain because you fucked up your drive?"

"Neither, by god. I'm going to take a mulligan."

"Bull shit, Buck ... you get a mulligan on the first and tenth holes only."

"Whose rule is that?

"It's the American Legion rule."

"There's no such rule, you asshole."

With that retort, Buck stormed off the tee box, shoved his driver into his golf bag, jumped into the cart, and headed in the direction of the clubhouse.

J-Rat realized just how chagrined Buck was. Otherwise, he would never have left a one-dollar golf ball lying in the woods without attempting to find it. J-Rat hobbled after the cart, screaming every curse word he had ever learned as a sailor and shaking his John Daly driver in Buck's direction.

Buck was out of range of J-Rat's ranting but soon cooled down enough to realize he did not wish to forfeit a forty-dollar greens fee. He turned the cart back around and returned to the number two tee.

The perfect companions resumed their game, with J-Rat agreeing that Buck rightly deserved to take a mulligan because of J-Rat's ill-timed, but well-meaning, remarks. He conceded that it was not good golf etiquette to broach the subject of pussy in the middle of your playing partner's backswing—a major concession by J-Rat.

The head-to-head death match continued without further controversy except for reaction to an occasional poorly timed "Oh fuck!" or "Oh shit!" It would be difficult to determine who held the edge in the emanation of these disconcerting eruptions—all part of a normal day on the golf course with Buck and J-Rat.

In the clubhouse, after play was completed, the gentlemen turned their attention and conversations away from the mundane elements of golf toward lofty ideals about the meaning of life, female companionship, and, of course, pussy. Buoyed by the afterglow of five or six beers, they happily agreed the time had arrived to have a thoughtful discussion on the latter subject.

"I'm telling you, Buck, you can meet all kinds of women on the net—lawyers, teachers, strippers, porn gals."

"Pole dancers?"

"You want pole dancers?"

Buck pulled the long-necked Miller Lite away from his lips and laughed. "I want one that knows how to ride that pole. Know what I mean, J-Rat?"

J-Rat nodded that he did and kept right on talking. "Some of those twenty-year-old gals will knock your eyeballs right out of their sockets." Beads of sweat formed on his forehead as he envisioned the young porn queens he had recently visited on prettylittlepussies.com. and beautifulyoungwhores.com.

No doubt, J-Rat had gotten his friend's undivided

attention and piqued his interest. Buck leaned closer and lowered his voice, "Any local stuff on the internet?"

J-Rat pushed back the Jack Nicklaus ball cap and scratched his head. "Depends on what you want, Buck. You looking to get screwed, or are you looking for a wife?"

"Me get married? You suffering from sunstroke?"

"No. I'm just saying you can find any kind of woman you want on those websites. I'll send you a couple of links tonight so you can see for yourself."

Soon, Buck was speeding along the internet information highway between his gratifying stops at enticing porn and singles websites. Once again, he had everything he desired: a soft job, money, a valuable collection of military artifacts, a faithful dog, an understanding friend, and the occasional company of a beautiful young woman, albeit from a distance. He had become a practiced hand—so to speak—at internet sex. This might have been enough to keep Buck a contented man if he had not, shortly thereafter, stumbled upon a website, "perfect for empty nesters and those in need of companionship." And it might have been karma or sheer coincidence that led Melba Nancy Zimmerman, a forty-eight-year-old divorcée, to belonelynomore.com about the time William Lee Buckhorn was reluctantly paying his membership fee to that same social website.

Nancy—as she preferred to be addressed—and Buck each posted a flattering photograph taken nearly ten years earlier. Her studio glamour portrait, which had transformed an almost fifty-year-old Shirley Booth into a young Catherine

Zeta-Jones, was Cupid's shot through the heart of Bucky Lee. Buck's photograph, sans his omnipresent baseball cap, was clipped from a VFW convention group picture. His black suit and red tie added an enticing touch of respectability, enough to lure Ms. Zimmerman to the lovelorn website time and again. The somewhat long-distance courtship continued unabated while Buck's golf bag sat idle in the corner of his bedroom and his Harley Hog languished in the two-car garage.

After a respectable period of computer foreplay, the potential lovers agreed to meet on neutral grounds. They came face-to-face for the first time in a Ruby Tuesday restaurant on the southern outskirts of Fort Knox. One might normally expect consternation at the ravages of time upon their alluring internet visages. However, contrary to such conventional expectations, the lack of resemblance to their youthful photographs was not an impediment to a mutual romantic attraction. Two bottles of wine sealed the deal, leaving both parties giddy with infatuation.

When the check was presented, Nancy insisted on paying half to obviate any hint of obligation to her internet playmate. The gesture of financial independence immediately endeared her to Buck—a woman, able and willing to pay her own way—was truly a woman after his heart.

A two-week, flesh-on-flesh courtship ensued. It simmered then sizzled, soon erupting into a flaming crescendo one Saturday night, in the king-size, four-poster bed of Nancy's boudoir. After three more weekends of unbelievably satisfying sex, Nancy—who had marriage in mind—talked of the desire to meet Jezebel and spend a weekend in Buck's Elizabethtown bungalow.

At this point, Buck began to ponder how he might solve the pungent piss problem without unduly bruising the feelings of Jezebel. As usual in such sensitive situations, he consulted his best friend. Although J-Rat was feeling somewhat peeved—having been ignored for more than two months by Buck—he realized how desperate his pal was and agreed to assist.

A plan was devised whereby Buck would spend the week with Nancy while J-Rat supervised the fumigation of Buck's kitchen and the replacement of the floor tile. J-Rat proposed placing Jezebel in a kennel while evidence of her indiscretions was being eradicated from the bungalow on Oak Street. However, Buck rejected that element of the plan.

"I can't leave her in a kennel, J-Rat."

"Why the hell not?"

"She'll be heart broke."

"What do you suggest?" J-Rat braced himself for Buck's response.

"You keep her, buddy, until the kitchen is finished."

"Let her piss on my floor?"

"Just take her out morning and evening to do her business. Then she won't piss in the house."

"All I can say, Buck, is that she'll be a dead dog if she pisses one little piss."

The fumigators began their tasks on Monday. Unfortunately, J-Rat fell asleep that evening while watching a triple-X porn flick and did not awaken until seven a.m. By then, Jezebel had urinated on J-Rat's living room Persian rug and was poised to dump a load on his hallway hardwood when he rubbed the sleep from his eyes.

His first instinct was to lob a grenade in the direction of the oversized mongrel. But his humane instincts took hold, and he limited his aggression to a swift kick in the ass and a sharp command to vacate the living room. "Get your dumb ass outside before I shoot it."

As Jezebel sat peering through the glass door, looking forlorn and puzzled, J-Rat's allegiance to his friend waned and wandered. He struggled with his conscience, searching for a solution that would save his friendship, but not risk having his house smell like Buck's kitchen. If he did nothing, Buck would surely marry Nancy Zimmerman, putting an end to his golf outings and his mountain rides with Buck on their Hogs. If he failed to give Jezebel the care Buck expected, he would also alienate his golfing buddy forever. He was caught between that ubiquitous rock-and-a hard place.

"Why the hell am I doing all this? He directed his rhetorical question in the direction of the sliding glass doors separating him from the rottweiler. Suddenly a new plan of action came across the intuitive mind of J-Rat, "I'll put an end to Miss Zimmerman's romantic notions for good.." He plucked the cell phone from the table by his chair and dialed Good Scents Fumigators.

"This is Jerry Ratcliff. Stop all work at the house on Oakwood. Immediately. Do not remove the tile."

He called Lowe's and cancelled the order to replace the kitchen tile. There was no longer a pang of conscience as he dialed Buck's cell phone number. "Yeah, Bucky, everything is fine here. The house will be ready for you and Nancy by Friday evening."

He whistled while loading Jezebel into the back seat. He sang the words to "Anchors Aweigh" almost in tune, as he drove across town. The beautifully noxious odor of stale urine greeted him as he opened the door. "Ahhh," he sighed, "Ammonia never smelled so good."

"The house is all yours, old girl; piss your heart out." He patted her side as he removed the leash from Jezebel's collar. As J-Rat pulled his car away from the curb, he envisioned Melba Nancy Zimmerman gasping for air just before she ran screaming from the house. He heard the unmistakable roar of Harley engines as Buck raced with him along a scenic mountain road. He saw his drive land twenty yards ahead of Buck's, straight down the middle of the number one fairway.

Soon things would be right with the world again.

20

THE UNLIKELY SAVIOR

When two people have spent their adult lives sharing success, failure, happiness, and disappointment while growing old together, it seems fitting that a merciful God would allow them to leave this world at the same time. With no children of their own, Jacob and Agnes always hoped they would take their last breaths holding hands, reminiscing about their forty-eight years of marriage. But Agnes died quietly in her sleep at seventy-two, her passing undetected by Jacob until he had finished his first cup of morning coffee, the discovery leaving him distraught and lonely, pondering the wisdom and ways of the deity.

For weeks following his wife's passing, Jacob, bitter and broken, spent most of each winter day alone by the fireplace. His eyes were drawn frequently to the mantle and a plain burnished copper urn, upon which were inscribed the words, *Adored in Life, Missed in Death, Agnes Ann Finley 1927-1999*. Except for a daily walk to the mailbox at the end of his driveway and an occasional trip to the Cornucopia Food Market, Jacob's universe shrank to one room of his six-room home. His shoulders slumped, noticeable in the mirror, and his spry step deteriorated to a discernible slow shuffle.

In the midst of his despair, Jacob's thoughts turned momentarily to his younger brother, Charles, to whom he had not spoken or written for more than twenty years. Reasons for the estrangement seemed insignificant now. It would be good to hear his brother's voice again. Jacob reached for the phone, then hesitated as his mind searched for words that might bridge the gulf between him and his sibling. He sighed, settling back into his chair. *He probably doesn't want to hear from me; best let things be.* Tears welled as he reflected on a life no longer holding joy or purpose. Resigned to inevitable loneliness, he turned his eyes to the urn on the mantel, then to the place alongside it where he hoped to soon join Agnes.

But it is written "we see through a glass darkly; we know not what the future holds." As Jacob would eventually realize, life and death are matters best left for God in His own good time. Understanding each of us, He works our miracles through might or gentle persuasion as suits His purpose. He sends our saviors in forms we often fail to recognize or appreciate until after we have given them over as sacrifices.

~

Jacob Finley's unlikely savior lay shivering on the doormat, a mass of hair, floppy ears, gangly legs, and a shaggy tail, much too long for his slight body. He stirred and whimpered when Jacob forced his arousal by partially opening the storm door.

"Where in the hell did you come from?" Jacob peered up and down the street, looking for someone who might claim the amalgamated mongrel now making himself at home on Jacob's front porch. "Go on home." The dog wagged his tail and shivered in response.

Jacob squeezed through the partially opened doorway. He picked up his morning paper, then looked again in all directions to see if his neighbors might be witness to his gathering dilemma. He slipped back through the sliver of doorway, scolding the pathetic cur once more, "You can't stay here. Go on now."

He poured a cup of coffee and settled into his easy chair, intending to pass the bulk of the day by intently perusing the morning edition of *The Milton Metropolitan News,* including the want ads, obituaries, and letters to the editor—anything to pass the time. He found his concentration in disarray, getting no usual comfort from his glances at the copper container on the mantel. Nothing in the paper could hold his attention nor keep him from rising from his chair and going to the window at near-regular intervals to inspect the shivering canine lying outside his door. By noon, an uncharacteristic urge to ease the dog's plight overcame his reluctance and he allowed his unwelcome guest to take shelter in the garage.

The evening meal of chicken potpie stuck in Jacob's throat, and after three or four swallows, he opened the door to the garage and set the remainder of his dinner on the floor beside a bowl of fresh water. The dog, with his unkempt brindled coat, looked up through soft hazel eyes and gave a grateful wave of his tail. His charitable act notwithstanding, Jacob was determined to remain aloof. He issued a veiled threat, summoning a semblance of his once baritone voice, the one that resounded to the rafters when called upon to read scripture in church, chilling sinners and causing the devil to slink away. "You better eat, you pathetic cur . . . it's the first and last meal you're getting from me."

The next morning, Jacob did not risk further emotional attachment to the unwanted stray. At 8 a.m. sharp, he dialed the local SPCA shelter. He informed the lady who answered the phone of his involuntary acquisition and asked if he could bring the dog to the shelter for possible adoption.

"I'm sorry, Mr. Finley, but we are overflowing right now, and the city shelter is full too. Can't you keep him for another week or so? We should have a spot by then." The lady sighed, obviously pained at the prospect of acquiring another animal for which a home probably would not be found. "So many animals have been abandoned . . . it's difficult to find people who want them."

Although he had no desire to become responsible for a wandering discard, he could not turn the dog out into the cold.

"What happens to the animals if you can't find homes?"

"We have to put them down."

Jacob wearily stroked his chin. "How long do you keep them before . . . you know . . . you kill them?"

"Ten days to two weeks, depending on how full the shelter is, and the likelihood that someone will adopt."

Jacob weighed the lady's words for a moment, his eyes going to the urn on the mantel, seeking the wisdom and strength of his life partner—but no answer came. He pictured the scruffy mixed breed outside the kitchen door and realized the dog would never find a home.

He became aware again of the lady speaking on the phone and moved the receiver closer to his ear.

"Are you still there, Mr. Finley?"

"Yes, I'm here."

"Can't you keep the dog for a week or two?"

Jacob thought for a moment, torn between his humane sensibilities and his desire for simplicity in his daily routine. He could no longer tell himself that he found real joy in living—nor was it joy that he any longer expected from life, but rather solace and contemplation. These, he found sitting before the fire, sharing his thoughts with the essence in the urn. He intended to say to the lady on the phone, "I'm sorry, but..." Instead, these reluctant words formed on his tongue: *One week. That's it. I'm too old to change my life now for a stray mutt.*

As he drank his next cup of coffee, Jacob wondered why —of all the houses on the block—the dog had chosen his front porch to seek asylum. He pictured a car door opening at the corner and the animal being pushed onto the curb. *Go on, you mangy hound.* Jacob could feel the cruelty of the man's words. He visualized the dog watching the car drive away and finding himself alone and hungry in the freezing cold. Confused by his unfamiliar surroundings, he made his way to the nearest door.

Jacob shivered at the thought of frigid temperatures predicted for the night. He pushed back his chair from the kitchen table and went to the garage. Kneeling by the dog, he stroked its head. "You poor bastard; you're so ugly, only a mother could love you. The folks at the shelter won't ever find you a home." Jacob opened the door to the backyard and watched as the bizarre canine—perhaps fearful of being abandoned into the cold again—cautiously ventured outside.

While the dog explored the backyard, Jacob went to the basement and returned with a large wooden crate, in which he made a bed from old clothing destined for the Goodwill drop box. After several minutes, the dog scratched at the door, and Jacob allowed him to return to the garage.

That evening, the fireplace spread its warmth across the living room. The flickering light occasionally illuminated the copper urn, reminding Jacob of his good fortune to have shared his life with Agnes Ann Finley. He had loved her to the exclusion of everything else in his life, and, alone now, he missed everything about her. What would she have said of the unfortunate animal, curled into a ball, attempting to keep warm in the garage? He heard her unmistakable voice: *Let him inside, Jake.* He went to the garage and moved the crate into the laundry room. The dog followed, then sat by the crate, his grateful eyes searching the old man's face. Jacob patted the dog's head. "If we are going to be together for a whole week, I guess I should give you a name. How about Fred? You look like old man Fred Kemper, the ugliest human being I ever saw; and you certainly are the ugliest dog I've ever laid eyes on." Jacob smiled, wishing he could share the moment with Agnes.

It is for good reason that a dog is known as man's best friend—nothing is more faithful or unselfish. Whatever love is shown to a dog is generously returned, and wrongs are eagerly forgiven. A dog loves freely and unconditionally; he is faithful, even to those who are not faithful to him. Fred must have sensed in Jacob a capacity for love that the old man did not know he still possessed. The dog followed him throughout the house, seldom leaving his side. He waited patiently by closed doors and gleefully greeted Jacob with each reappearance. In the evenings, he lay at his new master's feet, and each night, slept at the foot of Jacob's bed. By the end of the week, the odd couple had found their way into each other's hearts, and thoughts of the SPCA shelter faded far from Jacob's mind.

In the days and weeks that followed, the old man often spoke of his departed wife, sharing his deep hurt and sense of loss at her passing. "I wish you could have known her, Fred. You would have loved her as much as I do." Whether by the fire in winter or in the park on long summer walks, Jacob told the dog of his love for the woman in the urn. Fred always listened, sharing his friend's palpable pain, showing his understanding by a whimper, a wag of his tail, or the touch of his nose against Jacob's hand.

As summer turned to autumn and leaves of yellow, brown, and gold drifted across their paths, Jacob and Fred began their morning walk in the park. Winds blowing across the surface of the lake brought with them the first hint of winter. The nip in the air caused Jacob to pull his scarf tighter about his neck. At the nearest park bench, he stopped walking and sat down, gasping for breath, his face ashen. Jacob stroked Fred's head reassuringly. "It's okay, boy." After a moment, he attempted to get to his feet, but slumped forward onto the ground, one hand clutching involuntarily at his chest, the other reaching for his dog.

Jacob lay motionless. Fred nudged at his master's hand, whimpering impatiently. He sat on his haunches and lifted his face toward the sky, letting go an agonized howl that pierced the air. Nearby joggers converged on the crumpled form of the old man. One attempted CPR while the other ran for help. Soon, calls for an ambulance echoed across the park. Fred sat steadfastly at Jacob's side while the undulating wails of emergency vehicles sounded in the distance.

Jacob awoke to pastel shades of pea-green walls and the pale blue scrubs of ICU nurses. He slowly became aware of the array of hoses and wires connected to beeping monitors at the foot of his bed and drip bags hanging from the metal tree. His surroundings told him he had cheated death—an end he would have welcomed one year earlier while in the depths of mourning for Agnes. But now, he didn't want to die. He had a reason to stay alive. He had Fred. He raised his hand and motioned for a nurse to come near enough to hear his labored whisper. "How long have I been here?"

"Three days, Mr. Finley. You had a heart attack, but you're going to be fine now."

"Where's my dog?"

"I don't know about your dog."

Jacob struggled to sit up, but the nurse placed her hand on his shoulder. "No, Mr. Finley."

"I want to know what's happened to Fred."

"Fred?"

"My dog."

"We'll find out, Mr. Finley." She rubbed his arm reassuringly. "Get some rest now."

"Call the shelter, please." Jake closed his eyes, holding back tears as he pictured Fred, living out his last few days caged and trembling in fear, awaiting his turn to receive an injection ending his life. Or perhaps he was wandering the streets, disheveled and hungry, hoping to be taken in.

THE FIRE FLICKERED, occasionally throwing its light upward to the ceiling and reflecting off the copper urn on the mantel. For three weeks, Jacob had lingered in the hospital, clinging to life, expecting to be taken to be with Agnes. But for reasons known only to God, his life was spared, and he returned home to recuperate.

Now, in his unhappy solitude, Jacob felt the bitterness of the past overwhelming him. He called to the lady in the urn, expecting a small token of solace. "What am I going to do, Agnes? I don't want to live my life alone." But the urn exuded only cold silence.

He thought of the .38 Magnum in the drawer by the bed. *I'll have to arrange things, make sure I don't leave a mess; maybe call Charles before I do it—no, can't do that. Killing myself would be a victory for him. I'll call 911 when I'm ready.*

Jacob rummaged through the night table drawer, took out the pistol, and checked to see that it was loaded. He spread two bed sheets onto the kitchen floor, walked to the mantle, and removed the urn which he took to the kitchen and set on the sheet near the gun. He fell to his knees and attempted to say the Lord's Prayer, but his mind was flooded with words from the twenty-third Psalm: *The Lord is my shepherd, I shall not want; He makes me lie down in green pastures; He leads me beside the still waters; He restores my soul.* His mind lingered on those last four words as he reached for the phone to dial 911. *Please, God, restore my soul.*

Jacob heard barking coming from the porch. Startled, he got to his feet and made his way to the front door. Through the storm door, he saw Fred, sitting on his haunches, his long tail flickering, his tongue hanging from his mouth. Jake hurried onto the porch. "Fred, Fred, where have you been?" The dog stood, rising on his hind feet with his front paws on Jacob's stomach. The old man dropped to his knees and threw his arms around Fred.

"Dingo, Dingo," a young boy shouted as he made his way from the front gate to the porch. He was out of breath as he sank to the top step.

Jacob tried to comprehend what was happening. "You bring my dog home to me? How long have you had him?"

Between gasps for breath, the boy spoke. "I'm sorry, Mister, but this is my dog.'"

"No, son, you don't understand. I lost him when I went to the hospital."

"No, sir, he's my dog. I've had him since he was a puppy. He ran away last year but came back home three weeks ago."

"Why would he run away?"

"We don't know. He jumped the fence one day and disappeared. I looked every place for him."

Jacob dropped to his knees again and stroked the dog. Fred licked the old man's face, then moved closer to the boy. "I guess he's yours, Son, but how did you know where I live?"

"I followed him here. I let him outside for a while, and he jumped the fence again. I ran as fast as I could to keep up with him."

Tears filled Jacob's eyes. "He's a wonderful dog, my only companion for nearly a year."

"I'm sorry," the boy said again. "Thank you for taking care of him."

"We took care of each other, Son, Fred and I. I mean Dingo and I."

"His name is Dingo; but from now on, I'm calling him Fred."

"What's your name, young man?"

"Joey; Joey Wilson."

"You must be a fine boy, Joey, to be loved so much by a dog like Fred."

The boy turned to leave. "I'll bring Fred by to see you sometime if you would like."

"I would like that very much, Son."

As the boy led Fred toward the mailbox, Fred tugged at his leash and broke loose. Dragging his tether, he ran to Jacob and sat, looking apologetically into his old friend's eyes. Jacob bent and stroked the dog's head then picked up the end of the leash. "It's okay, boy, you belong with Joey."

Jacob watched as Fred and Joey disappeared around the corner at the end of the street. He returned to the kitchen. Kneeling by the urn, he found the words to the Lord's Prayer and said them aloud, tears rolling down his face. He thought of Fred, somehow knowing an old man needed him. He visualized the dog jumping a fence, making his way to the front door, giving Jacob new purpose in life. He looked at the gun beside him on the floor, pushed it aside, and thanked God for sending Fred and Joey to save him once again.

That evening as Jacob sat before the fire, he cast his eyes upon the urn. It occurred to him that he had not told his brother of Agnes's passing. He wondered how he and Charles could have allowed a family inheritance to come between two brothers who were once so close. Nothing of material value could truly take the place of love—Fred had taught him that. If his life could be changed by the simple love of a dog, surely a small act of contrition, a simple offer of forgiveness could change the relationship between two brothers. He picked up the phone and dialed. After a moment, he heard his brother's voice on the answering machine. He waited, hoping someone would pick up. When the beep sounded, he hesitated for a moment, gathered his emotions, then spoke. "Charlie, this is Jake. Call me, please. I just want to tell you that I love you."

Still holding the phone, his eyes turned back to the urn. "It's all right, honey. I'll call Charles again tomorrow."

He dialed again and waited. The receptionist answered, "SPCA."

"Yes, ma'am, this is Jacob Finley. I want to adopt a dog."

"What kind of dog are you looking for, Mr. Finley?"

"I want the one no one else wants—the next one scheduled to die."

21

TRIMMING TREES FOR GOD

A sprawling live oak reached skyward, its roots no more than twenty feet from Edward Tinsley's back door. It was one of many such trees populating his sixty-acre estate. The hundred-year-old limbs provided an umbrella of shade over the back yard. The trunk was the altar at which he gave thanks to a mythical being each morning as he and Bowser, the dog, peed against the mighty oak. Mr. Tinsley was not a pious man. He did not attend church regularly. However, once each year, he donned a suit and tie for the annual Christmas play at The One and Only True Baptist Church of Galaxy, Mississippi. He also accompanied his demure little wife, Juniper, to the sunrise service every Easter Sunday. As far as Edward was concerned, this was almost enough to get him into heaven, if there was such a place—this and his generous contributions to the church.

The Baptist absolutes, instilled in him from childhood, had mutated into dubiousness over the years. Even so, Edward's doubts had not entirely silenced the small internal voice occasionally reminding him that a greater power than he was still in control. He had no desire to evoke God's wrath and was determined to compensate for the burgeoning agnosticism gradually anchoring itself to his religious thought. By giving generously to the church through his proxy, Juniper, he attempted to assuage any possible ire directed at him from Jehovah. If the Good Lord accepts secondhand devotion, then Edward's salvation was assured by Juniper's representation. She attended church twice on Sundays, prayer meetings on Wednesdays, and choir practice two other nights of the week. She was active in all manner of volunteer and fundraising events for the poor. Edward was content in the good works of his saintly wife and happy to provide a monthly tithe to the church that exceeded all its collections from other sources. He also donated a large portion of the mortgage payment each month for the training hall being erected as an adjunct to the church.

While Edward may have questioned his own eternal salvation, there were no such doubts in the mind of Pastor Elvis Goodfellow, who would never look a gift horse in the mouth. And although he might have viewed Mr. Tinsley as a queer sort, his nouveau riche financial support and petite little wife were highly valued by the reverend. It was perfectly fine for Edward Tinsley to play golf on Sunday morning while the church accepted his tithing and prayed for him in absentia. However, unbeknownst to everyone, a fateful event was about to occur that would throw a kink into the cogs of this smoothly functioning arrangement. Following a Sunday morning golf outing, Edward turned his AM radio dial toward the sounds of the station, Classic

Country Music. Mistaking the nasally voice of the announcer with that of his favorite country disk jockey, he stopped searching and listened to Brother Jimmy Swindle's Trimming Trees for God Ministry. As the organ rendition of "All Is Well with My Soul"—played by the preacher's wife—faded, Brother Jimmy began to speak. "We," he said, "are like those giant live oak trees you see growing all over this part of our state. They are magnificent indeed, but like every one of us, they are not perfect. Limbs die, branches grow excessively long, and carpenter ants invade their trunks. Like us, dear friends, they need an occasional trimming; they need to be treated to kill those destructive ants. I am coming to you over the radio this afternoon, doing God's trimming, to tell you what you need to do to prune your unsatisfactory life. I'm telling you how to cut off those dead branches. I'm coming to you to tell you how to find salvation today." Edward listened, taking stock of his own life. He even lifted an arm skyward, examining it for dead branches. *Is my tree in need of trimming?* He settled back into his oversized easy chair, sipping on a beer, and listened to the remaining ten minutes of Brother Jimmy's sermon. "Let me ask you, dear friend, did you find time to attend church this morning or did you find some other diversion? Did you fritter away God's Sunday morning doing something selfish for yourself? Did you ignore God's law that says this is his day?" Edward nodded. *He's preaching to me. That man can see right into my soul.* He hastily downed the last ounce of beer, walked over, and turned up the volume on the radio. Brother Jimmy continued, and after several more minutes, wound down his sermon with an inevitable plea for donations. "Friends, if my message touched your heart today and you feel called to send a donation to support this weekly ministry, the address is Brother Jimmy Swindle, that is Brother Jimmy Swindle, S-W-I-N-D-L-E, Post Office Box 222, Galaxy, Mississippi. " Edward felt the calling deep within his heart. He quickly jotted down the address, then turned his attention back to Brother Jimmy's final words. "I am grateful for the donations this ministry receives. But most of the costs of this broadcast are paid from the proceeds of my tree-trimming business. So, if any of you have large trees, such as live oaks or pecans, call me at 228 666 5656. If those trees have dead limbs or have grown too large and need shaping, call that number, 228 666 5656."

Edward thought of the spreading oak right outside his back door and the hundreds more like it on his property; most of them needed trimming. He reflected on the generous contributions he made each week to The One and Only True Baptist Church. As any good businessman would do, he contemplated the return on his investment. He did not discount the piety and satisfaction Juniper realized from the donations made on her behalf. But Pastor Goodfellow had never delivered a sermon that touched Edward the way Brother Jimmy had that afternoon. It seemed fitting to consider an equitable adjustment based on the relative benefit derived from each preacher. Without further deliberation, he decided to give equally to the two ministries. Thus, he would reduce his donations to The One and Only True Baptist Church by half. To say that this decision did not sit well with the dainty little Juniper would be a massive understatement. She burst forth with expletives highly unbecoming of one so steeped in religiosity. When she saw that Edward was unflinching, her ire turned into self-pity.

She bemoaned the ill effects a reduction in the weekly stipend to Pastor Goodfellow would have on her elite standing in the church. She then resorted to the wiles of ordinary women, climbing upon her husband's knee and cooing into his ear. But Edward was unmoved and continued sipping his beer. Finally, she ran up the stairs, slammed the door shut, and fell onto her bed, crying. Her shrill voice penetrated the solid oak bedroom door. "I hate you, Edward Tinsley. I hope you rot in hell." Bowser curled up in his dog bed and covered his ears with his paws. Edward popped the top on another *Miller Lite.* A pall settled over the household at 2100 Thousand Oaks Drive. Hardly a word was exchanged by the occupants during the next week. Edward slept in one of the guest rooms and kept a respectable distance between himself and his seething spouse. And Bowser walked on tiptoes in the presence of Mrs. Tinsley. When Sunday morning rolled around, Edward met his golfing buddies for their 8:15 tee time. Juniper dressed for church and climbed into her Jaguar XK, looking ravishing as always. Inside her purse was a check signed by Edward P. Tinsley, payable to The One and Only True Baptist Church for half the usual amount. She was prepared to explain to Reverend Goodfellow the temporary nature of the downsized donation and the steps she was taking to restore the full amount. After golfing, Edward opened a beer, turned on the radio, and settled back for the afternoon sermon by Brother Jimmy Swindle. The message was particularly poignant considering the state of affairs between the Tinsleys.

"Good afternoon, friends. This is Brother Jimmy Swindle coming to you over WWPZ radio in Galaxy,

Mississippi. The Trimming Trees for God Ministry is on the air again today thanks to the many supporters who have sent in their donations. Special thanks go out to Mr. Edward Tinsley of Galaxy, who has helped us mightily with his generous donations. All this past week, we trimmed and pruned the great oaks on Brother Tinsley's property. We hope today's sermon will help him and all of you, dear friends, trim your tree of life."

Edward set down his beer and cocked his head to take in every syllable spoken by the evangelist. Brother Jimmy continued. "Today's message is taken from Ephesians 5, which I read in part: "Submit yourselves one to another in the fear of God. Wives, submit yourselves unto your own husbands, as unto the Lord. For the husband is the head of the wife, even as Christ is the head of the church."

Before Brother Jimmy could begin explaining the theme of his sermon, Edward's mind had seized upon the Bible reading. A nascent resentment at being locked out of his bedroom by his wife began taking shape. He was convinced that the hand of fate had turned his radio dial to 960 kilohertz, where the tree-climbing preacher broadcast his message each Sunday. It must have been ordained by a higher power that Jimmy Swindle would show him the way, the truth, and the light.

The evangelist preached. "Now, friends, I know there are some modernists out there who will take offense at the basis for this sermon. They will say that the word 'obey' should be removed from marriage vows, that men and women are entirely equal. But you and I know what the 'Bible says. It is clear: 'Women submit to your husbands.'"

Edward lay back on his chair listening intently, unaware the Miller Lite can in his left hand had been sucked dry.

From Galaxy, Mississippi, the deliverer of God's message continued: "It is the man who is head of a happy home. You want to find trouble between a man and wife, just ask: *Who wears the pants in this home?* If there is trouble in the bedroom, friends, you will find that the wife is in control. But is she happy? Is the husband happy? No, friends. And why not? Because God says that the man is head of the household, the woman is to submit to him."

Edward nodded in concurrence. He smiled with satisfaction as he scurried to the kitchen to retrieve another beer, keeping his ear cocked to hear every word spoken by the bold country preacher.

"Listen, all you husbands, if the branches on your tree of life are growing out of control, if they are reaching into your home, into your bedroom, maybe it is time for a trimming; maybe you need to discuss these matters with your mate—come to an understanding that is pleasing to God, and you will have a home pleasing to both the husband and wife.

"If you want to know why there are so many divorces—there I have said that nasty word, divorce, d-i-v-o-r-c-e—just take stock of the way we are living today. The wife does her thing; the husband does his. That leads to too much independence and to trouble, trouble at home, trouble in the church, trouble in the bedroom."

As the sermon neared its end, Edward reflected upon his marriage. Maybe the current estrangement between Juniper and him was not entirely her fault. Perhaps he could have been more diplomatic in his approach, let her down easy; he should have been firm but gentle, and still not yield his position as head of the household. He met his wife at the door when she arrived home after church and enfolded her in his arms. "Honey, we need to talk."

Startled, she extricated herself from his arms, recoiling like a viper watching its prey. "About what?" *Firm but gentle,* he thought. "Our untenable situation."

"Does that mean you have changed your mind about the church tithing?"

"Not entirely, but we can't let that come between us. We need to agree on our roles as husband and wife. Have you ever read Ephesians 5?"

"Have you been listening to that tree trimmer again?" She turned her back and walked stiffly from the room.

Edward followed, thrusting his finger toward the back of her head. "Yes, and you might learn something from him instead of drinking that swill down at your church. Elvis Goodfellow wouldn't know a meaningful sermon if it bit him in the ass."

His comment brought fire to her eyes. Speechless, she turned for the stairs. That night, she locked the bedroom door, leaving the head of the home muttering to himself and vowing to cut off all donations to The One and Only True Baptist Church. Bowser pounced through the doggie door and took shelter in the swimming pool cabana.

The interminable week passed without one verbal communication between the Tinsleys. When they met on the stairs, Edward gave Juniper a menacing scowl which she avoided by looking straight ahead. She attended prayer meeting on Wednesday. At Tuesday and Thursday choir practice, she sang soprano like a bird, her voice joyfully rising above the rafters. As usual, Sunday found her before her mirror, preening and powdering in preparation for the 11 a.m. service.

Edward bowed out of his scheduled morning golf match. He called his longtime partner to complain of a strained back muscle. Although he would never admit it, the disagreement with his pretty little wife was beginning to prey upon his mind. Juniper's continuing rigidity was entirely unexpected. He might have to consider a modification to his unflinching position for the sake of harmony. Perhaps he would offer to restore the tithe to The One and Only True Baptist Church to 70 percent of the original amount. *That should appease her and make life a little more pleasant around here.* He smiled at the thought. Edward reached down and patted Bowser's head, then reclined his chair. He settled back for a nap before the start of Brother Jimmy Swindle's radio sermon. The dog stood and whined obediently at the knee of the man of the house. No doubt, Bowser appreciated the message from Ephesians 5 much more than Juniper did.

That was about the time Sunday school was ending at The One and Only True Baptist Church. The main chapel was beginning to fill. The choir, in their flowing robes, sang "Great Is Thou Faithfulness." Notably missing from the harmony were the high soprano tones of Juniper Tinsley.

Assistant Pastor Dan Forthright took to the pulpit. He raised his arms in praise, then stood in silent prayer as the choir sang the last verse. "Friends, as you can see, Reverend Goodfellow is not with us this morning and neither is Sister Juniper, whose sweet voice is missing from our choir."

There was a buzz and a low rumble of incredulity that moved like an ocean wave across the chapel.

"It pains me to tell you that Reverend Goodfellow will not be returning to our church."

The rumble from the pews was louder and there were lots of *I told you so* looks exchanged by the members.

Assistant Pastor Forthright continued. "Reverend Goodfellow asks for your forgiveness and prayers as does Sister Tinsley. I have a short letter here." He held it up, waving it briefly near his microphone. "I will read it now, and I ask that you be charitable in your judgment of our Pastor and Sister Juniper. I also ask that you pray for Mrs. Goodfellow and Brother Edward Tinsley."

THE PHONE RANG at the Tinsley home a few moments before the scheduled start of the Trimming Trees for God sermon. Edward ignored the ringing and turned up the radio to hear the message from Brother Jimmy Swindle, which was about to start.

The introductory organ music began with "Nothing but the Blood of Jesus." After a moment, the announcer spoke. "Hello, radio friends. As you may have learned already, Brother Jimmy Swindle fell from a pecan tree this past week. He is critically ill in Swan River Hospital with a broken back and neck. He will probably never walk again. His great voice for God may be forever silenced. Please pray for Brother Swindle. But the Trimming Trees for God Ministry must go on. Obeying the will of God and her husband, Sister Swindle will bring you the message today."

For the first time in his life, Edward Tinsley felt lost and alone. He missed his wife. He got up from his chair, clicked off the radio, and turned for the stairs. At the top, he opened the bedroom door and looked in. A small pink envelope, propped against the pillows caught his eye. He sat on the edge of the bed, opened it, and read Juniper's short note.

> Edward:
>
> God controls our lives, sometimes leaving us without our own free wills. He has seen fit to make me fall in love with Elvis Goodfellow. It is God's will, and is beyond my control. I doubt that you will miss me. You have much in your life to make you happy. I have only Elvis.
>
> Be sure to water the plants in the sunroom.
>
> Juniper

The man of the house sat for several minutes, slowly turning to view everything in the room. His attention was drawn to the arched doorway to the bath and steam room. On the right of the entrance was Juniper's walk-in closet, filled with dresses, shoes, handbags, and accessories that made her the envy of her female acquaintances. *Maybe I gave her too many material things.* The lights from her dressing table shone through the doorway. Edward got up and flicked off the switch. He could almost hear her voice as she sat before that mirror, singing while she prettied her face. He left the bedroom and closed the door. Bowser lay at the foot of the stairs. He stood and licked Edward's hand, then followed his master outside.

The sun shone brightly with scattered shards of light flickering through the leaves of the giant oak. Edward looked up through its branches. *I wonder how high Brother Jimmy climbed before he fell.* He struggled against the oak, attempting to climb to the notch where the tree branched into two separate trunks. Bowser whimpered. Edward stepped away from the tree. For a moment, he admired the symmetry of the recently trimmed oak. Bowser whimpered again. Edward bent and stroked the dog's head. He glanced back to the top of the tree. "You're right, boy. That would be a stupid thing to do."

Bowser raised his leg and urinated against the trunk. The man of the house smiled, unzipped his trousers, and peed alongside his dog.

22

THE BOY IN THE MIRROR

There once was a very beautiful boy by the name of Narcissus. He fell in love with his own image. Many young nymphs and goddesses sought his affection, but he rejected all of them because none were as beautiful as he. Enthralled by his own beauty, he sat by a pristine pool adoring the face looking back at him from the water. He longed to kiss and embrace the young man in the pool, but each time he attempted, the water was stirred, and the image disappeared. Narcissus pined away his life beside the pool and died.

— FROM GREEK MYTHOLOGY

In the loneliness of his room, fifteen-year-old Devin found someone with whom he could laugh and cry and share his innermost secrets. The boy in the mirror was always there whenever Devin needed a friend.

~

William was drunk again. He reeled on his heels and leaned toward Devin, grasping his arm, spitting vitriol with every stinking breath. 'Where you been, you little runt?"

Devin's stomach convulsed, propelling the taste of the bologna sandwich he had eaten earlier in the day into his mouth. He squirmed to get away from his stepfather, but William reached for Devin's shirt collar and held on tightly. Devin raised his arms above his head to ward off the blows he thought were coming. "I been delivering my papers."

"You 'sposed to been home an hour ago. You been down to that library on the computer again, I know damn well."

"No, honest, I haven't. I collected today."

"You got money then?"

"No, I had to pay Benson."

"The hell you say. You lyin' to me, boy." His hand went to the sheath on his belt holding a mock-pearl-handled hunting knife. "You don't pay the paper man 'til tomorrow. Think I don't keep track?" His eyes followed his hand to the knife as if to reinforce his unspoken threat.

"No, sir, I paid him this evening." Devin stood stiffly, his eyes now fastened on the knife at William's side.

"Why'd you do that?"

"He helped me collect—drove my whole paper route with me." Devin looked toward the kitchen, hoping his mother had not left for work at the Silver Star Diner, and would come to his rescue. "Where's Mama?"

"Your mama's workin.' Why you ask? You think she's goin' to save your ass?" He raised his eyebrows, shook his head, and laughed—a menacing chortle. "Ain't no way she's goin' to save your ass if I want it, boy. Why you lyin' to me?"

"I'm not lying. Honest, William, my boss helped me collect this evening. He kept what we collected. "

"You been to that library again." He yanked on Devin's shirt, pulling the boy's face closer to his own, his breath strong as ammonia, stinging Devin's nostrils. "If you collected, you got money. Come on, boy, give it over." William clenched his fist against Devin's chin. "Cough it up."

Devin fastened his eyes on William's reddening face, anticipating a blow to the side of his head from the unsteady drunk. Anything Devin might have said would have fallen on deaf ears. When inebriated, William was angry at the world. There was no use talking to him. Devin might have explained how layoffs at the local fabric plant were affecting his customers' ability to pay on time; he might have told William that Benson agreed to drive the route and help collect; but none of that would matter to William—his only concern was getting enough money for another beer or shot of whiskey.

William tightened his grip on Devin's shirt causing his head to snap backward. "You mean you ain't got nothin' left?"

"A quarter." Devin reached into his pocket and displayed the twenty-five-cent piece on his upright palm.

William snatched the money with his free hand, shoving Devin backward across the room. He sprawled near the landing at the foot of the stairs.

William pocketed the quarter then staggered toward the door, looking back at Devin, who had now risen to his feet. "You better not be lyin', boy, 'bout that money; else, I'll beat your ass when I git back tonight."

At the top of the dark stairs, Devin opened the door to his room. He plucked a five-dollar bill from his shoe and pulled the bottom dresser drawer out of its slot, revealing an envelope, postmarked Raleigh, North Carolina. He opened the flap and placed the bill into the envelope. Fingering the six or seven other bills concealed there, he was reminded of the bus trip he would soon take to Raleigh. The thought made him want to read the letter again, probably for the hundredth time. Nevertheless, at that moment, he needed to relish the reassuring words from the friend he had never met:

> Dearest Devin:
>
> Devin, Devin. What a beautiful name! It rolls sweetly off my tongue.
>
> I am so pleased I found you, pleased that we found each other. Yet, I am sad because you are unhappy, for your unhappiness makes me unhappy too.
>
> You sound like such an interesting and wonderful young man. I hope to get to know you better very soon. You are welcome to stay with me in Raleigh. I have a large apartment. Of course, my student instructor duties and my work toward my doctorate keep me busy. But we will still have time to do the things we can enjoy together such as listening to classical music, going to theater, etc. Do you like chess? I'll teach you to play chess.
>
> I will talk with you soon on the Internet. I hope you will answer my letter. I do so love receiving letters.

It will be wonderful when I finally see you in person.

Much love,

Sean McGuire

Devin folded the letter and placed it back inside the envelope. He crept back to the stairway and listened for sounds from downstairs, making certain William had not returned to the house. He placed the envelope into the open slot, then slid the dresser drawer into place, concealing the letter and money beneath the closed drawer. One day soon, he would leave for good, and no one would know where he was going. Only thing was, he feared for his mama and what might happen to her after he left home.

DEVIN PULLED THE CHAIN, turning on the light above his bed. For a few moments, the single bulb swung on its cord, a slow-moving pendulum, casting its shadow on the walls. He lay on a pillow, his hands behind his head, his eyes following the shadow—a swinging hangman's noose—until the motion ceased. Out of the side of his eye, he found his reflection in the mirror. He turned his head away, not wanting to see futility in the face of the boy looking back at him. After a moment, he gathered the courage to look again; this time the boy beckoned him to come closer.

He slipped from the bed and moved across the room. Dropping to his knees, he knelt before the mirror, his arms resting on the dresser top. The boy wiped the last vestige of a tear from his eye while a wistful smile formed on his lips. He consoled Devin. *That's better; everything will be okay when you get to Raleigh. Just wait and see.* Now they were both smiling, moving their heads in unison, Devin admiring the handsome features of the young man behind the glass.

It was a familiar friend Devin found looking back at him, one he sought often in his moments of loneliness or despair. He could no longer turn to his mother for comfort and protection from William the way he once could. Her work shift ended at ten each evening, but a deliberately slow walk home assured her William would be sleeping or passed out by the time she arrived at eleven. Most evenings, Devin avoided William's drunken spates by withdrawing to the solitude of his room, alone except for his alter ego in the mirror.

He missed the warmth of his mother's embraces, the smell of lilacs when his face touched her hair. He thought of the feel of nylon against his skin, the way it was when his mother used to hold him each night, promising things would get better. He heard the swish of her nightgown across the floor as she walked to the door, turning then to blow a goodnight kiss. "I love you, Son." His hand reached out to her, touching the cold of the looking glass. Startled, his eyes met those of the boy in the mirror as he clasped Devin's hand.

Their smiles broadened then faded to flirtatious pouts. Devin moved his head closer to the mirror, examining every feature of his face. He admired the dark hair covering the tops of his ears and falling gently on the back of his neck. He tilted his head, smiled, frowned, and laughed, his emerald eyes watching the light reflect off perfect white teeth. A fragrance of lilac wafted through the open door. "Mama?" He rushed to the landing but saw only a glimmer of light at the bottom of the enclosed stairway. He stood for a moment and listened to the sounds of silence from downstairs. An unmistakable scent of his mother penetrated his senses, drawing him into her bedroom. Kneeling before a bureau, he opened the drawer and removed a long crimson gown, which he slipped over his head. He smoothed the gown down the length of his body, relishing the cool sensuality of the nylon, imagining it silk. He returned to his room and sat before the mirror. The boy looking back at him nodded approvingly.

Engrossed by the beauty of the boy in the mirror, Devin sat, quietly admiring his features. His dark hair and green eyes contrasted perfectly with the crimson hue of his mother's nightgown. He flashed a smile, turning his head slowly from side to side, tilting it first one way then another, assessing the aesthetic features of his face from every angle. His hands reached out and touched the cold surface of the mirror. Bewildered by the reality of his uncharacteristic actions, he jumped to his feet and began to remove the gown. He turned toward the door and saw William standing there.

William reached for the gown, pulling it from Devin's grasp. "What do you think you're doin', you little pansy?"

"Nothing." He might have attempted an explanation if he understood himself. "I don't know, William."

"Wait 'til your mother sees what a little queer she has made out of you, treating you like a baby."

"I'm not a queer."

"You got a smart mouth on you, boy."

William swung his arm upward, striking Devin with the back of his hand, sending the boy sprawling across the bed. By the time Devin sat up, William had removed his leather belt from its loops, the hunting knife falling to the floor and skidding under Devin's bed. William struck the boy again and again with the belt. Devin curled into a fetal ball and stoically absorbed the punishment from his stepfather.

Devin lay quiet for several minutes after the beating ceased. He pulled the quilt tightly about him, hoping the warmth of the cover would relieve the throbbing welts raised on his back by William's belt. The bedsprings creaked in unison with arrhythmic sobs racking Devin's small frame. An occasional whimper eked from his lips, despite his efforts to suppress the need to cry. If he showed the slightest signs of weakness, William would stagger up the stairs and beat him more. For now, he would quietly endure his agony. He would endure it until—until when? Devin didn't know but was sure of one thing: if he couldn't run away, someday, he would have to kill William.

Morning brought with it a resurgence of confusion and pain as Devin fumbled to comprehend the events of the previous evening. He buttoned his shirt, pulled up his trousers, and tied his shoes, mindfully avoiding the face of the boy in the mirror, fearing the truth he might see in the boy's eyes. Devin was eight years old when he began to suspect he was different from other boys, but he never understood the implications of those differences, whatever they were. Their mystery had always plagued his conscience. And now, with the vagaries of puberty, his young mind struggled to understand those differences, perhaps embrace them. There was something liberating about such thoughts—liberating, yet terrifying. Devin raised his head, his eyes meeting those of the boy in the mirror. The boy's face was expressionless, offering neither reassurance nor disapproval. Devin turned away and slipped quietly from the room, down the darkened stairs, hoping to leave the house before either his mother or William awakened.

Halfway down the stairs, a board creaked. Devin stopped and listened. Shortly, he heard his mother's bare feet walking toward the stairs. At the top landing, she looked down at him, his face barely visible in the shadows.

"You all right, Son?"

"Yes, Mama, I'm fine. Why?" He couldn't tell her about William. It would only bring up issues he didn't wish to discuss with his mother or anyone else.

"I'm worried about you," she whispered. "You and William."

"No, it's all right."

"You would tell me, wouldn't you, Devin?"

"Sure, Mama. You know I would."

She took two steps toward him. "Want me to fix you some breakfast?"

"No, ma'am. I don't feel like eating this morning." He walked down the stairs.

"Love you," he said quietly over his shoulder, wondering if she heard him, knowing it would change nothing. She would be gone when he arrived home that evening, and William would be drunk by then.

"Excuse me, William." Devin looked up at the disheveled man blocking the doorway. William offered a sardonic smile as he stepped aside, allowing the boy to enter the house.

"Your mother's comin' home early tonight." There was a mocking tone to William's voice. "She told me to tell you." It was obvious that he wasn't quite drunk, but that observation gave Devin little comfort—William's words could be biting and cruel even when he was stone-cold sober.

At the stairs, Devin acknowledged his stepfather's condescension. "Did she say what time?"

"No, just that she would be home early; yes, she did say she would bring home something to eat." William slumped into a chair, the television remote in hand. "Good thing. I'm starved. Had a helluva day at work."

"I'm sorry, William."

"You done somethin'?" William smiled derisively. "What've you got to be sorry about, boy?" He put a can of beer to his mouth and swilled down the contents.

A few more beers and any thought of rational conversation with William would be futile. Devin walked upstairs. He closed the door to his room and pressed his ear to the door, listening for sounds of William's boots on the stairs. Hearing nothing, he sat on the edge of his bed and removed a five-dollar bill from his shoe. The boy in the mirror watched uneasily, his countenance changing from concern to terror as Devin squatted before the dresser and pulled the bottom drawer from its slot.

Devin's cries of pain were answered by William's footsteps on the stairs. He kicked open the door. Standing with his back against the doorframe, he held up an envelope, "You lookin' for this?"

"You bastard." Devin rushed toward the door, reaching for the envelope, which William now waved above his head.

He held Devin at arm's length, pretending to read from the letter. "Devin, Devin, Devin. Your name rolls sweet off my tongue." He wiped the back of his hand across his mouth. "Now don't we have us a little queer boy on our hands?"

Devin stretched to get hold of the letter, desperation in his voice. "Please, William, give me my letter and my money."

"You're a lyin' little queer. Wait 'til your mama reads this." He clenched his fist, bringing it crashing against Devin's ear, knocking the boy onto the bare wooden floor. Devin lay near the bed, his arms stretched underneath. His hand touched something. His fingers explored the handle of William's hunting knife. He struggled to his knees as William lunged toward him. Holding the knife upward, he thrust it toward William's gut, feeling it plunge into the soft belly of the hulking man. William gasped, mouth open, agonizing disbelief contorting his face. He slumped forward to his knees, mouthing incomprehensible words. Devin pushed the knife in deeper. William pitched forward, his face landing with a thud against the floor.

Devin lay stunned for an eternity of seconds, trying to understand the enormity of the past few moments. He pushed William's limp arm aside and looked into his placid face, now devoid of menace and hatred. He watched William's eyelids flutter and settle half-closed as life drained from the man Devin had come to fear and despise. But he didn't want him dead. He wished he could undo what he had done.

He got to his knees and crawled to the dresser. The boy's

bloody face peered from the mirror. Devin cringed at the sight of the knife still in the boy's hand. He scowled at the image in the mirror. "Look what you've done now!" The boy smiled sadly. *I did it for you, Devin.*

Devin plucked the letter from beneath William's boot. He got to the stairs and started down. An aura of lilac penetrated his senses, drawing him to his mother's room. He knelt before her bureau and pulled the crimson gown from the drawer. He slipped the gown over his head, then stood for several minutes admiring his image in the mirror.

He heard his mother open the front door. After a few moments, she called his name. "Devin?" He listened as she came to the foot of the stairs. "Devin? You up there?"

"Yes, ma'am," he whispered.

"Devin, you up there?"

"Yes, ma'am," he shouted back.

"You seen William?"

"No, ma'am."

"Come down and eat. I brought you burgers and fries."

Devin smoothed the nylon gown with the palms of his hands as he walked toward the stairs.

"I'm coming, Mama."

It was the first time he had been happy in days.

23

THE TENANTS

She cracked open the door just enough to cast one bespectacled eye on me as I hurried up the marble steps into the vestibule. I suspected she had lain in wait, knowing that I got off my after-school job at seven.

Turning on the furnace for our landlady in the cool of the fall Friday evenings had become a weekly ritual. On Saturday mornings, I would knock on Mrs. Bjork's door so she could allow me to turn off the furnace for the day. Her Jewish orthodoxy forbade her to light or extinguish fires between sunsets on Friday and Saturday in observance of her Sabbath. Before leaving, I would dial the phone so she could talk with her son, Joseph. I would listen to one side of a conversation in Yiddish and broken English. Mrs. Bjork would spit and sputter for four to five minutes before handing me the phone to replace in its cradle.

"Marvin." She opened the door all the way and crooked her finger in my direction. "Come here, boy."

I glanced at the diminutive old woman as I stepped

through her doorway. A washed-out patterned dress hung around her fragile body, the hem striking her mid-calf. Pale beige nylons rippled like slow-running water, the wavelets gathering at her ankles. Her graying hair was pulled into a bun at the back of her head with loose strands over her ears. The years had not been good to her. "Can I help you, Mrs. Bjork?"

She motioned again with her finger, and I followed to the basement door. She opened it and pointed to the switch on the wall above the stairs. "Turn on the furnace for me." Spittle formed in small white deposits at the corners of her mouth. The tip of her tongue protruded with each syllable as if she required some great effort to speak. Although I never asked, her broken English told me she was from Hungary or Poland, or maybe Russia.

She closed the basement door, then walked back down the hallway, her body shifting on bowed legs, rising and falling like a penguin on ice. She held open the door. "Thank you, Marvin . . . you're a good boy."

"You're welcome, Mrs. Bjork. I'm glad to help you." I started up the stairs to my family's apartment on the third floor.

"Marvin."

"Yes, ma'am?" I stopped and turned to look down at her.

Waving a finger at me, she shook her head in benevolent disapproval. "You mustn't kiss your girlfriend on the front stoop anymore. People will talk."

"Yes, ma'am."

"You're a good boy, Marvin." "Thank you, Mrs. Bjork. "I smiled, knowing her compliment was intended to soften her chastisement.

Her door closed as I continued up the stairs

Muffled sobs penetrated Maggie Miller's door. I hurried past on tiptoes, attempting to conceal my proximity. Hearing the fortyish Miss Maggie cry was usual fare most evenings since Mr. Tom Hatfield, a salesman at Johnny's Used Car Lot, stopped calling on her. For more than a year at 9 p.m., the dapper Mr. Hatfield climbed the stairs to the second floor. But his hour-long visits ceased altogether right after Labor Day. That was when the effervescent laughter emanating from Apartment 202 ended. Now Miss Maggie's frequent weeping could be heard most evenings by anyone pausing near her door.

I slid my hand along the banister rail, hoping she had not heard my footsteps on the stairs. As I stepped onto the landing leading to the third floor, a sliver of light from Maggie's living room burst into the hallway. I stopped and stood quietly waiting for her to appear at the door. "That you, Marvin?" she asked without showing her face.

"Yes, Miss Maggie. You need something?"

She opened the door wider and wiped at a tear with the tips of her fingers. "You have a minute to talk?"

"Sure. I suppose I have a few minutes. I have to meet Rebecca at eight." I walked back toward Miss Maggie and followed her into the apartment.

"She's a lucky girl." Maggie motioned for me to take a chair. She sat on the end of the sofa nearest me.

I laughed. "I don't know about that. I think I'm the lucky one."'

We sat looking at each other for several minutes. She sipped on a glass of wine while I shifted nervously in my chair. I cleared my throat. "What would you like to talk about, Miss Maggie?"

"I don't know, Marvin. Just . . . I'm so lonely . . . I need a kind face to look at for a moment or two."

"I'm glad to talk with you, Miss Maggie. You should know that."

"Sure, Marvin." She moved to the arm of my chair, still holding the wine glass. "Want a sip?" She tilted the glass toward my lips.

"Better not. I might get you into trouble. I'm only seventeen."

"One sip can't hurt a big boy like you." She forced a laugh as she ruffled my hair with her free hand.

"All right, then. One sip and I gotta go." I put the glass to my lips and tasted the wine as I got up from the chair.

She took my hand. "Don't go, please. I can't be alone tonight."

"What about Mr. Hatfield? Why doesn't he come to see you anymore?"

She scowled. "Please don't mention his name to me."

"Why? What did he do?"

She began to cry, concealing her eyes with her hand. "He's married." She wiped away the tears.

She was a pretty woman, slim, with warm hazel eyes, probably close to my mother's age. I wanted to comfort her without overstepping boundaries, but I had no idea what to say. After a moment of awkward silence, I said, "I have to go now."

She clasped my hand. I thought she would cry again. "You really have to go?"

"Yes, but tell you what. I will check on you later tonight after I take Rebecca home."

That brought a smile to her face. "Promise?" She held my hand tightly, her palm moist and warm. "I promise."

Maggie stood with her back to the door, preventing me from opening it. She closed her eyes slowly then asked seductively, "Pinky promise?"

"Yes, I will see you a little after eleven tonight. I promise."

She stood on her toes as she pressed herself against me. She kissed me desperately, her passionate lips pursuing mine as I attempted to back away. "Please," she pleaded, "don't let me be alone tonight. I'm afraid of what I might do."

"I won't, Miss Maggie. I promise."

"That you, Marvin?" Winton Simpson grabbed my ankle when I attempted to step over his prone body. He lay face up in the second-floor hallway, apparently unable to stand. Ruby, his wife of twenty years, had been considerate enough to toss a pillow out her door, not quite within Winton's reach. Instead, his head rested on an empty Rebel Yell bottle.

It was almost midnight, and I was hoping to sneak by Miss Maggie's door without being detected. But with the uproar the Simpsons had just created, the success of that endeavor was doubtful. I kept my voice barely above a whisper and at the same time, trying not to laugh out loud. "Yes, Mr. Simpson, it's Marvin. Don't you recognize me?"

He almost opened his eyes. “Tell you what, Marvin, I can’t see a damn thing; can’t feel anything either.” Only my previous experience in conversing with an inebriated Mr. Simpson enabled me to comprehend his slurred speech.

The door to apartment 201 opened, and an ample portion of RubkyRuby Simpson stood defiantly over the threshold. She might have been inclined to reveal more of her imposing figure, but the doorway was only forty-two inches wide. Regardless, I saw enough to convince me to remain aloof from the Simpsons’ domestic dispute. She offered an unmistakable warning that my better interest dictated no assistance or solace to the hapless drunk on the hallway floor. “Leave that worthless bum right where he is. Comes home again, no pay; spent it all on horses and booze. You leave him right where he is.” “Yes, ma’am, Mrs. Simpson. I’m just passing through, going upstairs.” A demure smile momentarily found its way to her lips. I stood motionless, my back against the banister. Her smile quickly faded, and her face resorted to its natural scowl. I saw that she had removed her false teeth for the night. At that moment, I realized why the man on the floor was drunk.

“I hope someone steps on him during the night.” She backed into her apartment and slammed the door. The deadbolt clicked shut. Mr. Simpson was doomed to another night as a homeless drunk. It was not his first, and almost certainly, would not be his last.

Winton mumbled something unintelligible. I bent close to hear. “What was that, Mr. Simpson?”

“Skippa My Lou in the sixth.”

His stale whiskey breath made me stand erect. “I don’t know what you mean.”

"The goddamn horse came in last. Led to the quarter pole then walked the rest of the way to the finish line. Thirty to one, the sonofabitch."

"You bet on him?"

"Not him, Marvin. She is a filly. Don't ever bet on a goddamn filly."

He made an effort to sit, but his head slid onto the floor with a loud *kerflump*. The bottle scooted across the floor and bounced down the stairs. I chased after it, catching up at the bottom landing. All hope of avoiding Miss Maggie ended with the clamor on the stairs. When I reached the top, she was standing in the doorway, her svelte figure silhouetted in the dim light behind her.

"It's after eleven, Marvin. When're you coming to see me?"

"I'm sorry, Miss Maggie." I set the Rebel Yell bottle down next to Winton Simpson's head. He didn't move. "He needed help."

"He seems to be all right, now—sleeping peacefully."

"He's passed out."

"Let him sleep it off." She tugged on my hand, urging me to come into her apartment. When she leaned with her breasts touching my chest, I knew my good intentions had all been in vain. I put my arm around her trim waist and pulled her tightly against me. We stood in the doorway, locked in each other's arms. She turned her pleading face upward, and I kissed her. She sighed contentedly.

Mr. Simpson suddenly sat up. "What the hell is going on?"

Maggie pulled me into the apartment and closed the

door just as my mother called from the third floor. "Marvin, you down there?"

Maggie stood against the door and put her finger to her lips. "Shh."

Mother called again. "Is that you, Marvin?"

I held Maggie aside and opened the door. "Yes, Mother. I'm just helping Mr. Simpson. I'll be right up."

Maggie tenderly touched my face. "Guess you better go home, young man. Your mother's calling. I was about to make an awful fool of myself anyway."

We stepped into the hallway. Ruby's abandoned husband was on his hands and knees crawling toward us. The obvious solution to the problems of two unfortunate people popped into my head. "Mr. Simpson needs a place to sleep. Can you put him up tonight, Miss Maggie?"

"Why not?" she said. "Any port in a storm, I've always heard."

That night, my mind ran rampant with visions of the sexually deprived woman downstairs. A little imp at the foot of my bed kept right on telling me, *you are an idiot, Marvin Kaspersky*. Finally, my thoughts turned to Rebecca, and I thanked God for my mother's midnight curfew. I fell asleep hoping Winton Simpson would get the hell out of Maggie's apartment before Ruby awoke the next morning. But at least Miss Maggie Miller would not be alone this Friday night

I LEFT for work early the next morning after turning off the furnace for Mrs. Bjork. As I stocked supermarket shelves that day, the budding romantic triangle, which I facilitated to

some small degree, was coming apart at the corners. Mr. Simpson did not awake earlier than his lovely wife. In fact, as she prowled the stairways the next morning, she heard Winton's unmistakable snoring coming from Miss Maggie's apartment. When Ruby's modest knocks were ignored, she became enraged and put a hefty shoulder against the hollow-core wood panel, splintering the door.

I arrived home moments after Mrs. Bjork's son pulled his Cadillac Seville to the curb at 1600 Eutaw Place. Joseph was a short, balding man of about fifty. He was the problem solver for his mother, visiting the apartment building only on rare occasions. The demolition derby on the second floor did not happen every day, and thus, qualified as rare. Joseph was there to investigate, assess damage, and assign—blame and financial responsibility.

I attempted to scoot by the congregation in the second-floor hallway as if they all were strangers. However, as I crouched to be less obtrusive, Ruby Simpson quickly identified me as the instigator of the salacious affair. Thankfully, she had rescued Winton from a wanton woman. She held him close, her chubby arms protecting him as if he were precious china. She pointed her finger at the nose of her accommodating neighbor and uttered the word, "harlot." Believing the term to be a little harsh, I suggested the more euphonic, "seductress," with which all parties to the dispute concurred, with the possible exception of Ruby. Through the entire inquisition and finger-pointing episode, Miss Maggie remained above the fray. She endured Mrs. Simpson's accusations with grace, occasionally placing a reassuring hand on the arm of Joseph Bjork. With each touch of her hand, Joseph moved closer to Miss Maggie until it was obvious where he stood on the matter. Maggie invited him into her apartment where she could explain the situation in a calmer environment. Since the damaged door provided little privacy, it was necessary for Joseph's investigation to convene in Maggie's bedroom. Needless to say, she was eventually held harmless (if not innocent) in the whole affair.

But it was also good news for the Simpsons. Although Ruby was obviously responsible for the destruction of private property, Mr. Bjork—out of the kindness of his heart—declared he would pay for all the damage.

Now there is a solid oak door on Maggie Miller's apartment. The new lock had two keys.

24

THE HERMAPHRODITE HORSE

"I'll shoot that lyin' sons a bitch." Ed had been drinking his own moonshine. He swept his arm behind him and without looking back, picked up the double-barrel 12-gauge standing in the corner near his chair. Holding the gun against his shoulder, he sighted down the barrels as he ranged across the room, the point of the gun passing two feet in front of my chin.

I was barely sixteen but experienced enough to know that Ed could be mighty careless with a gun. He shot off two of his toes less than a month earlier, and I assumed, his foot was rotting away under the dinghy, yellowed bandage that probably had not been changed since the day of his accident. "Watch that damn gun, Ed! You could hurt somebody."

He laughed, then broke the gun open at the breach. "It ain't even loaded, son." He reached into his weathered coat pocket, pulled out two shells, and loaded them. He pointed the gun again, this time toward the ceiling. "You do me a favor, son?"

"Yeah, Ed, 'course I will."

"You tell that sons a bitch, Laud Mullins, the next time he calls my horse a morphidite, he's a dead man." Ed scowled, set the gun firmly in the corner, and motioned for me to come closer.

I moved cautiously near his chair. Ed was beginning to scare me, talking out of his head about killing someone. That was in between his crying jags about his wife, Tillie, having left him. And why he made such a fool of himself over that dilapidated old mule—it wasn't even a horse—was beyond me. Maybe it was because the mule was the only thing in the world he owned besides his shotgun. But it most definitely wasn't worth killing anybody. And Tillie? Hell, I knew she wasn't going far away. She might want to, but she had no one else but Ed.

He looked up at me as he placed his arm around my waist. Tears welled up in his eyes. He was old beyond his forty years. "Where'd Tillie go?"

Ed was my father's first cousin. He came back from the big war shell-shocked and never got over it. I had seen him go crazy before. In fact, every time he and Tillie had a tiff, Ed sort of lost half his mind. But I knew he would recover as soon as she came back with Ed Junior, their four-year-old son —and she would eventually. The problem was that I had no idea where she had gone this time.

I stepped back quickly. "I don't know, Ed."

"Hell, you don't," he sneered. "If anybody does, you do."

Ed's assertion was not without basis. Tillie and I were close. She liked me because she could tell me all her secrets. Of course, she had her own reasons for confiding in me, one of which was my awareness of Ed's flirtations with the

McPherson girls, especially Justine, who had just turned eighteen. Tillie's suspicions were mostly unfounded, but she still quizzed me each time we were alone in the house. I couldn't help but wonder if I had said something during one of her inquisitions that heightened those suspicions and wondered if I had played any part in her leaving Ed this time. No one could have guessed how crazy Ed might get before the night was over. It wasn't going to be a good evening to be in his company.

I looked at him over my shoulder while moving toward the door.

"Where you goin'?"

"I have to get home."

"The hell you say, boy. You got to help me sell the shine tomorrow."

"I can't stay, Ed. I told my mother I'd be home before supper," I lied. I had planned to spend the night with Ed, but there was no way I wanted to be around him when he was drunk, and he was already on his way to mental oblivion.

"Goddamn, son, I been countin' on you to help me."

"Tomorrow, Ed. I'll help you tomorrow."

"Don't let me down, boy. McPherson is holding the cock fights tomorrow in his arena. I got no way of gettin' hooch down there if you don't help me." He hesitated for a moment, then chopped the air with his finger, and pointed in my direction. "You see Tillie, tell her to get her half-breed ass back home."

Tillie was half-Cherokee Indian, and when they fought, Ed always reminded her of that fact.

I nodded, then pulled the door closed behind me. I started down the rocky path toward McPherson's dirt farm that lay in the valley a quarter of a mile or more from Ed's run-down clapboard shack.

Ed's half-starved plow mule, Jessie, stood at the edge of the pasture, its head hanging over the top strand of barbed wire.

I walked over, patted the emaciated bag of bones on the forehead, then squatted down to peer between the mule's front legs, my eyes searching for equine genitalia. The only evidence of mule masculinity was a withered piece of skin drooping beneath his belly. Drops of urine clung to a strand of hair protruding from the end of the skin. *For Ed's sake, I am glad to see old Jessie once had a pecker.* I laughed out loud at the thought. *Maybe Ed would be justified to shoot Laud Mullins for maligning his hapless mule.*

The sun was sinking fast behind the hills to the west. Two miles of woods lay between me and home. I stood and patted the animal again. "I hope Ed remembers to feed you, you poor bastard." I began running as fast as I could down the hill toward the McPherson farm. As I ran, I looked for Justine. Maybe she would see me and follow me a little way into the woods.

An hour later, I burst breathlessly through the kitchen door just as Mother was finishing the supper dishes. I had run the last mile to get home before dark.

She wiped dry the final plate, set it on top of the stack inside the cabinet, and closed the door. "What are you doing home? Ed drinking again?" Mother draped the dish towel over the back of a cane-bottomed chair and breathed a long sigh as she sat down.

I pulled up a chair next to her. "Anything left to eat?"

"Ed didn't feed you?"

"No, ma'am. Ed's drunk. He won't even be cooking for hisself tonight."

"Himself," Mother corrected me. She was a self-educated woman and pushed her three children to learn everything they could in school. Her ears always perked up when she heard one of us mangle the English language and couldn't resist setting us straight. My father was the only one in our house whose grammar went uncorrected.

"I hope Ed remembers to feed that damn old mule."

Mother slapped my hand. "Don't you use that language in front of me, young man." She got up from her chair and brought back a plate with a pork chop, some poke salad, and a piece of cornbread left over from supper.

I began to eat. "You know where Tillie is, Mom?"

She nodded as she set a glass of milk next to my plate.

"Where?"

"I'm not saying. Ed'll get it out of you."

"She coming back?"

"Maybe, but not until Ed comes to his senses."

"That won't happen soon. He's still talking crazy. Says he's going to kill Laud Mullins."

Mother scoffed. "Ed's a lot of bull. He couldn't shoot anybody." Then she laughed at an apparent afterthought. "Except himself. Why does he want to kill Laud?"

"Cause he called Ed's mule a morphydite."

"You mean *hermaphrodite*?"

"I guess so, but Ed isn't very happy about it either way."

"Whether it's a hermaphrodite or not, Ed still makes a living with that old plow horse."

"It's a mule, Mother, not a horse. And it is not a morphidite." I picked up the pork chop by the bone and chewed off the last morsel of meat.

"How do you know?"

"'Cause I've seen up that old mule's rear end more than once, and tonight I looked him over real good. He's got what used to be a mule pecker under his belly." I laughed and got up from the table.

As I turned to leave, Mother swatted me across the back with her dish towel. "Get out of here, you nasty thing."

I turned and hugged her.

She hid her smile against my shoulder.

THE SUN HAD BEEN UP for almost an hour when I arrived at Ed's place the next morning. The mule was standing by the fence where he had probably waited all night for Ed to throw something into his feed box, but apparently, Ed had not sobered up long enough to realize that the mule was slowly starving to death.

On the back porch, I found two burlap sacks filled with ears of husked dried corn and carried an armload to where Jessie stood. He whinnied then settled into a low grunting bray—I assumed, his way of saying grace—as I dumped the ears of dry corn into the feed box. I watched for a few moments while the mule methodically chewed the corn off the cobs.

Ed opened the front door and stood on the top step as I approached the house. "You worried 'bout old Jessie?"

"Yeah, he's half-starved."

"What's wrong with grazin'? He's got two acres of grass in that pasture." Ed pointed down the side of the hill behind the old mule.

"Grass? ... I don't see anything but rocks and ragweed." By then, I had taken a seat on the lower step and was looking back over my shoulder at Ed.

"You're too smart for your own good," Ed said without a smile. "You're too much like your mother. What you need is a little bit more of your daddy in you, boy."

I stood and turned to face Ed. "Just be glad my mother doesn't know I'm going to help you sell moonshine today. 'Cause if she had any idea 'bout that, I wouldn't be here." I walked up the four steps, past Ed, and into the house.

He followed me, then limped to the corner of the room where a curtain had been hung to conceal three five-gallon jugs of moonshine. It was the last shine he had distilled before shooting off his toes. His small still was a mile further up the ridge above his house, concealed by a rock overhang and heavy brush. He pulled two boxes containing empty pint and half-pint bottles from under the bed. "Help me, son." He nodded his head toward the boxes.

I pulled the boxes away from the bed and pushed them with my foot across the floor in the direction of the door. Afterward, I rolled a moonshine jug to the doorway where I could see to fill the bottles.

He handed me a rusted tin funnel.

"Are we going to wash these bottles, Ed?"

"No need," he said. "They're clean. B'sides, alkyhall will

kill any germs that might be in them bottles." He smiled for the first time that morning. Ed limped over to a worn-out stuffed chair and fell into it, looking exhausted. He shivered as he pulled his coat lapels close against his chin.

"You alright?"

"Yeah, just a little chilly in this old house, I guess."

I knew better than that. It was mid-June, and already past seventy-five outside. I lay the flat of my wrist against his forehead. "Damn, Ed, you're burning up with fever."

"Might be my foot infected. Got no feeling in my toes, and my whole foot hurts like hell."

"Let me see."

"No, you get down the hill with that shine. It's already after nine, and the fights have started by now."

"Will you be okay?"

"Yeah, I'll be okay. Fix me a drink 'fore you go."

I poured half a glass of moonshine, added a spoon of sugar, and then filled the glass with water. I stirred it the way I had seen Ed and my father do it a hundred times before.

"Aahh," he said, after taking a swig. "Just right." He shivered again. He reached for a folded quilt on the bed and pulled it over him.

I shoved two pints of moonshine inside my shirt and slipped a half-pint in each front pocket of my trousers. "Take it easy, Ed. I'll be back soon."

He nodded as he pulled the cover closer to his chin. "I'll be all right. Maybe Tillie is coming home today."

"Maybe she is." I patted his arm reassuringly.

~

Jessie was just finishing the last of his corn when I came out of the house. He followed me along the fence to the bottom of the hill.

I walked over to him and slapped him lightly on the flank two or three times. "You are a lucky old bastard, Jessie. What do you have to worry about in this world? Nothing. No matter what, someone is going to feed your dumb ass. Maybe getting your nuts cut out wasn't much fun, but other than that, you've got nothing to complain about."

She startled me with her laugh. "Who are you talking to, Jimmy West? That old mule? "

Justine stepped out of the bushes. She sat down the bucket she had just filled from a freshwater spring.

I walked over to her and put my arm around her waist, pulling her tightly against me.

"I gotta get home," she said, not making any attempt to move away.

I lifted her dress and slipped my hand down inside her panties.

"It's sweaty," she said as she pushed herself firmly against my cupped hand.

"You hot?"

"Yeah, but I can't do anything right now."

"Why's that?"

"'Cause I'm ripe."

"Ripe?"

"Yeah, dummy, ripe."

I must have looked puzzled.

"I can get pregnant this time of month." Shaking her head in apparent disbelief, she pulled my hand from her panties and pushed down her dress with authority. "Where you goin'?"

"To the pit."

They won't let you in there to see them roosters fight. You're still a kid."

"The hell you say." I pulled one of the pint bottles from my shirt and held it out for her to see. "They're waiting on this stuff."

"Can I have a drink?" She moved closer until her breasts were touching my shirt.

Thankfully, I remembered Ed and the pain he was enduring up there on the hill in that house alone. I stepped away from her. "I'll give you some later."

We walked together to the McPherson house. She went inside. I continued toward the barn that served as a cock fight arena. Five minutes later, all four bottles had been sold, and I climbed back up the hill to give Ed his sixteen dollars.

He was sleeping in his chair. I placed the money on the eating table and selected four more bottles which I hid inside my shirt and in my pockets. By noon, I had made a dozen trips up and down the hill. One of the five-gallon jugs had been sold, netting Ed more than two hundred dollars.

I sat in the doorway, my feet resting on the top step, pondering whether to wake Ed.

Moments later, Justine's head appeared above the crest of the hill. She came to the steps and sat next to my feet.

"Where's old Ed?" she giggled.

"Sleeping," I said. "Ed isn't feeling very well."

She looked up at me coyly as she walked her fingers up the naked part of my leg just above my ankle. "Want to fuck?"

I noticed then that Justine was a pretty girl. "I thought you were ripe."

"That was just an excuse. Girls do that all the time." She pushed her long brown hair behind her ears.

"You mean lying?"

"No. 'Course not." She gave me a look that told me she possessed superior knowledge. "It's an excuse they use, you know, like, I'm on my period when they really ain't."

"So, you're not ripe?"

"Sorta," she said, "but I'm still willing."

"That you, Tillie?" Ed stirred, mumbled, and turned onto his side in his chair.

"No, Ed," I said, leaning back into the room, but he didn't hear me.

"Can I have a drink of whiskey?" Justine placed her hand on my thigh as I sat up again in the doorway.

"Sure." I was confident now where it was leading.

I went into the house and brought back a half-pint. I walked down the steps and continued toward the back porch with Justine following. We sat on the porch with our legs dangling over the edge and passed the bottle back and forth. After three or four swallows each, I rolled over onto the porch and pulled her on top of me. By the time I unbuttoned my fly, she had already removed her panties.

THE SUN WAS BEATING DOWN on the back porch when I opened my eyes to find that Justine was gone. I buttoned my trousers and pulled my belt through the buckle as I walked to the front steps.

Ed was still sleeping. It had been more than three hours, and he hadn't moved off the chair.

I shook him by the shoulder.

He opened his eyes, shivered, then pulled at the quilt. "Where's Tillie?"

"She's not here, Ed."

"Thought I heard her."

"No, it wasn't Tillie."

"How much you sell, son?"

"One whole jug. The money's on the table."

"Fights over?"

"No, Ed. It's just a little after twelve. I got to get back down there." I didn't want to stick around for him to quiz me about Justine during one of his lucid moments.

"How's the fever?" I placed my open hand on his forehead. "Christ, you're still burning up."

"To tell you the truth, boy, my leg is killin' me, throbbin' all the way to my hip."

"You need something for that pain. You got any aspirin?"

"No," he said. "Fix me a drink."

He held his whiskey with both hands while I attempted, unsuccessfully, to roll up his right trouser leg. The lower leg was too swollen, and Ed was in too much pain. With a kitchen knife, I cut through the hem of the trouser leg and then ripped it to his thigh.

The stench from his foot made me gag before I had removed the first bandage. I carefully peeled away each layer of gauze. Pieces of dark flesh clung to the bandage as I removed the final layer. I ran for the door and vomited on the ground beside the steps.

After a few moments, I returned to the unpleasant task

of examining Ed's right foot. The two smaller toes had been shot away. The middle toe and half of Ed's foot were dark brown, nearly black, and oozing a smelly yellow discharge. I forced myself to continue ripping away his trouser leg. I could see that the remainder of his foot had turned dark brown. The skin was cracked open from his toe to his ankle, with dark purple streaks running to his knee. I suppressed the urge to vomit again.

"I think you've got gangrene, Ed. You need to get to a doctor." I didn't know exactly what gangrene was, but I had heard my dad talk about it.

"Don't matter," he said. "I'd rather die than live with just one foot."

"I think it's more than your foot. I think you're going to lose your leg, Ed."

"Get me another drink." He was shaking badly.

I fixed the drink. "Let me do something to clean up your foot. You got any bandages?"

"No."

"I'm going for help, but I can't leave you like this."

In a bureau drawer standing against the wall, I found a worn-out bed sheet and ripped it into strips. I remembered that there was a wash basin on the back porch. After retrieving it, I set it close to Ed's chair. Straddling his leg so that I was holding the foot out in front of me, I poured a pint of moonshine over it. I bandaged the foot and pulled the cover back over Ed.

"I didn't mean that, boy."

"Mean what, Ed?"

"What I said about you being too much like your mother. She's a good woman."

"It's okay. I know you didn't mean anything bad." I turned for the door. "Got to get you a doctor, Ed."

"It don't matter, son. I'm dyin'. Get me Tillie. I want to see her 'fore it's too late."

"I don't know where she is, Ed. Honest, I don't."

"You can find her, Jimmy." Once in a blue moon, Ed called me Jimmy. "Take Jessie and go find her."

"Sure, Ed." I wiped tears from the corners of my eyes. "You're going to be all right. I'll find Tillie and get you a doctor up here."

The mule was in the middle of the pasture. When I whistled, his ears perked up. Slowly, he came walking in my direction. When he got to the corner of the pasture, I reached across the fence and took hold of his halter. I led him to the gate and threw a saddle blanket over his back. Ed didn't own a saddle.

I led Jessie to the bottom of the hill and then climbed on. As I approached the McPherson house, Justine came running toward me.

She looked up. "Where you goin'?"

"Find Tillie."

"Can I come with you?"

"No. Go check on Ed. He's bad off."

I clicked at Jessie and jerked on the reins. He took off at a trot, past the cockfight arena and onto the worn path leading into the low hills. Half an hour later, we emerged from the woods less than a mile from my house. It was nearly three o'clock when I tied Jessie's reigns to the fence post.

"Where's Tillie?"

My mother looked puzzled. "She doesn't want Ed to know right now."

"He's dying, Mom. He's got gangrene all up his leg." I began to cry. I hadn't realized before then just how much I loved that old man.

She bent over me and kissed my cheek as I sat at the kitchen table. "I'll get your father, and we'll take Tillie to Ed. You coming with us?"

"I have to get Jessie back to Ed's place. If I get started now, I won't be very far behind you and Dad."

When Jessie and I came out of the woods near the McPherson barn, the cockfights were just breaking up. The cars were moving slowly down the muddy wagon road toward the main highway. One of the cars slowed, and the driver rolled down his window. It was Laud Mullins. He laughed. "What are you doin' on Ed's morphidite horse?"

I jumped to the ground, ran, and caught up with Laud's car. Putting my face near the partially opened window, I said, "You call that horse a morphidite again, Mr. Mullins, and I will shoot you, you son of a bitch." I got back on Jessie and rode toward Ed's house.

My father's car was parked at the bottom of the hill.

At the gate, I dismounted and removed the saddle blanket. I shut the gate and pulled Jessie's bridle over his ears.

My father was standing by the front steps with his arms around my mother. I knew I was too late to see Ed alive again.

Tillie came out of the house, leading Junior by the hand. "He's gone," she said in a voice depleted of emotion.

"Did you get here in time?" I asked.

"I said goodbye. I hope he heard me."

I put my arms around her while she cried quietly against my shoulder. "I'm sorry, Tillie. He was asking for you."

"I know. I heard him call my name, but I think he was already out of his head by the time we got here."

"Did you find the money he left on the table?"

"Yes." She handed me a note written on a piece torn from a brown paper bag. "And he left this for you."

I sat on the lower step and slowly read Ed's barely legible words:

Thanks, Jimmy. Take care of my horse. He ain't no morphidite.

25

ORBITING THE MOON

Some relationships are up and down, never quite reaching a comfortable plateau. They are fatally flawed, but the parties either refuse or cannot recognize the truth. That is how it was with Nell and me. We orbited through scintillating apogees and disheartening perigees that kept us circling the moon but never landing in the Sea of Tranquility. She seemingly, could not let go of me completely but was reluctant to commit the way I wanted her to. And, despite myself, I could not stop loving her.

The vagaries of our relationship had inspired the lyrics to several love songs, which I wrote for the acoustic guitar. The most recent, entitled "To Hell with Nell," was intended to be the last one provoked by the vixen from Columbia. But a few days after my ship returned to the Charleston Navy base, I received a phone call from Eloise Matthews, Nell's older sister. Little did I know her call would be the genesis of another blockbuster heartbreak country ballad.

"Nell wants to see you. Can you come up to Columbia this weekend?"

Nell and I had called it quits six months earlier, and I had not heard from her since. Our breakup ended a three-month torrid reunion, the second that year. The problem was that Nell's old boyfriends kept worming their way from the woodwork at inconvenient moments. Since I am, by nature, a very suspicious person, I continually accused her of cheating. She grew tired of my jealousy and told me to hit the road. I swore, then and there, that I had made my last trip from Charleston to Columbia—but, by the time Eloise called, that vow had faded from my mind.

"Tell her I'll be there Saturday before noon."

My pulse quickened at the thought of making love again to the most beautiful girl in South Carolina. All the potential problems associated with that possibility were discounted by me as I prepared for my romantic romp in Columbia. By Friday afternoon, I was chomping at the bit, ready to get on the road. By four-thirty, I was headed out the main gate. Images of Nell floated around in my head while I envisioned her surprise at seeing me a day early.

The front tires on my old 1978 Buick Century were dangerously bald and unsafe at any speed, but I thought they might have one more trip to Nell in them if I took it easy. Anticipating a flat tire at every turn, I limped all the way from Charleston, taking the old highway to avoid freeway driving.

Eloise greeted me at the door with a sisterly hug and kiss. "Thought you weren't coming up until tomorrow."

I looked past her. "Where's Nell?"

"They called her into work. She gets off at midnight."

"Damn." I felt my blood settling back into my heart. "I thought she would be waiting for me."

"She couldn't get out of it. Anyway, we will see her at Elrod's when she gets off work."

Elrod's was a nightclub on the other side of the city, one of the favorite hangouts for country music lovers. Its clientele included an overpopulation of drugstore cowboys and unbridled fillies. I met Nell there two years earlier. Afterward, we spent many Friday and Saturday nights locked in each other's arms as we scooted across the dance floor while listening to a Merle Haggard or Marty Robbins wannabe.

This night, of course, I was dancing with Eloise and thinking of Nell. But after half a dozen long-neck stouts and a dozen turns on the dance floor with Eloise pressed against me, I was beginning to forget she might be my future sister-in-law. We danced until after one. By then Nell hadn't shown, and Eloise was displaying the effects of too many Pink Ladies, so we headed back to the apartment.

In the car, she massaged my thigh as I drove, working me into a state of excitement and confusion. As soon as we closed the apartment door behind us, we began depositing our clothing on the floor. By the time we reached the bedroom, both of us wore only what God gave us. And no more than thirty minutes later, we lay exhausted in each other's arms with me wondering what in the hell I had just done. Thankfully, the effects of the beer took over, and I fell asleep, thereby escaping any further pangs of conscience.

I awoke about 10 a.m., sick and sober, realizing the full extent of what had happened. I retrieved my clothing from the floor, donning them one piece at a time. As I pulled my belt tightly around my waist, I spied a note pinned to Nell's bedroom door. I walked over, focused my bloodshot eyes, and read:

> Johnny Hurt,
>
> You are a no-good bastard. Get out of my life and stay out.
>
> Don't bother saying goodbye.
>
> Nell

Well, there was just no way that I could leave without explaining to Nell how my bedding down her sister came about. I was prepared to blame it on my extreme disconsolation at not seeing Nell upon my arrival in Columbia the previous evening. Of course, I thought of several variations to my story, including the assertion that I passed out on the kitchen floor, where Eloise undressed me and carried me to her bed. I would claim that nothing happened between us. With these vague ideas in mind, I knocked on Nell's door.

"Go away, you bastard."

"Not until I see you," I yelled with my face almost against the door.

"Damn you."

I heard her feet hit the floor. Moments later, she unlocked the door, cracked it open, and poked her nose and mouth through the opening.

"You've seen me. Now go."

"Nell." I reached through the opening to touch her face. "Open the door."

She pulled away.

I pushed with my knee against the door, but she blocked it with her foot. It suddenly occurred to me that she had a reason for keeping me out of her bedroom.

"Who in the hell you hiding in there?"

I lunged at the door with my shoulder. Nell stepped back just as I made contact. Stumbling full-bore across the threshold, I flipped over the footboard onto the bed. Floundering around in the opaque light, my hand landed on the hairy chest of someone sleeping in her bed.

He grunted and rolled onto his side.

I stood up in the middle of the bed, pointing down at the dormant walrus at my feet. "Who in the hell is this?"

"Rocky."

"Rocky?"

"Yes, Rocky."

"Jesus Christ! That's my competition?"

"Believe me, you are no competition."

"Then, why in the hell did you ask me to come up here?"

"If you remember, Johnny, it was Eloise who called you —not me."

"And you didn't know I was coming?"

"Yes, I knew, but I thought you would be coming up today, not last night."

I stepped over Rocky onto the floor. As I walked by Nell, I said, "You can have Rocky tonight too, because I won't be staying."

I stuck my head into Eloise's room. "'Bye, Eloise."

She pulled a pillow over her head and waved me away from her door.

In the confusion of the moment, I hadn't realized how much Nell's betrayal hurt. Mine could be excused because I had succumbed in a terrible moment of weakness and intoxication. As I drove toward the freeway, I was overcome with an urge to cry. Tears flowed freely down my face. I knew I would never see Nell again.

For the first thirty miles of freeway, I was unaware of everything around me. I could only think of what might have been between Nell and me. At seventy miles an hour, I began to hum a tune that originated somewhere in my head. Before long, the words to a brand-new country song emerged. Oblivious to the other cars on the road, I began to sing:

Our love wasn't meant to be from the start
But I couldn't tell that to my heart
I said I didn't love you
But lying wouldn't do
I can't tell my heart I'm not in love with you

The explosion came from where the right front tire once was. The steering wheel jerked in my hand as I careened down the freeway. I had the good sense not to brake suddenly, and slowly brought the car to a stop next to the drainage ditch along the right side of the road.

I got out and stood in front of the car, now heeled over like a kneeling camel.

"Fuck you, Nell Mathews. Fuck you. I hope I never lay eyes on you again." My rage was interrupted by the urge to heave whatever was inside my stomach, which I did with abandon. Then I cursed Nell Matthews some more, throwing Eloise in once for good measure.

After solving the mystery of how the jack worked, I managed to raise the car and put on a spare tire that was balder than the one that had just evaporated. When I finished, I drove to the next exit and took the old highway back to Charleston.

It is a well-known fact that country songwriters savor heartbreak. Count me among them. And the two-hour drive gave me an opportunity to work on the lyrics Nell had inspired. At least for all my pain and suffering, I now had a new country song in my repertoire, even if she and I were through for good.

Back on the ship, I hit the sack and slept for the next three hours. I was awakened by the quarterdeck messenger shaking me.

"Hey, Hurt, I got a phone message for you."

I rolled over and sat up. "Who was it?"

"A girl named Nell. She said to tell you she's sorry and wants you to come back to Columbia."

"Christ," I said. "I guess I am destined to crash right into that goddamn moon."

The messenger scratched his head and turned for the door, leaving me mumbling expletives about never setting eyes on that bitch again.

When I was through cursing and fuming, I curled up into my favorite fetal position. It would be easy to go back to sleep, knowing how much Nell Matthews was missing me.

26

THE MYSTERIOUS PEG-LEGGED MAN

Most small towns have a bogeyman, a non-conformist, someone outside the mainstream who is misunderstood and feared and sometimes a target of derision. In the town where I grew up, our bogeyman was a recluse, whom my friends and I called *Peg-Legged Caldwell.*

His right leg below his knee was carved from the limb of an oak tree, the steel-capped end of the crude prosthesis protruding from the bottom of his frazzled trousers. He leaned onto a wooden crutch, causing him to lurch forward when he walked. With each step, he grimaced and grunted as the weight of his plentiful body shifted onto the artificial appendage. From behind his scruffy beard, he squinted through two blurred eyes obviously in need of spectacles. On his shoulder hung a dirty canvas bag, which evoked conjecture as to its contents. Rumor was that among the bag's mysterious inventory was a .32 revolver with which Peg-Legged Caldwell murdered prying meddlers.

At the head of the hollow, Mr. Caldwell's twenty-foot trailer sat on a spit of land, almost encircled by the flowing waters of Mackenzie Creek. He seldom ventured away from his trailer, but on occasion took a laborious two-mile walk into town to shop at the company-owned grocery store.

He always walked along the railroad track that paralleled the creek bed behind our house, his dark, amorphous figure taking a near-human shape and revealing itself in detail as he approached. His manner of dress never changed. Crammed on his head was a weathered brown hat, stained and faded by the seasons. Over his plaid shirt and denim overalls, he wore an aged leather vest. His comings and goings were announced by the succession of dog barks emanating from houses up and down our street as he traversed the tracks. He seemed to pay the dogs no attention as they heralded his appearance and acknowledged his slow, gradual disappearance back into the woods of Mackenzie Hollow.

A few times, I ventured into our back yard to witness Mr. Caldwell's painful progress along the track. I watched him in awe and fear, but he never looked my way nor acknowledged by word or gesture that he saw me. All the while, my imagination attributed horrendous misdeeds to this solitary, mysterious being, and I breathed a sigh of relief when he was gone.

"What are you doing, Son?" my mother called to me from the open kitchen window one afternoon as I stood mesmerized, watching the old man until he was safely out of sight. And before I could answer, she continued, "Why were you watching Mr. Caldwell with such interest?"

I walked toward the back porch, still looking up at her. "He scares me."

"Why? He's a harmless old man."

"No, he's not; he kills people."

"Who told you that?"

Mother turned away from the window.

I sat down, halfway up the steps.

Behind me, I heard the screen door open then close and realized I was about to be lectured for my insensitivity. I was the third and youngest of three children, and the beneficiary of my mother's experience of having raised my older brother and sister. Mother had acquired a unique ability to anticipate and understand my thoughts, even before they had formulated in my brain.

She came to the top of the steps and stood, looking at me for a moment as she silently wiped her hands with the kitchen towel. "Those are awful rumors, Tim, and I don't want you repeating them."

"Everybody says it ..."

"Well, don't say it anymore. Truth is, Mr. Caldwell is probably more afraid of you than you are of him."

"What do you mean, Mom?"

"I mean that he doesn't trust people. He's been ridiculed too much and prefers to live alone rather than to be subjected to more hurt."

"How do you know that?"

"I just know," she said. "Nobody likes to be ridiculed."

I sat on the steps, looking across the creek toward the railroad track along which Peg-Legged Caldwell had just walked. I searched my mind for something to say to my mother, but nothing seemed appropriate. Shortly, I heard the screen door open and close again, and I was alone with my thoughts, feeling a bit remorseful, but not entirely convinced the scruffy old man was harmless.

More than a month passed before I saw the peg-legged man again. One late afternoon his ominous figure approached, an apparition looming out of the western sun's glare. He came toward my friends and me as we played near the railroad spur at the edge of the woods.

"It's Peg-Leg," one of the boys yelled, pointing down the track.

We scattered, looking for hiding places, safe from the old man.

I watched suspiciously from behind a poplar tree as he passed not more than twenty feet away.

In one hand he gripped the straps of a small shopping bag; in the other, he held onto his crutch. With each step, he grunted under the burden of his weight and the load he carried. At the end of the track, he stopped and dropped the bag to the ground. Removing his hat, he wiped the back of his arm across his sweating brow.

One of the boys tossed a pebble that landed near the old man's feet. Suddenly, a barrage of pebbles followed, falling all around him.

As the stones got closer to him, I could see the fear and confusion in his face.

He covered his head with his hands and slid to the ground to shield himself from the attack.

I moved from my hiding place and ran toward the old

man. "Stop! Stop!" I yelled in the direction of the other boys. I heard them running through the bushes and realized that I was alone, face-to-face with Peg-Legged Caldwell.

He sat up, picked up his hat and placed it on his head. He pulled himself up with his crutch, and looking me over, said, "Hey, boy, come here." He motioned with the arm that rested on his crutch.

I trembled as I approached. "Yes, sir,"

"Your daddy Morgan Miller?"

"Yes, sir." I attempted to disguise the quiver in my voice, digging deep for a manly timbre.

"Your daddy's a good man."

"Yes, sir, I know."

He lifted his chin with the dignity of the unvanquished, and with a determined look, turned to face the long trail ahead. "Tell him I said so."

"I will."

I watched him until he was out of sight before heading home. I thought about the old man's words, his simple expression of admiration for my father. He had paid me a high compliment, if only obliquely, by letting me know that he saw my father in me. I quickened my pace and walked a little taller the remainder of the way home, proud to be my father's son.

"That poor man," my mother said, looking up momentarily from her dinner plate. "Those boys should be ashamed."

"You did a good thing, Tim." My father reached across

the table and gently grasped my wrist. "Mr. Caldwell has not had an easy life. I'm sure he appreciates your kindness."

"How did he lose his leg, Dad?" I had thought about that many times but had never bothered to ask.

"Vietnam ... Battle of Khe Sanh, I think. That right, Louise?"

My mother nodded without looking at me or my father.

After a few moments, she placed her hand on mine. "Eat now, Timmy," she said in a quiet but firm tone that told me I should not ask any more questions.

We finished our meal in silence.

That night as I lay on my pillow, I thought about Mr. Caldwell in a different light. He was no longer a menacing figure in my mind. Rather, I saw him as a pathetic old man, recoiling from his attackers as he lay near the railroad track unable to defend himself. As much as anyone else, I had helped foment fear of the peg-legged man among my friends, and I felt responsible for their actions. Before falling asleep, I vowed to make amends.

A LONG-EARED MONGREL crawled from under the trailer and set up a howl before I had gotten closer than fifty yards. As I moved nearer, he began barking incessantly.

I approached slowly. "C'mon boy, c'mon boy."

He stopped barking and sat on his haunches, eyeing me suspiciously.

"Good boy." I stayed a safe distance away, but close enough to see a chain attached to his collar.

The dog sat near the steps, daring me to approach the door.

"Mr. Caldwell," I called, then waited. After several minutes, I called again. "Mr. Caldwell."

A curtain fluttered behind a small window at the end of the trailer. Moments later, Peg-Legged Caldwell opened the door and held it. He stepped onto a small platform at the top of the steps, appearing much larger and more formidable than he had during our last encounter. "What do you, want, boy?" He leaned against the doorframe for support.

"Nothing," I said timidly. "Just paying you a visit."

"What for?"

"Can I do anything for you, Mr. Caldwell?"

"No."

He pulled the trailer door toward him, stopped, and opened it again. "Who sent you?"

"No one. I just thought you might need some help with something."

I stepped forward.

The dog stood on all fours, growled, and moved toward me until he strained at his chain.

"Quiet, Copper," Mr. Caldwell said gruffly.

The dog whimpered and returned to his bed under the trailer. He lay with his chin on the ground, eyeing me as I took a few more steps toward the trailer.

"I don't need help, boy. Your dad send you?"

"No, sir. He doesn't know I came. No one does."

"Well, I don't need help."

"Can I bring something from the store for you?"

"No, I just want to be left alone."

"Can I stay and talk a little while?"

For a moment he eyed me without speaking, appearing to mull over my proposition. Then he reached behind him and pulled a straight-back wooden chair to the door. He sat down inside the trailer with his one good leg and his prosthesis resting on the platform outside the trailer. Without his hat, even with his unkempt appearance, he seemed younger, no older than my father.

"Talk," he said as though he had more important things to do.

I ventured closer and took a seat on a small wooden bench. "I don't know what to say except I'm sorry."

"For what?"

"For everything ... for the way me and my friends treated you."

"You've already apologized. Them other boys don't matter."

His statement seemed to put everything into perspective for both of us. There was not much more we could say that would change our tenuous acceptance of each other. We sat in silence.

I squirmed uneasily on the bench, not allowing my eyes to meet his.

"Thank you for coming," he said, getting up from the chair. He stepped abruptly back inside the trailer and pulled the door closed.

Copper crawled from under the trailer and posted himself at the bottom step. As I got up, he warned me away with a series of menacing growls.

Reconciled to failure at befriending Mr. Caldwell, I began my solitary walk down the dirt road that would lead to the trail through the woods. Whatever grievances or fears he harbored would remain known only to him. There was nothing I could do to penetrate the shell he had enclosed around him, and I wouldn't try again.

The gun blast startled me. I stopped and listened but heard nothing except the rippling of Mackenzie Creek as it flowed steadily by. A second blast, seemingly louder than the first, split the air like thunder. I ran toward the source of the gunfire.

Copper had taken refuge under the trailer, apparently terrified of the blasts he had just heard.

"Mr. Caldwell! Mr. Caldwell!" I called frantically and waited for him to open the door.

After a moment, I moved closer, keeping my eyes on the dog as I approached.

Copper didn't move.

"Mr. Caldwell. Mr. Caldwell, you all right?"

Torn between a lingering fear of the old man and the possibility that something terrible had occurred inside the tarnished walls of the trailer, I started up the steps. Something—perhaps my curiosity, perhaps my compassion—overcame my fear, and I cracked open the door.

"Mr. Caldwell," I called, almost whispering. After a moment, I pulled the door toward me and stepped onto the landing. Peering through the doorway, I could see that the trailer was in disarray with papers and trash strewn about. On a worn stuffed chair was the canvas bag that Peg-Legged Caldwell always carried on his shoulder. Its contents had been emptied onto the chair.

I stepped cautiously into the trailer and turned toward the far end. The ceiling above the door to a small bedroom had been blasted away. Mr. Caldwell lay face up with his legs extended in my direction. A shotgun was on the floor near his body. His left hand clutched a dingy, flowered curtain that had been pulled from the doorway as he fell. A portion of the blood-soaked curtain lay across his chest. I got close enough to see that his face no longer existed. The bedroom walls and ceiling were splattered with blood and pieces of flesh.

I stood frozen, unable to grasp the magnitude of the scene before me. I thought of running to find my father for help. Instead, I stood looking at Mr. Caldwell, unable to make my legs move. I remember muttering his name over and over before I regained my sensibilities. I staggered back through the trailer. Steadying myself by a small bureau near the door, my eyes were drawn to a corroded metal picture frame with a black-and-white photograph of a young girl. In the lower corner were scribbled words that I could not read in the dim light. My instincts told me that I had seen the picture before.

Squinting in the sunlight that shone through the open door, I read the faded words scrolled across the bottom of the picture LOVE ALWAYS, LOUISE. Next to the photograph was a faded envelope. It was addressed to PFC John Caldwell, US Army, US Army Surgical Hospital, Dong Tan, Vietnam, APO San Francisco, California. Reluctantly, my eyes moved to the return address on the envelope: Louise Hall, General Delivery, Dunham, Kentucky.

Holding the envelope and picture, I found my way out of the trailer and fell on my knees by the steps. As I cried uncontrollably, I felt Copper at my side.

He whined. I patted his head then wiped the tears from

my face. I ran down the dirt road, not stopping until I reached home.

Mother was sitting on the front porch swing, reading. I sat down beside her and handed her the picture and envelope.

"John Caldwell is dead," I said. "I think he would want you to have these."

27

SCOTTY

We buried him without ceremony or tears. He was ten, seventy in dog years, I was told. His dying was merciful, not only for him but also for Tommy, my little fox terrier, who now had the few available table scraps to himself. Winter was unusually cold that year, and our dogs slept outside under the house. Old age, an empty belly, and bitter temperatures made death easy for Scotty to accept. Alone on a burlap bag, on the ground below the kitchen, he closed his eyes and surrendered the ghost, sending it, I am sure, to that place where all good dogs go.

"Dogs belong outside," my dad always said when either Scotty or Tommy stuck his muzzle through the opening in the doorway. My dad wasn't cruel; that's just how he was raised. He believed dogs had a purpose: hunting, fetching the cows, and signaling when strangers approached. House dogs were something that people of means had, but not dirt farmers and coal miners in southwestern Virginia where I was born and raised—we had outside dogs. I think Scotty was aware of our meager existence and understood he would never rise above his station. He seemed resigned to that fact and was happy until he slunk away to die alone.

I was four when my uncle called from the front porch of my grandparents' home, holding a four-week-old brown and white puppy up for me to see. "I have something for you, TE," he called and waved his arm for me to cross the road.

I was breathless when I reached the foot of the steps. Uncle Nolan placed the dog against my chest, securing both my arms around him. "Don't drop him," he cautioned.

"I won't. Is he mine? Is he mine?"

"He's yours. What are you going to name him, TE?"

"I don't know. I'll ask Mommy."

"OK," he said, "Now, be careful." He put his big hand on my shoulder and walked with me back across the road to our front yard.

“Have I Told You Lately That I Love You” by Lulu Belle and Scotty was playing on the AM radio when I pushed open the kitchen door, my puppy clutched to my chest. They were my mother's favorite singers, especially when they sang “Have I Told You Lately.”

"Scotty," she said. "We'll name him Scotty. “It was a little more than ten years later, just two days after Christmas, when Scotty succumbed to the inevitability awaiting all of us. His life had been uneventful, steady, and predictable. Every evening, he fetched the cows at milking time, never waiting for my dad's signal to go into the pasture and bring Jersey and Mildred home. Powerful shoulders and hindquarters made him a formidable foe to any dog attempting to breach his territory. He fought with ferocity when challenged. Yet, he generously accepted Tommy's intrusion into his life the year before he died, sharing his food and shelter without a trace of animosity. Scotty's genial demeanor endeared him to our family. We all loved him, but I think none of us were aggrieved to see him go. It was time.

The first snow fell in mid-November the year Scotty died, portending an early winter and bitter temperatures that would make his life not worth living. The snow was swept away a few days later by dry, billowing winds, swirling continuously up the valley, eager to beat mercilessly against the mountainsides and walls of our three-room clapboard house. The wind beat just as relentlessly against the cloth jackets my older brother, Joe, and I wore as we dug coal from a bank two hundred feet up the hill. The coal kept the fire burning in the cooking stove and single fireplace that heated our house.

That year had not been kind to my family. Mother miscarried her fifth child in March—a blessing for mother and child in retrospect. Jersey, our reliable old milk cow, died while birthing a stillborn calf. The union voted to strike Black Star Coal Company in May. By September, we were penniless, surviving on the few canned goods my ailing mother had preserved that summer. We sold Mildred, our other cow, for twenty-five dollars. A contract was signed in October, affording my father and his coworkers a ten-cent per hour pay increase. Union activities took Dad away for extended periods. He found other reasons to prolong his absences, often not coming home for several days. Sometimes, for hours, my mother stood by the kitchen window, weeping, watching for my father to walk up the road toward home.

"We ought to have a tree," my mother said as if she had somehow solved a dilemma with a less-than-satisfactory solution. She had spent her tears and exhausted her spirit that Christmas Eve. "We'll put it there." She nodded toward the window of her sparsely furnished bedroom, which held, in addition to her bed and cedar armoire, a Stewart Warner console radio, tuned to WSM, Nashville, Tennessee. Three straight-back wooden chairs circled the hearth and fireplace. The radio crackled while Hank Williams sang "Lovesick Blues." "It won't seem like Christmas without a tree."

Joe said nothing, but donned his jacket and walked outside into the biting cold. He was gone for an hour, returning with a scraggly pine barely his height. He stood by the fire warming his hands.

"It was the best I could find, Mother."

"It will do, Son," she said. "We'll make it do."

Joe nailed two crossed boards to the bottom of the tree trunk then nailed the boards to the floor. As I watched, he said to me, without looking away from the pitiful tree or rising from his crouched position. "Have you fed your dogs, TE? They followed me. I think they're hungry."

"Yeah, Joe, I gave both of them soup beans and cornbread too. They may still be hungry, but there's nothing else."

"Ok." Joe stood to inspect his handiwork. "Guess they'll just have to wait 'til tomorrow."

Mother popped corn on the stove. We watched as she strung the popcorn with a needle and thread. After completing a dozen or so, she handed the strings of popcorn to my sisters and me. We painstakingly wrapped them around the tree while Mother cut stars and bells from brown paper bags. She colored the largest star red and climbed onto one of the chairs to place it at the top of the tree. Her body shook with sobs as she stepped down from the chair onto the floor where no presents would be placed.

From the armoire drawer, my mother removed a small bag of hard candy. She laid out four white socks and divided the candy evenly, crying silently and wiping away tears as she placed one of our names on each sock.

My father did not come home that night or the next.

It began snowing two days after Christmas. Winds from the north whipped our house, almost shaking it on its fragile foundation. When our supper of water dumplings was over, I cleaned off the table, collecting scraps from our plates and the cooking pot. I stepped outside and called the dogs for feeding. Tommy emerged from beneath the house almost immediately. I assumed Scotty's arthritis had slowed him more than usual. I whistled for him and waited impatiently. After a few moments, I filled Tommy's dish and watched him devour its contents in voracious gulps then sit looking wistfully at me for something more to eat.

"Sorry, buddy. The rest is for Scotty."

It was unlike the old dog to miss a feeding. I knew something was wrong but didn't want to face the possibility of his dying and could not gather the courage to crawl under the house to see for myself. Shivering in the wind, I leaned against the house, cursing myself, my father, and the world.

Joe called from the kitchen door. "TE, you OK?"

I walked around the corner of the house to see him. "Something's wrong with Scotty. I think he's dead."

Joe got on his hands and knees and crawled toward the spot where Scotty made his bed. After a few minutes, he returned, grim-faced. "He's dead. I'm sorry, brother."

Evening shadows had already fallen across the yard. "We'll have to bury him tomorrow," Joe said. "It'll be dark soon."

The next morning, he pulled Scotty's stiff remains from beneath the house and placed them on a small wooden sled. With the frozen grass crunching beneath our feet and the sled, we dragged our burden up the hill to a flat place behind the old cow shed. There, we dug a grave long enough and deep enough to hold his emaciated body. As I tilted the first shovel of dirt toward his once faithful head, I searched for something appropriate to say. "I can't do it, Joe. I can't put dirt on his face."

He took hold of the shovel and gently removed it from my hands then, with one arm, hugged me close.

"I hope he didn't die feeling unloved," I said.

"Don't worry, TE. He knew you loved him."

"But why can't I cry?"

"'Cause there's nothing to cry about. He's better off dead." Joe stood, looking into the grave, his eyes glistening. He began shoveling dirt until Scotty's head was no longer visible. "We'd all be better off dead."

Joe continued shoveling until the old dog was covered completely and the mound of dirt was beat firm with the flat of the shovel. We walked back toward the house in silence, pulling the empty sled behind us.

28

LUNCH WITH FRAN

From my cubicle, I watched the girls go giggling on their way to the office in the back corner of the engineering department. That was where my good friend, Chase Collier, held court for half a dozen or so office cuties every morning before the starting bell. I was the straight arrow in our department and wouldn't have strayed on my wife for love nor money. But Chase and some of the other guys couldn't overcome the temptations thrown in their paths by young divorcées, neglected wives, or single young ladies looking for an experience with an experienced man—and Chase Collier was of that reputation. My self-imposed straight arrowness did not diminish the pleasure I got from ogling the pulchritudinous pretties parading by my desk each morning. Nor did it preclude me from relishing the titillating tidbits of office gossip pertaining to Chase and Fran Dubois, newly separated-potential-divorcée, who had joined the daily parade. But let me say at the start, that what I am about to relate to you is not based on such gossip. It is based on my own observations and Chase Collier's unembellished accounting of his ill-advised dalliances with Fran—and you can take it from me, he would never have lied about such things. I always knew when Chase was in the shits at home. His assigned parking space was adjacent to mine. And on those mornings when all of his prized personal possessions and clothes were piled into the back seat of his 1995 Ford Thunderbird, it meant that he had left home in a hurry, raiding his closet on the way out the door. In the trunk would be his Navy sword—the remaining symbol of his twenty-plus years of service, a shaving kit, and his Yamaha acoustic guitar. The guitar was especially prized by Chase because it had saved his life by coming between him and a steel barbecue fork thrown by his wife. The fork embedded itself just above the top E-string with a frightening *thwong*. He had looked up just in time to raise the guitar over his heart and blurt out the words, "Are you crazy?"

Fran was a diminutive beauty with short dark hair and sparkling green eyes, the bright light of an otherwise dull accounting group. Every morning when she swished by, she left a trail of Parfum des Violettes wafting in her wake. If any woman could have shaken my determination to remain chaste, Fran might have been the one. However, I never got more than a "Hi, Bob" out of her as she passed my desk. And when I learned that Norm Dubois was 6'6" and two hundred forty pounds, I was thankful as hell she kept on walking.

I had a premonition that Fran might be Chase's femme fatale, but who was I to say? After all, he was the undisputed champion in triangulation of the heart, while I had been to bed with only one woman in the past twenty years. So, I demurred in the presence of the master.

Fran's tight little bottom had just rounded the corner as she headed back to the accounting department.

"I'm going to nail that stuff tonight, Bob." Chase leaned over and thumped his fist on my desk.

That morning, I had noticed his guitar and clothes in the Thunderbird and took for granted Chase would be on the loose that evening.

"Why don't you join us for a drink over at the Poodle Dog after work, Bob?"

"No can do. Momma has dinner on the table promptly at six-thirty." I patted my stomach that was in the first stage of protruding over my belt. "Haven't missed a meal yet."

Chase laughed. "Me neither. I just eat out a lot."

The next morning, while I was putting my brown bag lunch into my desk drawer, Fran passed by. "Hi, Bob." She waved a little wave. I waved back. She was smiling when she opened the door to the corner office; she was smiling more broadly when she came out.I don't know if it was envy or the quest for vicarious pleasure that made me get up from my chair and walk back to Chase's office, but I just had to find out what in the hell happened the previous evening.

"You're not going to believe it, Bob." Chase began laughing.

"Yeah?"

"A half dozen of us were there, Bigsby, Shelton, Marylyn, and Roberta..."

"Roberta?"

"Yeah, from Blueprints. You know, the one with the big tits."

I nodded, eager for Chase to get into his story.

"After a few drinks, Fran began rubbing her hands up my thighs. Man, that didn't last long. I got up, and she followed me out to my car, parked by the BFI dumpster. Things were getting hot and heavy. She unfastened my belt, then unbuttoned the top button of my trousers. I unzipped my fly and waited for the most sensational blow job of my life."

If I wanted graphic details, they were on the way, and I was ready to hear them.

Chase continued. "Suddenly, my car started shaking violently from side to side. I thought, *damn, this is going to be good.* I looked up to see a wild-eyed face pressed against the driver's window. I thought: *Holy shit.* Then I shoved the door open and slammed the Sasquatch-sized son of a bitch against the dumpster."

By then, I was bent double with laughter.

Chase continued. "That's not the half of it, Bob. When I got out of the car, my pants fell down around my feet. I struggled, walking like a penguin while wrestling with a Godzilla I didn't even know."

I was sitting down, holding my head in my hands, roaring at my friend's dilemma. "How in the hell did you get out of that, Chase?"

"Well," he said, "I heard Fran yell, "It's Norm," just before she cranked the car and backed it all the way across the parking lot. I hoisted my trousers as I watched her turn the car toward the exit. Thank God he ran after her, chasing my car and Fran until all three were out of sight. The only thing I could think was *I hope she doesn't let Norm fuck up my guitar.*"

Not long afterward, Fran hired a lawyer and filed for divorce. Armed with a restraining order, she apparently had no compunction about her morning strolls to Chase's corner office. He had taken an apartment in town providing a temporary safe haven for his guitar and sword. Around the office, it was known that Chase and Fran were now a couple. The story might have ended there except for Norm's persistent pursuit of the woman he claimed to love.

Flowers for Fran arrived every other day at the office—not one dozen, but two or three dozen brilliantly colored roses, with notes attached that read: I love you. Please forgive me. The ploy worked, and before long, Fran allowed Norm to come back home. Chase was not heartbroken, but he missed her enough to attempt to get her back into his bed. She turned down his invitation for drinks at the Poodle Dog or trysts at the Holiday Inn after work. But the poontang king from the corner office didn't give up either. Finally, Fran agreed to have lunch with him, but only if a third party accompanied the two of them. And like a damned fool, I accepted the invitation. I thought that with three of us, things would appear innocent enough to Norm.

Just before we left the parking lot, Chase turned his head to look at me sitting in the back seat. "Keep your eye out for Norm."

"Norm? What the hell? What kind of car does he drive?"

"Who knows?" Fran said. "But his regular car is a Chevy Impala—light blue." She chose that moment to tell me Norm worked at a used-car dealership and might be driving anything from the lot.

Chase took a couple of unfamiliar streets, made a precautionary turn, then headed up the hill toward a little restaurant that people from our office sometimes frequented. Elliot Ness would have had a hard time following our circuitous route, but not Norm. Near the top of the hill, just before reaching the restaurant, Chase looked into his rearview mirror. "What's that goddamn Volkswagen doing right on top of my ass?"

Fran looked through the back window. "Couldn't be Norm. He wouldn't be found dead in a VW."

By now, I was watching the little car that was following no more than two feet away from our back bumper. "Can you believe there is a gorilla driving that VW?"

Fran looked again. "Oh my God, it's Norm. He's probably got his gun with him."

Now I was thinking: *Oh shit! I'm closer to him. He'll get me first.*

Chase went right through the intersection, kicked the Thunderbird in the ass, and left the VW sitting at the stop sign. He drove past the restaurant and turned down a residential street that eventually ended in a cul-de-sac. The turnaround was made without braking, still doing thirty miles an hour, and we were headed back in Norm's direction.

My head was swinging back and forth like a gun turret as I watched for the dark green Volkswagen. "There it is." I pointed down the street. In front of the stop sign, the VW sat crosswise, blocking our exit. Bent across the hood, with a long-barrelled pistol pointed in our direction, was a behemoth by the name of Norm. Now I was happy to be in the back seat, where I was unlikely to take the first bullet.

Chase stopped the car and leaned over the steering wheel. After a moment, he sat upright and looked straight ahead, gritting his teeth. "You son of a bitch." With his foot on the brake, he revved the engine, powering up like El Toro pawing the ground just before charging the matador.

I scooted down with only the top of my head above the front seat back. "Holy shit, Chase. What are you doing?"

"Fuck him," he said, still looking straight ahead. "Fasten your seat belts, boys." The wheels whined and the engine roared as we laid rubber halfway down the block.

Fran screamed and hid her face in her hands. I closed my eyes waiting for the collision. The tires screeched as our car slid around the corner onto the main street. I looked back to see that Norm had pushed the VW onto the crossing street just in time to avoid getting squashed by the Thunderbird.

Our car was doing eighty by the time we made the freeway, and the VW was nowhere in sight. Moments later, I heard a thump, thump, thump as the car leaned, ever so slightly to the right. "Think you got a flat tire."

"Damn." Chase slowed to forty, but the thumping continued.

A pint-sized VW appeared in the rearview mirror. Moments later, it had grown into a voracious green monster as Norm gained on our limping Thunderbird. By now, sparks were flying as the rubberless rim ground into the blacktop. Chase slowed to twenty, and Norm easily came alongside to our left. The madman behind the wheel of the VW rolled down the right window and screamed a profanity in our direction. I couldn't hear him but read his lips. "Pull over, cocksucker."

Chase lowered his window and yelled back a profanity of his own. "What the hell do you want, you crazy fuck?"

Norm pointed in Fran's direction. "I want her."

"Follow me." Chase motioned with his left arm then rolled up his window. Now the Thunderbird limped along at no more than ten miles per hour, with the VW taking up a position less than a car length behind. At the next exit, Chase turned down the ramp and headed, at a crawl, toward the Poodle Dog. But to my surprise, he drove right on past, two blocks further down to the McDonald's drive-through. Norm followed right behind.

Now, Fran was laughing. Chase too, but I failed to see the humor. "You crazy bastard; you're going to get us killed."

"No one gets killed in the McDonald's drive-through." Chase moved up to the window.

A sixteen-year-old girl leaned toward us. "May I take your order please?"

"Yes," Chase said cheerfully. "Three Big Macs." He looked around at Fran and me. "Anyone want fries?"

Neither of us moved our lips. Whatever appetite I once had was lost way back behind me in the cul-de-sac.

"Three fries," he continued calmly.

The Volkswagen horn sounded. "Anything to drink?" the sixteen-year-old asked sweetly.

"Yeah, three medium Cokes." Chase chuckled as he handed the girl a twenty-dollar bill.

The Volkswagen horn sounded again.

Before moving away from the drive-through window, he defiantly unwrapped a burger, moved it to his mouth, took a bite, and chewed slowly.

I was ten seconds away from exiting Chase's car and running like hell back to our office. "Geeze, Chase, what the hell are you doing?"

"I'm having lunch with Fran, by god."

He pointed across the street to a sign that read: PENDLETON POLICE DEPARTMENT. The girl in the window leaned out to see where he was pointing.

"Call the police station," Chase said. "Tell them there's a crazy man in that green Volkswagen behind us. He's armed and dangerous and wanted by the FBI."

Chase pulled his limping car on through the drive, creeping toward the filling station on the corner. As police sirens wailed, he parked the car, and we all chowed down on Big Macs and fries and downed our Cokes. I looked back toward McDonalds. The green VW was flanked by two police cars with blue lights flashing.

Sadly, Fran did not get flowers that afternoon.

29

THE ARAPAHO WARRIOR

"He's a half-breed from the Arapaho tribe." She smiled and held up a paperback novel. *The Arapaho Avenger—Dianne Silver* blazed across the front cover. A muscular man with American Indian facial features and shoulder-length dark golden hair stood astride the body of a fallen westerner. In the warrior's raised right hand was a blood-stained tomahawk; the other hand grasped the waist of a beautiful auburn-haired white woman, struggling to get free.

"I know it doesn't interest you," Melanie said as she tugged at the pillows behind her shoulders.

"Should I raise you up a little?" I reached for the button controlling her hospital bed.

She shook her head. "No, I'm okay."

I pushed myself back into the chair and watched as she brushed her unkempt hair away from her face.

"I'm a mess," she said.

A thousand thoughts flashed across my mind, bits and

pieces of a relationship that could only be considered cordial at best. It had taken eight years after our divorce to reach even that accommodation. "No, Mel, you look fine," I lied.

Earlier that week, our son, Kevin, called from San Bernardino to tell me his mother was in hospice and not expected to survive more than a week or two. "Will you go see her, Dad?"

"No," I said without hesitation.

I could visualize Kevin, his eyes closed as he let the urge to call me a sanctimonious bastard pass. After a few seconds, he asked, "Why not?"

"It's too hard, Kev. I don't have anything to say to her."

"Christ, Dad, you two were married for fifteen years. You have three kids. Surely, there is something you can say that she would want to hear."

"Nothing that would comfort her, Son."

"You know, you were not blameless in what happened."

"I wasn't the one who found a lover. It was your mother who went looking for someone else."

"Are you going to hold that against her forever?"

"No, Kev, I've been over that for a long time—put it behind me, but I don't want to open up old wounds."

He let go a plaintive sigh. After a moment, he said something to me, perceptive beyond his twenty years. "Dad, I have always thought you were a brilliant man, much more intellectual than Mom. She enjoyed simple things; she was without pretense or guile. She was easy to love. You never were. You always held that against her. You thought you were too sophisticated for her."

"I think you are being a little unfair, Son."

"Think about it, Dad. I hope you change your mind."

~

"So, how's the book?"

She smiled weakly and held it up for me to see. "Like most of the others. You know, the Indian brave captures the white woman and makes her his love slave—the kind of stuff you always ridiculed." She let the book fall onto the bed.

"Nothing new?" I was searching for something we could discuss while I kept her company.

"Maybe a few things," she said. The hero's name is White Wolf. He's a half-breed and became chief of one of the Arapaho bands."

I listened, occasionally nodding that I understood.

"Am I boring you?"

"No, no. Go on. Tell me about the exploits of White Wolf."

"Promise not to laugh if I tell you something very personal?"

I held up my right hand.

"I've seen him here in this room, watching me."

"Who?' I was amused, almost to the point of smiling, but kept a straight face.

"White Wolf. Sometimes he stands by the door or at the foot of my bed. I've even seen him sitting right there in that chair, where you are."

"That's amazing," I said, attempting to sound sincere. "Does he speak to you?"

"No, just sits there."

"But says nothing?"

"Night before last was different. I was just closing my eyes when he came into the room. He startled me, and I struggled to sit up. He reached out his arms toward me. He stood there for the longest time, beckoning. I finally settled back on my pillows and fell asleep. When I awoke he was gone. He hasn't been back."

"I don't know what to make of that," I said, attempting not to sound skeptical.

She closed her eyes. I was prepared to see tears rolling down her cheek. After a moment, she smiled, picked up the book, and continued her synopsis.

"White Wolf's mother was raped by one of Colonel Chivington's soldiers during the Sand Creek Massacre. She was a chief's daughter, only fourteen. Growing up, her son was an outcast because his father was a Union soldier. Later, White Wolf became a great hunter, strongest of all the young braves, and at eighteen, was made chief of one of the Arapaho breakaway bands. He began raiding army supply wagons. During one of those raids, he killed a senior army officer and captured his young daughter, Maureen."

She stopped to catch her breath and, I suppose, to give me time to express my derision of the story.

When I said nothing, she continued.

"You know how it ends, Dan. Maureen falls in love with White Wolf. They disappear into the Colorado Mountains and were never heard from again."

"Damn, I was hoping for some great sexual feats. Don't these stories usually have that?"

"Yes," she said. "This one does too. Don't laugh though. You know you always do."

I chuckled. "Not this time; I promise."

"Okay. There's this one scene where they want to take a bath, but the river is frozen over. White Wolf breaks the ice with his tomahawk and carries Maureen into the stream. While she is bathing him, he becomes so aroused they have sex right there in the icy water."

I burst out laughing.

She laughed too. "You promised me you wouldn't."

"I couldn't help it. That was just too good. Must have been some tomahawk."

When our laughs subsided, we sat looking at each other. I think neither of us knew what to say next. After a moment, I stood and took her hands in mine. "I have to run now. Maybe I'll get a chance to drop by again in a couple of days."

"It's all right. You've come; that's what matters."

"You going to be okay?"

"Sure," she said. "I'm made of pretty tough stuff."

"I know, Mel. I learned something about you during fifteen years of marriage."

She grasped my hand. "Can you forgive me, Dan?"

"Long ago." I bent, kissed her brow, then walked to the door. I turned around to wave one last goodbye. A brawny Indian warrior stood at the foot of her bed, legs spread, muscular arms folded defiantly across his chest. He nodded in my direction but never changed expression. I started down the hall but was compelled to return to the door. When I looked in, he was seated near the bed, his eyes steadily set on Melanie. She was sleeping peacefully.

At the elevator, I suppressed an urge to sing. I knew the warrior would carry her safely across mountain streams.

30

ANTS

Glimmers of the morning sun slipped through the curtains in room 2019 of The Grand Castille Hotel. I sat up and looked around, taking in the opulence of my unfamiliar deluxe accommodations. *You have finally made it, you lucky son of a bitch.* I pulled open the drapes and looked down on the early morning streets of Los Angeles. On the sidewalks twenty stories below, people scurried in all directions. Industrious little ants, part of the colony. Worker ants. I could imagine one of them looking up at my window and seeing me peering through the drapes—just another ant. That might have been true a few days ago, but no longer; my fortunes had changed. Jonas Mallory, soon-to-be renowned playwright, had broken free of the colony.

None of those people, none of those ants knew anything about me. They had no idea that, for twenty years, publishers' rejection letters filled my mailbox or that one week ago, I was on the brink of suicide. My best screenplay,

The Misunderstood Man, had been turned down by a dozen or more publishers. My funds were exhausted, and my wife had left me, taking our two teenage boys with her. In the throes of despair, I planned to end my failed life.

Moments after I sat down at the table to write a farewell note, the phone rang. That evening, salvation came in the words of Tolliver Sullivan, a literary agent in Los Angeles. "I've got terrific news, Jonas. Thomas Goodsoul of Practical Pictures likes your play. He wants to talk to you about making a movie out of it."

Elated, I pushed back the poisonous pills and sank into my chair. After a moment of silent celebration, I thanked God for the reprieve and recovered my ability to speak. "Great ... great news. When do we meet?"

"As soon as you can get out here, my man."

"I'm a little short right now. ...Don't see how..."

"Tell you what, Jonas, I feel pretty solid about this. I'll front you for your plane and hotel."

"You're a good man, Tolly." I don't know why I assumed that familiarity, but at that moment, he seemed like a brother to me. The tears that I had suppressed during the five-minute conversation flowed. I had no desire to wipe them away. Five days later, I was on a plane bound for LAX.

Now, as I prepared for an 11 a.m. meeting with the moguls at Practical Pictures, I envisioned a new beginning, a life of prominence and comfort. I slipped a ready-made tie over my head and adjusted the Windsor knot. As I touched up my neatly combed hair, I congratulated myself for my persistence and determination. "Impressive," I said to the man in the mirror.

With an hour to kill, I unlocked the briefcase holding six

copies of my manuscript. Opening one of the binders to the front page, I read: *The Misunderstood Man, A screenplay by Jonas Mallory.* With a sense of pride and satisfaction, I turned to the introduction: "Calvin Pierce is an accomplished pianist. He has just received an invitation to perform a concert at Carnegie Hall..."

The phone rang.

"Mallory here."

"Jonas, you sitting down?" It was Tolliver Sullivan. "We have a little setback, but I think we will be all right."

I dropped the manuscript to the floor. "What..."

"Thomas Goodsoul had a heart attack last night. Died on the operating table this morning."

"Damn.... What about the meeting with Practical?"

"Off. ... It's off for now."

"What does that mean for us?"

"The man's dead, Jonas. What can I tell you? I think I can get us another shot in a month or so."

My eyes fell onto the manuscript on the floor. *I don't have a month.*

"Maybe you will, Tolly; maybe you will," I mumbled as I hung up the phone.

Checking the inside pocket of my coat, my fingers found the return ticket. With my bags sitting by the door, I walked to the window for one last look at the streets below. The ants were still there. Surely, one more ant by the name of Jason Mallory would go unnoticed among them. I pressed the button for the elevator and waited. It made a slow transit from the fourth floor, went past, and lingered on the twenty-sixth before stopping in front of me. I stood motionless, staring at the well-dressed gentleman holding open the elevator doors. Obviously irritated by my failure to enter the elevator, he asked, "Going down?"

"Yes," I said, "but I forgot something."

I turned away from the elevator and walked toward the exit door leading to the roof. A dozen stairsteps later, I was gazing down at the street from the rooftop. Below, the ants scurried up and down the sidewalks, back and forth across the streets, in and out of buildings. No one below realized that a failed playwright was watching from above, envious of their apparent satisfaction with their own mundane lives, and unaware that a desperate man, high above them, was about to leap to his death. I wondered if those ants down below would notice me during my eight-second plunge to the sidewalk below. Jonas Mallory was about to rejoin the colony.

31

THE CENSUS TAKER COMETH

Having produced and sent out into the world two progeny, Mary Belle, nineteen, and Norman Ray, twenty-two, and having outlived a like number of golden retrievers, Gladys and Melvin (Bubba) Chance had watched dispassionately as their marriage dissipated into a mutually grudging acknowledgment of each other's existence. In the waning days of their civility, only smoldering ashes of a once fiery love life remained. Intercourse consisted of the exchange of seductive sexual innuendos when they met in the hallway each morning: *Fuck you, Gladys. Fuck you, Bubba.*

This sorry state of affairs between Bubba, age forty-seven, and Gladys, age forty-four, did not happen overnight. Rather, it evolved over many years as their idiosyncratic habits—so easily tolerated during their courtship and early years of marriage—matured into screeching sources of irritation. It came to a decisive head when Gladys informed Bubba that she no longer found him sexually desirable and would henceforth remain chaste until the day she died. However, her assertions of celibacy were blown to bits when Bubba found, hidden under the mattress, a well-worn male phallus, dwarfing the instrument Bubba had exhibited with pride wherever and whenever the occasion called for it. Needless to say, he took umbrage at being replaced by a piece of electrically stimulated twitching plastic, no matter how real in appearance.

Gladys's renouncement of her conjugal obligations came at a time when Bubba was considering unholy inclinations toward Wanda Wilcox, the wife of his best friend, Claude. Bubba was confident that Wanda's lingering touches and seductive glances happened too frequently to be unintentional. Now that he had been rejected by his own wife, he thought it time to explore possibilities with wild-eyed Wanda, ten years his junior. His suspicions of her potential promiscuity were confirmed one evening when he dropped in unannounced at her apartment, knowing full well that Claude worked weekdays from four until midnight. She proved only too happy to restore his confidence in his manhood, sending him home well-worn and with a new spring in his step. Following this encounter with Wanda, he found the courage to inform Gladys, in no uncertain language that he no longer gave a fiddler's fart whether he ever again had sex with her and that she was, and always had been, a *bum fuck.*

Normally, such a rebuke by one's marital mate would stimulate an immediate move toward permanent dissolution, but this was not the case with Gladys. Her mind worked in its own peculiar fashion. She had never coped well with rejection and needed for Bubba to be miserable and longing for her affection—fat chance with Wanda waiting around a few corners, up a few streets, less than fifteen minutes away. As Gladys's suspicions grew, Bubba became more and more adept at inventing excuses for getting out of the house several evenings each week.

"I suppose you'll be going for your evening walk after supper." Gladys cast a knowing eye at the top of Bubba's head on which the hair was beginning to grow thin like lawn dying out after the first frost.

Bubba looked up from his beef stew and noodles. "Yeah, guess so."

"Why the sudden interest in physical fitness?"

Bubba stood and patted his rotund belly, protruding just slightly over his cowboy belt buckle. "Gotta stay in shape. Don't wanna get that middle-aged spread."

"Guess you don't mind if I come with you. I'm startin' to put on a few extra pounds."

Bubba suppressed a tendency toward a smart-ass snicker but thought a whole lot better of it. "You sure? I hadn't noticed."

"Give me a few minutes, and I will get my tennis shoes on." Gladys left the table and headed for the hallway closet.

Bubba grabbed the kitchen phone and frantically dialed Wanda's number. "Can't make it tonight, doll. Gladys is on the prowl."

Bubba played it cool for the next few days but grew restless as the weekend approached. With wanton Wanda waiting impatiently, his mind churned to devise new reasons for getting out of the house. "Gladys, I think I'll run up to the filling station and top off my tank."

"Why tonight, Bubba? Why can't it wait 'til morning?"

"Gotta be in early tomorrow. So thought I would fill up tonight. I'm about on empty."

After observing that Bubba filled the tank at least three times during the next two weeks, Gladys's suspicions mounted. The next time he mentioned a trip to Mr. Zip's Gas and Go, she decided to tag along.

"Give me a minute, and I will go with you. I need cigarettes."

Damn. Bubba hurried to the bedroom and dialed Wanda. "Can't make it tonight, doll. Gladys is on the prowl again."

Although Gladys viewed Bubba's sexual prowess with amusement, almost certain no other woman would want him, there still was a small portion of her brain that suspected he might be hankering to slip his weenie into another bun, and she was not about to let that happen. She decided it was time to stow her dildo—for which by now, she had developed great affection—in the bottom dresser drawer and coax Bubba back into her bed.

Her uncharacteristic decision created a dilemma for Bubba: should he give up wicked Wanda once and for all for the sake of domestic tranquility? Or could he summon his once youthful exuberance, keeping both ladies sexually sated and unsuspecting? It would have been entirely out of character for him to choose the saner course of action. So, while Gladys regained confidence that the marital crisis had passed, Bubba dreamed of wayward Wanda and waited for his first opportunity to get out from under Gladys's watchful eye. That opportunity came one Monday evening when she was glued to the television watching George Hamilton on *Dancing with the Stars.*

Knowing that nothing could tear Gladys away from her favorite program for the next hour or more, Bubba made a daring proposal. "We're out of bread, honey. Think I'll run down to the Mr. Zip's to grab a loaf. Want to come with me?"

Gladys stuffed her mouth with potato chips and mumbled something akin to no, never taking her eyes off the flat-screen TV.

Ten minutes later, Bubba's 4X4 Ford F350 screeched to a stop, bumper against the garage door, in the Wilcox driveway. Grateful that the gods of fornication were smiling down on him, he hopped to the ground and bolted up the front steps. He knocked and waited in anticipation until Wanda cracked open the door. The surreptitious lovers fell into each other's arms. Wanda threw her legs about Bubba's waist in a scissor lock as he frantically worked the buttons of her shirt (actually, it was Claude's white Sunday shirt, the hem striking Wanda's thighs just above the knees). Bubba staggered toward the living room couch, holding onto Wanda who clung to him like a suckling chimpanzee. Depositing her onto the sofa, he dropped his trousers, preparing to climb aboard the undulating love train writhing in anticipation beneath him.

"Hurry," she said breathlessly, "I've missed you, Bubba."

Bubba had always been a sucker for such sexy talk, and knowing how much Wanda wanted him heightened his excitement. She arched her back and thrust her body upward, toward him as he began to administer the coup de grace.

A knock at the door sent visions of shotgun blasts scurrying through Bubba's brain. *Christ, Claude's home early!* With his trousers about his ankles, Bubba penguin shuffled in circles, his eyes searching for a place to hide. Wanda shrieked, bounding from the couch as she pulled up her panties and smoothed down Claude's white Sunday shirt while moving toward the door.

"Yes?" she inquired, sweetly. "Who is it?"

"The census taker." An authoritative government voice boomed from the other side of the door.

Bubba stood, slack-jawed, his eyes transfixed in the direction of the doorknob. Wanda motioned with both hands for him to get on his pants, which were still mostly on the floor. Her hands trembled as she reached to open the door. Now fully clothed, Bubba sat down and stretched out his legs, presenting the image of a totally relaxed man, not one who was breathing a sigh of relief that he had not just inhaled a mouthful of buckshot from Claude's 16-gauge.

Wanda slid back the night latch and pulled the door wide enough to insert her face into the opening. "How can I help you?"

"I'm a census worker." The man held up an ID card showing a picture of a full-bearded grizzly bear. "You mailed in a census form, but I need to verify some information."

By then, Wanda was shaking as if she had developed palsy, relieved that Claude was still at work, but fearful she might be eaten by the beast standing at her door.

"May I come in?" The bear sounded less menacing.

"'Scuse my poor manners," Wanda stepped aside and gestured for the carnivore to enter. She extended her hand. "I'm Wanda Wilcox."

"I'm Mo Tally. It's good to meet you, Mrs. Wilcox." He turned to Bubba who sat, now dumbstruck by the course of events. "And you must be Mr. Wilcox."

Wanda intervened before Bubba could respond. "Yes, this is my husband, Claude."

Mr. Tally took a seat across from Wanda and Bubba, clipboard in hand, and began his interview. "Number of adults living in the household?"

"Two, just two." Wanda grinned and squirmed. Bubba stared into the corner, hoping he had lost his voice.

"Any children, and their ages?"

"Two," she replied, syrup dripping from her mouth, clutching Claude's white shirt around her knees, "but they're with their real daddy for the summer. I get them ten months out of the year."

"I'll bet you miss them. How old are they?" The census taker was proving to be entirely genial and understanding.

"We sure do. Twelve and ten." She reached across the couch and patted Bubba's knee affectionately. "Don't we, honey?"

Bubba cracked his knuckles and nodded his assent.

"Do you own or rent?"

"We rent now, but my husband wants to buy, dontcha, honey?" She patted his knee again.

Bubba almost smiled as he nodded in agreement.

"Now, this portion," the tallyman explained, "you don't have to answer if you don't want to."

Bubba welcomed the opportunity to stop the agony. Knowing he would never see Mr. Tally again, he raised his right index finger, signaling an end to the inquisition. "In that case, we don't want to answer any more questions." He opened the door and bade the grizzly goodbye. Bubba's eyes now turned to Wanda who lay on the couch with Claude's white Sunday shirt unbuttoned from top to bottom.

Bubba checked his watch. With ten minutes allotted for his transaction with Wanda and five minutes to pay for a loaf of bread at Mr. Zip's Gas and Go, he would get home before Gladys missed him. His arrival was timely, finding his wife bereft that George Hamilton and his partner were eliminated from the *Dancing with the Stars* competition. Bubba held her gently, offering consolation that only one's understanding mate can provide. Gladys responded to his comforting embrace by suggesting a romp in the sack. Unfortunately, because of his prior activities with Wanda, Bubba was unable to rise to the occasion and adequately supplant the electric plastic device now lying fallow in Gladys's bottom dresser drawer. This failure created serious doubts in her mind as she suddenly realized Bubba had disappeared for nearly an hour and returned with only a loaf of stale bread.

Bubba explained that he ran into an old Navy buddy from Joplin, Missouri down at Mr. Zip's. The two of them spent the next half hour reviving memories of high school football heroics and swapping sea stories. Of course, as he explained, he tried to break away, but his friend kept talking. For the life of him, Bubba couldn't recall the friend's name—pretty damned embarrassing.

Gladys reluctantly accepted Bubba's explanation, but she could not overcome her nagging suspicion her husband was up to no good. She vowed to get to the bottom of things and began monitoring Bubba's every move. He resorted to toeing the line, keeping his distance from the Wilcox abode. After several days away from Wanda, he considered intimacy with Gladys. However, fearing rejection by his wife, he waited for her to make the first move; and Gladys, wary of Bubba's apparent wilted condition, waited for him to do the same, wondering if he had finally succumbed to total erectile dysfunction. This impasse left the unhappy duo no choice but to spend their evenings watching TV game shows. It seemed they would live out their lives sitting on opposite sides of the room, tolerating each other, stuffing their faces with popcorn and potato chips. Thankfully, their humdrum lives changed with the ringing of the doorbell.

Happy for the unexpected interruption, Bubba rushed to the door, swung it open, and looked squarely into the face of Mo Tally., the census taker.

"Who is it, Bubba?" Gladys's shrill voice carried over a *Wheel of Fortune* contestant's sounds of "big money, come on big money."

Bubba shrank to the size of his penis.

"Well, Mr. Wilcox, we meet again." The census bear roared loud enough for Gladys to hear above the ear-splitting volume of the television set.

Hearing the name Wilcox, her eyes were suddenly opened. She grasped a small vase filled with artificial roses and flung it across the room. "You bastard." Milk glass exploded into shards as the vase struck Bubba in the back of the head. He crumpled to the floor. Gladys hurried to his prone body, his eyes open, showing only the whites. She placed her foot on his chest. "I should have known it was that damn hussy." Then she glowered at the census taker. "Who in the hell are you?"

Mr. Tally, apparently concerned for his own safety, stammered, "I'm Mo Tally, a government census taker." His demeanor was, putting it mildly, subdued. "I need to verify a little information if you don't mind."

While Bubba lay on the floor unconscious, unaware he was about to be counted twice in the US Census, Gladys explained the situation to Mr. Tally. He limited his questions to only three to which she provided succinct responses before sending the now domesticated bear on his way.

Gladys then turned her attention to her wounded mate whose memory had been tragically eradicated—a profound case of amnesia. His slow and painful convalescence was enhanced by a steady diet of game shows and soap operas, Gladys constantly by his side. Several weeks later, Bubba realized his memory was returning when he began thinking of Wanda and wondered if she had laundered Claude's white Sunday shirt.

One Monday evening while Gladys was lost in a game show, following the urges residing in his groins, Bubba dialed the Wilcox residence. To his consternation, Wanda did not answer. The following evening, Bubba tried with the same result. By Friday, his libido, enhanced with visions of winsome Wanda writhing beneath him, he made a now infrequent trip to Mr. Zips, stopping at the Wilcox abode on his way. An unfamiliar Ford Fairlane was parked in the driveway, arousing Bubba's suspicions. He knocked on the door and waited for his pulchritudinous paramour to open it. When no one answered, Bubba stooped to see through a slit in the venetian blind covering the front door glass panel. He saw Wanda buttoning Claude's white Sunday shirt and Mo Tally, the census taker, cowering in a corner, attempting to put on his trousers.

ACKNOWLEDGMENTS

I wish to acknowledge Frank Eastland, CEO of Publish Authority, for his patience and encouragement. I appreciate his team at Publish Authority, especially the talents of Raeghan Rebstock who worked diligently to create front and back covers that visually depict the essences of my stories. And I must recognize my editor, Janie Mills, who faced too many italicized words, but stubbornly produced copy acceptable to the publisher. My eternal gratitude goes to Shirley Adams, who served as my eyes, reading and rereading each story before compiling the original manuscript.

ABOUT THE AUTHOR

Travis Short is a successful author who has published several books in various genres. His latest novel, *Killers Can't Hide*, is now available online and in real-world bookstores worldwide. Originally from southwest Virginia, he served in the US Navy before retiring as Lieutenant Commander. Following his military career, he began working in management positions and eventually became a business owner in the shipbuilding and machinery manufacturing industries. After retiring from his second career, he now writes full time. Travis is a proud father of four daughters and three sons and currently resides in Moss Point, Mississippi.

For more about the author, his books, and his upcoming book events, you are invited to visit his website at TravisShort.com.

ALSO BY TRAVIS SHORT

Anna

A touching story from an autobiographical memoir written by Anna Marie Gamble, a tribute to a beautiful life of faith and courage.

Faraday Fox

An engaging story of a red fox traveling across the US, from Georgia to Washington state, meeting forest animals and facing perils along the way.

Killers Can't Hide

The hunt for the former beauty queen's killer rocked Cumbersome County. If they don't catch the former beauty queen's killer, the town is in peril. The suspects are many.

THANK YOU FOR READING

If you enjoyed *Corners of My Mind*, we invite you to leave a review online and share your thoughts and reactions with friends and family.

www.ingramcontent.com/pod-product-compliance
Lightning Source LLC
Chambersburg PA
CBHW060858210726
48293CB00006B/1867

* 9 7 8 1 9 5 4 0 0 0 8 3 4 *